I0535707

ECO AGENTS

SAVE THE PLANET

Space Opera Books
an imprint of
Regency Assembly Press
www.regencyassemblypress.com

ECO Agents
Save the Planet

By

D. W. Wilkin

&

D. J. Wilkin

SPACE OPERA BOOKS
Regency Assembly Press

REGENCY ASSEMBLY PRESS
HEMET, CA, USA

First Printing, July 2012
1 3 5 7 9 10 8 6 4 2

Copyright © D. W. Wilkin, D. J. Wilkin, 2012

ePublished in the United States of America
Printed in the United States of America

Without limiting the rights under the copyright reserved above, no part of this publication may be reproduced into a retrieval system, or transmitted, in any from, or by any means (electronic, mechanical, photocopying, recording, or otherwise), without the prior written permission of both copyright owner and the above publisher of this book.

PUBLISHER'S NOTE
This is a work of fiction. Names, characters, places and incidents either are the product of the author's imagination or are used fictitiously, and any resemblance to actual persons, living or dead, business establishments, events, or locales is entirely coincidental.

The scanning, uploading, and distribution of this book via the Internet or via any other means without the permission of the publisher is illegal and punishable by law. Please purchase only authorized electronic editions, and do not participate in or encourage electronic piracy of copyright materials. Your support of the author's rights is appreciated.

LICENSE NOTES
This ebook is licensed for your personal enjoyment only. This ebook may not be resold or given away to other people. If you would like to share this book with another person, please purchase an additional copy for each person you share it with. If you're reading this book and did not purchase it, or it was not purchased for your use only, then please return it and purchase your own copy. Thank you for respecting the hard work of the authors.

ECO Agents: Save the Planet is dedicated to

Daniel

for being a great example to his sons

ACKNOWLEDGMENTS

We would like to thank our families for supporting us in this endeavor. Susan, Cheryl, Ben, Brandon, Annie, and a lot of pets, too numerous to name.

We also thank Sadies Estella Yanes, Tram Ngoc Tran, Angelica Mae Revilla Pomares and Van-Hang Ngoc Hoang for being readers.

Last we thank the Brea Borders Writers Group and Valle Vista Library writing group for their encouragement in publishing and then refining this book. Deedira Bockhold, Elizabeth Durand, Anne Okamoto and Jennifer Martindale.

TABLE OF CONTENTS

-Chapter 1-

Watching the clock was something he was sure no one else did. It was in the upper right hand corner of Parker's laptop screen. As well as on the thermostat near his window; on a bookshelf across from his desk; and there even was a mantel clock on his desk. Parker also had a wristwatch and he was sure his tutor, Mr. Frakes, had a watch as well.

Mr. Frakes also had an alarm on his phone that rang when the lesson time was up and then could leave. Mr. Frakes was the math tutor and came three times a week for two hours in the early afternoon. Parker was home schooled and had seven different tutors that his parents paid to teach him.

Some, including Mr. Frakes said they could do so over the internet and did not really need to be physically present, but Parker's parents insisted. And so Mr. Frakes showed up. It was probably wise that he did so, otherwise Parker might not pretend to be so diligent.

At the moment he was just pretending to double-check his answers on the three tests that Mr. Frakes had brought over. It was summer and even the kids in the public school were out on break. Parker though was cramming to get extra work done before he left for his new school.

What Parker really was doing was working on material for the tutor for the next day. He had a current events report do, and it was nearly finished. Parker had three tabs of news open in his browser, along with the word processing program, and then the testtaking program that Mr. Frakes thought he was using. Parker was reading about how, "Z Corp Celebrates Zedidiah Carter's Birthday in Grand Style." Must be nice, Parker thought to himself.

Another minute ticked away, Parker noticed, by glancing at the corner of his laptop.

Parker had been accepted into the ECO Academy. It was one of the most prestigious schools for High School age students. Advanced students that were going to earn college degrees at the Academy before they would normally be able to go to college.

And everyone the same age as he was.

Clearing his throat Mr. Frakes said, "Nearly time, Parker. Are you ready to send me your answers so I can grade them?"

"Almost Mr. Frakes. Just need to check this. Here are the first two tests." Parker replied. Parker clicked enter and the email with the two tests attached went to Mr. Frakes. Not quite another minute had passed, but then when it did, he prepared a second email and sent it off to Mr. Frakes.

"Ah, good. Good. Well let's call it a day then. Your folks are out, but they said you are to play in the yard for an hour. Not to ride over to the park," The tutor said.

Parker nodded. That was fine with him. But he wasn't going to play in the yard. Mr. Frakes gathered up his computer and showed himself out.

His parents were out of the house and so entering his father's man cave could be done without anyone knowing. Parker was to leave for school in three days, so the punishment, even should he be caught, was not going to be too serious.

You had to weigh the risks with the rewards. His father was always saying that. It was one of the concepts about managing money that his father, the banker, was really concerned with.

The man cave was where the 80 inch television screen was.

And for today, Parker wanted every bit of resolution he could get.

Parker was going to play Call of Duty: Modern Warfare with his clan, the Lords MissRuled. They had a double s in misrule for Missouri. Parker was pretty sure all the other members of his clan were all over sixteen since they talked about cars and driving, and girls, and stuff like that while they fought, or in their private forum chats. He kept his own age hidden so that they did not know he was younger.

He had two hours before his folks came home and he was going to use every minute that he could to score some great victories for his team. He set a loud timer so he could go AFK with enough time to leave the battle and return the room to the way his father liked it.

Parker ejected his father's bowling disk from the PS3, and then put his own game in. He scrolled to his account on PSN to sign in. Fortunately his father did let him have an account on the PS3 in the man cave. Otherwise he would have had to do some hacking on his father's console.

A few minutes later, he and the other Lords MissRuled were in the game. Killing the enemy and wracking up victories.

After each mission he would look at the clock.

The punishment if his father caught him in the man cave without permission had always been severe. It was why he had to sneak in. Two weeks ago, Parker had asked to use it.

Prescott Thornton had looked like he was considering allowing him, "You know, I don't think so. Last time I let you in, you tracked mud on the carpet, and I don't really like that."

Parker hadn't though. His father had tracked the mud into the room, but he was blaming Parker again. So Parker knew it was better to not ask permission sometimes. Sometimes you just had to do what you had to do. And the Lords MissRuled were way ahead of anyone else they had battled so far. It was a good day.

Parker was able to put everything away, and even remembered to put the bowling disk back in the console before his folks got home. He was taking his own PS3 to school with him, but he did not know if he was going to get as much time to play as he had at his parents' home. He told his online friends that he would try to connect with them.

Parker knew every year it got harder to remember the times when he was a child. Kansas City, at least the neighborhood he had grown up in could have been right out of a TV show. Parker knew now that the house he grew up in the Roanoke Park section of town was a fake Tudor two story affair. Back then, it was just a great big home. Much bigger than his family really needed. He had no siblings so it was just his parents and he.

He had a lot more space for himself growing up then he had when he reached his away school. He could not really call it boarding school, even though he was boarding there. But he had been advanced to tenth grade and still was faster at everything then the other students. His parents had then been advised to take him out of school and have him home schooled where he could test above his grade and get his diploma. With online teaching, he could also start college work from home.

Parker just felt he didn't fit it. At least with the kids of the neighborhood, he could ride his bike and play in the park and there, school did not matter.

One of his first memories was Roanoke Park and his father training him to ride a bicycle. It was just after his birthday, and he had a hot blue two wheeler to celebrate. Riding a bike instead of a trike was what the big kids did. He was going to be a big kid. Though he liked to ride his trike up and down the street. His parents told him he could never leave the sidewalk with his trike and he always had to slow down at driveways.

With a bike he could ride all over the park and there were lots of sections without cars so he could go really fast. That would be way fun.

At first his father, the president of a small regional bank, had training wheels on the bike. They would run down the street and Parker could feel the air flow against him like wind. His father ran fast and Parker pedaled as hard as he could. Then his father would let go and the bike would be a bit wobbly but it was pretty steady.

His father, Prescott always said he had become a bank president not only because he was determined, but because with a name like Prescott, what else could he do. It was important, his father said, to live up to your name, and Thornton was a name that was at the bottom of the Declaration of Independence. Not that his father wanted to flat out tell everyone that they were descendants of a signer of such an august document, but it placed a great burden on the name.

Just as those that came over in the Mayflower felt they had some legacy to live up to. Or when you joined the Sons or Daughters of the American Revolution, and Parker was scheduled to become a member on his eighteenth birthday of that club. The Thornton name had a history and his father and mother told him he was to do great things because of his name.

They placed the first trophy he had earned on the mantel in the living room. His father had a whole lot of trophies in his man cave room. Parker's small collection would have been lost if it was placed amongst his father's collection.

Parker's mother Beth had ribbons and sashes, tiaras from when she was a beauty contestant. She had been runner-up to Miss Missouri when she had met his father. He had been first vice president at grandpa's three branch bank. Parker knew that because Grandpa Thornton always said that. That between his father Prescott meeting his mother, and then Parker being born a few years later, his father had made the small bank into eleven branches. It was over twenty-five branches when Parker left for school.

Parker knew now that made them pretty well off. Parker supposed another way he could tell his father did well, was they always had food to eat. The house was warm in winter. He got a great selection of toys for Christmas and his birthday, and special release sneakers from Nike and New Balance when they came out. Not to mention the entire team of private tutors. The only things he did not have were friends, or a brother or sister.

Or Parker knew they were rich was that his father was a banker and people tended to give bankers lots of money. And his father said he was smart about the money. Other bankers took on too much debt and made risky loans. His father didn't, Prescott always said. He took on solid loans in the community. He leant to homeowners with two jobs. His father also didn't sell the loans to other banks so the customers wouldn't look elsewhere when they needed their next loan.

His father said that these were life lessons. Learn about the people you needed to trust. In his father's case it was those he leant the bank's money to. For Parker, once his father accepted the fact that he was going to be a scientist and not a businessman, it was trust those he wanted to work with. Prescott had told his son that he had heard of a great many scientists who stole the work of their researchers to pursue such prizes as the Nobel, or other awards.

Parker thought what his father was saying was watch his back. His mother Beth, who was not the smartest of women Parker had come to realize (for her beauty pageant answer to the question of what she wanted most was the safe 'World Peace' answer), said that his father meant more than a trite modern slogan. He meant build a group that could be trusted. Trust was key. *Fide, sed qui, vide.* "Trust but take care whom." Parker had learned Latin when he was nine.

Prescott had several life lessons like that. Just like when he taught Parker to ride his bike. Trust.

Parker had trusted his father then.

"Okay Parker, I've got you. You did great before. You held her steady. Just do that again. No more training wheels. I know you're ready."

"No Dad. A few more times, please. The training wheels help." Parker had said.

"I've already taken them off," Prescott had said. "You saw me do it. Now come on, you're a big man now. You're five and you can do this. I know you can. Straight and steady just like the last time. I'll hold on to the bike all the way. I promise."

That was what Prescott had said. He promised. Father had said that he could be trusted. If only all those customers knew that his father lied. Not even half way down the block, his father had let go. It took a few feet, maybe his pedaling past two houses before he realized that his father was no longer with him. He heard his father calling, "That's it Parker! You're doing great."

And Parker turned his head and with his turning, so to did the bike, the wheel going way too sharp and the bike collapsing, tilting into the asphalt. Parker's leg coming down and the knee guard getting pushed off as the asphalt tore into his leg. And arm.

It hurt. Badly.

Even then at the memory, ten years ago, he could still remember the pain and rubbed at his arm where it had become scratched and bloody.

Life lessons. Know whom you could trust. And trusting your closest family was something you had to think about.

Parker found that he might not be able to trust people as much as he could trust science. He found that in science there were laws that held true. That he could set a hypothesis and prove it, or disprove it. That worked quite well.

People would lie.

Science did not.

Knowing that unlocked doors for him. He had been able to use his mind and never ride a bike again if he didn't want to. He spent so much time with his books and lab experiments, surfing the web for information, that if his parents thought he didn't play enough, all he had to do was show them his awards of merit. That got them to be quiet. After he studied some physics, (Stanford had podcasts of their lectures on his iPod), he tried riding his bike again and found that he could do it well enough. It was about balance.

Centering his gravity and pushing the envelope of speed faster than anything he could imagine. That kept him up and he went to the park and rode when he wanted. Though it was not as much fun as the lab he had set up in the basement. That was fun.

Kansas and Missouri had tornadoes and though he was too young to chase them, he learned as much as he could, especially how they were so destructive to the ground. How the wind could whip up so fast that it could tear buildings apart. The reason they had a basement was because of the tornadoes.

"Parker, there will never be any way that I shall let you become a storm chaser. And if you want to watch *Twister* ever again under my roof, you can only do it when your mother and I are out for the night. If I have to see Jamie Gertz whine her way through that movie one more time…" His father had said.

Parker's mother said, "Now honey, you know it has two Oscar winners in it, Seymour something. And the girl from that sitcom. If Parker watches it when we are out…"

"Yes, I know. But I just can't stand it any more. Parker, you know all the words. Don't you get bored with it? You are always talking about global warming. Why don't you look at what's going to happen when Antarctica sinks into the sea?"

"Dad, *Happy Feet* is for little kids. But, there's *The Thing*. Yeah, I can watch that!" Parker had said. He had said it to make his father get all wigged. It had worked too. Parker didn't really want to watch movies about Antarctica, but he began to study it.

Aside from it being so cold, it was probably the reachable last frontier. One day man might get under the sea and be able to understand the ocean. To live there. It was after all about 70 percent of the area of earth, and humanity was not taking advantage of it.

Certainly men and women were ruining it. The garbage patch in the Pacific was now twice the size of Hawaii. That was big and it was getting bigger every year. Then the overharvesting of fish not only put fisherman out of business, which one had to think of as being their own fault for overfishing and killing the geese that laid their golden eggs so to speak. But the whole oceanic ecosystem was in jeopardy. And should the icepack melt because of global warming... It was probably impossible to conceive what would happen to the Earth.

Parker's mind began to boggle at all the disparate thoughts that came as he began to look into Antarctica and what was happening there. Could he stand the cold? Could he venture forth to the last outpost of mankind? It would certainly be far from Kansas City and Roanoke Park. From his father and the family bank.

He was ten when his mother came home from a lunch with her girlfriends. They were all pretty ladies. Parker was able to see that. And his mama, the former Miss Missouri finalist, was the prettiest of all those ladies she had become friends with.

"Now Parker honey, are you sure about this science thing? You know your father will never say anything, but he sure would like you to help him at the bank."

"But mama, we don't need any more money. You are always saying that." He had learned that a good child remembered what his parents told him and said it back to them. That he should always be agreeable.

"Helping your father at the bank when you are older isn't the same thing as us making more money, though of course it could happen. There is nothing bad about money you know. We make enough of if, or your father does, that we can help a lot of needy people." His mother had said.

His parents gave a lot to charity. Parker knew that. On Thanksgiving, early in the morning, they went to a local homeless house, though it didn't look like much of a house. It was an old building. While there, he put on an apron and was given a pair of tongs and was told to put a biscuit on everyone's plate in a line that came by.

Other people who worked with his father at the bank were there as well with their children passing out food. After they went to Grandpa and Grandma's for turkey dinner. Grandma always said she cooked for three days before, but Parker had noticed that as he had grown up, Grandpa and Grandma had moved to a bigger house and now they had a maid, who also had a maid on holidays, always helping in the kitchen.

"But mama, dad always says that he doesn't need my help at the bank. That I am too young," Parker had responded to his mother.

It was a Saturday and his dad was down at the bank once again. They opened till the middle of the day on Saturdays. He also had lots of work opening up new branches, he always said.

"Yes, but you are way ahead in your studies about science. Why not study about finance and economics and see how you do? Janey's son has just gone to college to study economics. Your father thinks that if he does well, he could go to work at the bank."

Parker said, "Dad always wants other boys to work at the bank. He has never said he wants me to work there."

Parker's mother shook her head. "He just says that. He does want you to work there, like he worked at the bank with Grandpa. He really does."

Parker was not sure that was true, but he thought he would see if it were so. There had been a lot of news about home prices rising fast. Parker cut back on his time doing experiments and research from his study of Antarctica to see if anything could come of the rising home prices. He found that others believed that home prices were overheated and were shorting the sale of them, thinking that prices would crumble.

Parker was ten and so a lot of what he was finding he didn't understand and had to spend time with Wikipedia, and then YouTube to understand. He had to look at CNBC and read some books by writers like Jim Cramer, who was funny to watch on television also.

"Booyah."

What did that mean? And no one thought it was very funny when he said it at the park. He would ask his tutors, but they had little idea. And when he met with some of the other home schooled children nearby, they thought it was anti-religious. Most of the other children weren't home schooled because they were smart, and trying to get into a school like the ECO Academy, but because their parents hated the government or they wanted a religious education, or just thought they could do a better job then the teachers at the schools.

Parker had to meet up with the other children for physical education classes, but some days the religious ones were rather short sighted. They knew he was really smart about science, and would try to make him argue about Creationism. That was always a losing argument. Once a person of belief wanted to hold to their thoughts, no logical argument would do. Not even the part which pointed out their view of religion, on a world with seven billion others, was a minority religion.

Not that Parker and his family did not go to church. His father ensured that they dressed up for church twice a month. A bank president of the community bank had to be seen as a religious man. Well except during football season. If the Chiefs had a home game, his father had season tickets and Prescott took his biggest clients to the games. Prescott and Grandpa also went all over the country for the road games.

In late August and September, his father would go to all the baseball games on the weekend. Parker went with his mitt, but they never sat anywhere you could catch a ball. And waiting for a ball to even come near could be really boring. It took a long time for a ball to be hit near them. His father did buy him a lot of great food though. Hot dogs, peanuts, colas, ice cream. That was great.

Parker finished his study about the overpriced houses and showed it to his father. "Why this is pretty long, Parker. Have you been working on this for a while?"

"Mom said you wanted me to help with the bank. So, yeah. A couple weeks." He didn't want to sound like it was anything big. He actually had been working on it for three weeks.

His father shook his head and then quickly turned to the last page, "Fifty three pages. Single spaced?"

"Well there are a lot of charts and things. I got a lot of quotes from people too."

"I have economists who work at the bank who don't know how to write more than five pages. Okay, I'll look at it," his father said.

Parker's mother said, "Really? Parker did a lot of work on that and you must read it. You should be happy he is showing an interest in the bank."

Parker did not understand the look that his father sent his mother, but his father turned back to him. "Was this as exciting for you as when you work on your science and study Antarctica?"

"What? Oh no. This was so, so one dimensional. I think that is the word. All this stuff about housing is quite predictable. You can see what is going to happen. With Antarctica, we still don't know enough to see what is going to happen. Just that what we see now points to it being bad."

"I understand," his father said. He patted the report on the housing market, and then turned back to his paper.

A week went by and his father said nothing about the paper, but his Grandpa took him for ice cream. "Your mama gave me that paper you wrote. I thought it was very fascinating."

That was more than his father had ever said. "Really? It wasn't that hard. It's happened before in lots of other things for sale."

Grandpa had chuckled, "Like Tulips?"

Parker nodded. He had found out about the run up in Tulip prices in the 1600s. The first great bubble.

"Well I liked your report. Your father never wrote one of them for me like that when he worked for me at the bank. I don't think your father has ever written anything with so much depth."

Parker did not entirely understand. There was an obvious problem, and he had tried to cover all the issues regarding it.

"Well, I am going to talk to your father about the matter, and make sure we take precaution against these mortgages and the brokers who don't really check into the borrowers. I know we have purchased some loans that could be questionable in the last few years."

It wasn't the only thing that was in his report. It was clear that there were a bunch of people who did not check enough and packaged mortgages to the banks where there was no way the homeowner could afford the payments, when the interest rates climbed.

For the next few weeks after Grandpa had talked to him, things had become tense at home. His father was working longer hours at the bank. But then when the mortgage crisis hit, Parker remembered his father came home and rubbed his hair.

His father said, "We passed the stress test with flying colors. And Parker, it is because of you."

"What did I do now?" Parker wondered aloud.

Parker had been filling out his application for ECO Academy, which was really long that day. And he had to come up with a preliminary science study to show his worthiness. His father thought that anything about the Penguins or Polar Bears should be good enough for the school. Parker knew it would take a lot more than that. "Good enough" for ECO Academy had to be college-level material, or even more advanced. Not some playful study by most teenagers.

His father told him, "Oh, your suspicions had us double check all the loans we were making, both consumer and commercial, that were tied to the housing run-up. I had to get rid of one in six from people who were lying about their income, or for other reasons. But we have very little bad loans on our books given what has happened. Some people may be underwater when this is all done, who we have loans with, but we can help them refinance, and make sure they can afford new payments and even have equity after. No we are in great shape. And your grandfather, he's made a fortune. He invested in that fund that said everything was going to crash."

Parker didn't understand, "But what about those other people? The ones who can't afford their loans? What is going to happen to them?"

His father seemed a little heartless. "They may lose their house. They should not have bought them in the first place, or lied about how much money they were making."

"But you loaned them money. You're responsible too."

His father got mad, "I am not responsible. I have set up very strong guidelines at the bank. These people, or their mortgage brokers lied to us. We would never loan them money to buy a house."

Parker wasn't finished, "But those brokers, didn't they get paid right away? You take the money over thirty years, but the brokers have nothing to lose. They get paid when the house is bought. They have every incentive to lie…" Parker had learned that when he had written the report.

That Parker had found in his research. That was something his father had nothing to say to. He just nodded. "You're right. Grandpa said that we needed to only do loans through our own people. No independents, and I've cut back on all of those. Grandpa has me making the last of them into employees. I still have to pay them on commission, but if there is something wrong in the deal, I can fire those who do wrong."

Parker attributed it to another life lesson. Grandpa had read the report and what his father said back to him was what had been in the report. Prescott did what his father told him, and had not read the report. His father was not as smart as Parker was. If he had been, a few weeks work and he could have found out all that Parker had found out.

His father did not value what he had said. It even seemed that as he grew older, his father was pushing him to be a scientist. Not to help him at the bank. His mother, was more concerned that she had found her hair going grey and needed to use color to keep it the same sheen it had always been. Her latest craze had become Botox.

She and all her friends were having their lips and eyebrows done. "No wrinkles. I will not have any wrinkles," had become her mantra. Prescott didn't seem to care about the expense, or her desire to have such work done.

"What ever makes you happy darling. You know I love how you look," his father had said. It reinforced something that was not quite right. Parker supposed it was good that his parents were attracted to each other, but there should have been something more besides that for their marriage. But they were old and he had begun to notice the pretty girls he saw at the park, or on television.

Pretty was nice. But were they smart as well?

At ECO Academy they were going to be smart. That was a given. Since the first class went to the advanced school, only twenty young people had been admitted each year. Ten boys and ten girls. So that meant those that got accepted were smart. But amongst smart people, the pretty genes weren't always prevalent. It could be why smart people weren't often on the cover of the fashion magazines.

But Parker had a few of those genes from his mother. It would be a shame to let them go to waste if he didn't find someone pretty as well.

And since he was fourteen, he was thinking about pretty girls a lot.

He was sure that the girl on the *Big Bang Theory* had to be smarter than how she acted. When he got to California and to ECO Academy, if he got in, he was going to do his best to find out. And that Sheldon could not be as smart as he was supposed to be. Sheldon remembered too many different disciplines. That was way too Hollywood.

Parker was willing to bet that the man's physics were wrong too. Not that he wanted to go to CalTech. ECO Academy graduates did much better post-doctorate fellowships than those from Cal-Tech. CalTech let in far too many run of the mill high school graduates with no clear idea of a discipline to pursue. ECO Academy was a totally different premise and really catered to scientists who wanted to make the world a "Greener" place. That appealed to Parker, and getting out of Kansas City appealed as well.

Mostly though, the chance to meet people his own age who were just as smart as he, was what the biggest attraction was.

"Hey Parker," Kevin, a friend who lived a block away and whom he met at the Park every few days, said.

"Hi Kevin. How are you today?"

"Okay. What's going on? Are you really going to move away? I wish I could do that," Kevin said.

Parker responded, "Yeah it should be great. California, right above the beach. Dad says I should learn to surf. I think I would like that."

Kevin whistled, "Wow, surfing? That's so cool. And you're supposed to go to school? What a riot."

Parker snorted. He had never known anyone to be envious of him before. Kevin had a lot of friends because he went to the public school. Parker had few friends from school, though his Facebook page and his IMing list was quite large. He had met a lot of people interested in the science he studied. He used a picture of a Polar Bear since he didn't want anyone to know how old he was. But when he announced he had been accepted to ECO Academy, those who knew about the school then learned he was only thirteen.

"I'm pretty sure there is going to be a lot of studying. It seems like the kind of place that they make you study a lot," Parker said.

"I bet. Some rich guy runs it and Disneyland is right there." Kevin said.

Parker knew that most kids his age didn't understand. He was going off to an advanced college to study, and others his age were just about to enter High School. There was a world of difference and Parker could see that. Kevin was near his own age and did not know that Parker had completed everything that Kevin was about to study three years before. Parker was very far beyond anything that Kevin was about to learn, but Kevin had tons of friends from school their age, and Parker could not call any of the school children in his home schooled class that he shared physical education with 'friends.'

Parker hoped that being at ECO Academy with other children his age would change that. It was supposed to be one of the attractions. 20 children each year the same age, learning together, and learning separately to support their own interests and speeds. With others who were gifted like he was, he knew that the pace that things were taught at in local schools were designed for nearly the most stupid in a class. It left their minds too idle. A gifted child needed more stimulation, which led to even a greater thirst for knowledge.

Leaving for ECO Academy might be the best thing in the world for him, and perhaps he could learn to surf as well.

-Chapter 2-

His fingernails had been polished that morning by a manicurist as he had his weekly trim and a fresh shave. Though he used an electric razor every other day of the week, this once a week indulgence was certainly something he could afford.

"Mr. Carter, the senior staff are assembled sir." That was the voice of one of his three personal assistants. Michael. Not only did Zedadiah need three assistants, he also had several office suites throughout the world with secretaries, project managers, vice presidents, troubleshooters, all ready to jump and aid him in managing the world's biggest conglomerate.

Third biggest company by sales, behind Apple and Exxon Mobil. But a great deal more profitable that those two. ZED Corporation, or Z Corp for short, an affectation he had renamed the company when he had first obtained control of what had been the old E4A conglomerate.

Then the company had offices in Europe, America, Asia, Africa and Australia, and extracting commodities had been the business model. Zedadiah had started in the New York office at sixteen. He had used a fake ID that said he was twenty-one and a little computer hacking had created a paper trail to show he had graduated from an Ivy-League college. That was so long ago, he had forgotten which one.

Zedadiah had a few minutes as he walked to the foyer of the building floor. The 91st story overlooking London's Isle of Dogs. ZED Corp had built the largest building in the Canary Wharf section for its world-wide headquarters. Not only the tallest building there, but in all of Europe as well. If they had stayed in New York, they would have been one of many. Now they rose and towered above all others that could be seen. Size really does matter.

Zedadiah remembered when he had first applied at the old E4A company. Three floors then of a middling size skyscraper in Manhattan. The HR interviewer looked at him when she sat down, "You look quite young, which may be a difficulty for your co-workers, or you."

Zedadiah thought quickly, he had always been the youngest in any circle he had been in. His faked credentials had some basis in reality. He had completed his first year at college, a prodigy, he had enrolled three years younger than his classmates. But after one year, he knew more about economic theory than most who were graduating that year. Zedadiah certainly knew enough to hack the computer system and give himself all the documentation that showed he graduated.

"I have had that problem for as long as I can remember," Zedadiah had told the lady. Ms. Schmanski, he remembered. She was not a native New Yorker. He could tell that she had a great deal of the Midwest in her. Which was not a criticism, but he was a native of the tri state. "I put my head down, do my work, and then show that because I look young does not mean that I am not accomplished. You can see I interned last summer for your Boston office."

"Yes, I made some phone calls and they said that they remembered you."

He quietly snorted a laugh. He had found where all the other interns for E4A were as well as six other large companies. He had spent a day at each rotating through all the companies. He had been at the E4A offices for perhaps thirty hours, but he had glad handed as many people as he could. He had dropped his name, and then he had left them with reports that had been assigned to the interns to do. He also collected some nice cash from each company. Some of whom he had worked for throughout the school year as well.

Cash was always good. Only General Electric had figured out he had been absent more than he had been in attendance. Only IBM's computer security measures had been too challenging for him to pull the scam off.

"I am glad I made an impression," Zedadiah replied. "I hope they had favorable things to say."

"Bright, personable, your research was spot on. This is merely a formality. We would like to offer you a management trainee position, we start at 85 a year…"

The advantage to being able to hack computers was that you

could hack lots of computers. And he had already hacked E4As computers the previous year. He knew how high she could go, and what trigger her supervisor might come in to finish the negotiations. "I have already had an offer of over 100 from IBM. Are you sure you can't do better." Ten minutes later the supervisor came in and he finally got them to concede to their top number. 115 a year and three weeks vacation. "$115,000 a year, not bad for a 16 year old," Zedadiah though to himself. Oh how times have changed.

The money was not an issue, not really. It was access to information. That was what was going to make him wealthy. To learn about things before anyone else did, and E4A had people on every major continent. People who were only just beginning to understand that their computers could talk to each other faster than they could talk to one another.

Zedadiah knew that reminiscing was an indulgence. He had lived in the present since long before joining the company. And then leaving E4A a few years later.

Today was special. It was his fortieth birthday, officially that was. And the company was honoring him for reaching the milestone. Birthdays were great as a device he found for measuring how well he had achieved his objectives. This one was a year that many thought of as important. Born in 1972 and now it was 2012. The world had changed a great deal but fundamentals were all the same.

It was how much money and how much power you had that was important. At forty he was one of the five wealthiest in the world. Probably third, but the Forbes and Fortunes lists were never really quite accurate he had found as he became eligible for them. Especially since a great many of his assets he didn't report. Just like many of the things that ZED Corp owned or controlled wasn't mentioned anywhere. One needed their secrets in business.

Zedadiah could see his employees ahead, hundreds who worked in the building, many of whose names he didn't know. Several other employees of the conglomerate who had made sure they were in London for the day so they could attend and shake his hand. They knew, as he did, when he was much lower on the ladder, that getting the boss to notice you was the way to advancement.

His first years at E4A he had thought to do so, and his skills with extracting economic information from the corporate computers had made him very successful at that. That coupled with the money he amassed during his summer of multiple internships, allowed him to invest in the stock exchange. He not only traded company securities but as his account balance ballooned, he used options and futures, traded commodities, and rode the largest wave of capital creation that America had ever known.

His salary negotiation was like nothing that first day for after a month of access to not only E4As computers, but also many of the systems from the companies he had interned at, he had made more than a years pay on the stock market. Within six months he had amassed a net worth of over a million dollars, and still not even seventeen. By twenty he had more than ten million and it was time to use that to leverage up to even greater wealth.

Zedadiah left E4A then and opened his office in London, a few blocks from where he now was. The applause was starting as they saw him approach the foyer. People already were beginning to sing, 'For he's a jolly good fellow,' Pity they didn't remember he was born in New Jersey and sang Happy Birthday instead. But he had now lived abroad for many years.

Not that Zedadiah had cut his ties with the States. Zedadiah had more than a dozen accountants manipulating the tax codes of many countries to ensure that he paid very little in the way of tax. Keeping his US citizenship was crucial to that strategy. Even if he hadn't spent more than a couple months in the United States every year for the last decade.

When Zedadiah left to set up his own company, he started his own investment fund, still stealing information from the computers of those companies he had one time worked for and had hacked their knowledge. He only used computers from his flat in Kensington, but that made him seem like a genius to his employees when they would get phone-calls from him, or those emails to tell them to act upon one of his 'hunches.'

The company he formed was called Carter Investments, still a part of his conglomerate. His traders though had started to call themselves the 'Z-Men.' With his hunch, he had bought the majority interest in a French water company. The world in the nineties began to thrive on French bottled water. It was like minting money and he was able to purchase other commodities, and mineral extraction companies that he found at a discount, and then see rise to profitability.

There, on one of the tables off to the side of the marble encrusted foyer, were hundreds of bottles of ZED Corp water for the guests to enjoy. Everything now was a division of ZED Corp. Branding had become important and it bred loyalty amongst the mindless consumers. More of them trusted those that made the brand, then there own opinions to decide what they should use. What they should buy.

He snorted a laugh as he waved to the well-wishers and then began to shake hands. His most loyal lieutenants that he allowed to work alongside him in London. Others who managed the various divisions and companies that had flown in for the day. Someone handed him a glass of champagne and when he took it, there began a call for a speech. Soon the chorus calling for him to give an oration was all that could be heard. He held up the champagne glass until he could make himself heard.

"I am glad that you all could be here. A few drinks, some cake, and we will have marked the occasion quite appropriately. I am now, ahem, forty. That is an age that a man comes into his own I think. Passes the baton of being a young man, a firebrand, and able to take a much longer view of his accomplishments, achievements and what is yet to be achieved. Today, we have a very strong company, but we have barely touched the surface, so to speak, of what we can achieve. We have dedicated ourselves to making sure that all mankind's standard of living rises up, and I can attest that mine has these last forty years." He hadn't thought of his roots in Secaucus for a very long time.

His parents house was smaller than the two story flat he now had. Security was an issue in a place to live at present. He had a house being built on The Bishop's Avenue, alongside other billionaires. There, his Vice President for Company Integrity, assured him that he would be safe. Stefan Kutuzov was former

KGB. There was no need to hide the fact that he had been a Colonel working in Moscow before the Soviet Union broke up. But once it had, Stefan had decided that his services could be purchased and he could be comfortable.

Zedadiah had no qualms about hiring the man, and then within a year, promoting him to head the Protective Services Division of the company. It was also the part of the company that dealt with spying on their competition, as well as other governments, and Stefan was trained to do both. At headquarters, in the ninety-one story building, they had fourteen floors devoted to their operations, and to access those floors, Zedadiah had to not only do a voice and retina scan, but his face had to pass the newest technology in identification algorithms.

Continuing with his speech to the employees Zedadiah added, "When we started our strategy at Carter Investments and saw that we could make a difference in the lives of so many, we did not think that the rewards would be as great as they are now. We never thought that purchasing a plant that bottled, clean, pure water, would be the engine to propel us to a manufacturing empire. I wanted to buy a music label and promote Rock bands. Who knew we would go in a totally different way."

That last was an exaggeration. As a youngster in High School, before he went to college for that one year, he had always been pushed ahead one grade, two and then three. He was much younger than the other girls in the grade he had tested into. And the girls were very pretty. Most liking the schools football heroes or those in a band. At fourteen, he had not grown big enough to be on the football team, and he was all knees and elbows which made basketball out. He did however play a keyboard a little. Not well, he could think now, but enough to have dreams of being in a band and having something to talk to with a girl.

Dating once you were wealthy, and then very wealthy was not so hard. And he had an ex-wife to prove it. One who did her best to see to the raising of his two children. Two children who only wanted to talk to him when they wanted something. Something expensive.

"Water has been the key to our success, and the key to so many hopes and dreams. It is my intention, and what better time to make such an announcement then my fortieth birthday, that by my fiftieth, we can look back on these next ten years and say that we have solved the world's water problem. That we will have found the means to drill wells every place on this earth that man inhabits. I commit the resources of ZED Corp to ensuring free water for all mankind these next ten years. That we will be able to filter that water so it is clean and pure, and almost as great tasting as our very own Z brand of water." There was some laughter, "We want everyone to have healthy water, but we still want to provide ours and make a profit." There was no danger of that. No matter how many times they had raised the price of water, for one real reason, or for many phony ones, people bought it. And every year, every month, people bought more than they had bought before.

There was applause and even a few cheers. Zedadiah had never thought that people would cheer him as a leader. He had never thought to be a leader in front of everyone but to have made his wealth quietly. And certainly when Carter Investments had purchased the bottling company, that had not catapulted him to the public's awareness. Going head to head with other big beverage companies had raised his profile, but by then Carter Investments had made significant purchases in many other companies. Silver mines, Copper mines, Molybdenum mines.

Ores, water, and also food. By the time he had turned twenty five, his companies had tens of thousands of hectares under cultivation. Last year ZED Corp had even purchased a classic French winery. One they had said would never be sold, and yet when a family needed money, they sold. It was where the champagne came from that his guests, his employees were sipping.

Raising his own glass, "Now thank you all for coming, and lets have some cake!" Another cheer and then a second round of singing. Zedadiah felt like a jolly good fellow. But then why shouldn't he? He was rich and respected. He was doing great things that had made him so.

Perhaps many of the people who worked the mines, the farms, the manufacturing plant had no idea how well he lived. There were employees in Africa, men who made less that $200 a year, and his personal wealth grew by six billion the previous year. Six billion pounds not dollars.

But without him, that worker in the Congo wouldn't have that $200 job. Though to be fair his leveraged buyout of E4As assets had brought such a low earning person into the company fold.

Jerry Piedmont, the VP of Corporate Affairs, or the Conglomerates lawyer was making his way over. He looked determined, and had to have flown in from the New York office.

Jerry had been the chief council for E4A and had been so difficult when it came to negotiating the merger, that when it was finally done, and Jerry looked to be out of a job, Zedadiah offered him one. "Mr. Carter, I wanted to personally wish you a happy birthday."

Piedmont was a Long Island legacy. His parents had a second home in the Hamptons, and their parents before. With what Piedmont was paid, he could easily afford one as well, but instead chose to live in New York. "Thank you Jerry. I appreciate it, but I sense that there is more?"

"It's the bid for New American Steel. I got a call from my friend on the Joint Commerce Congressional Committee. We are hitting a snag there, and since it was your special day, I thought I would come over in person to talk about it."

Zedadiah knew what that meant. One of the Senators or Congresspersons wanted to be bribed. They needed money in their reelection coffers, or something more direct. There was no company stock to give them, as ZED Corp was closely held by principals, which really meant Zedadiah. "I suppose if we are creating the second largest steel company, there was bound to be a problem. Has this held up negotiations with ArcelorMittal?" They were the worlds largest steel concern, but they had challenges, managing as well as political. They were selling assets to ZED Corp.

"No, I got the information from my friend. No one knows about this but us," Jerry said.

"Best you stick around so we can discuss it. There is a small dinner later. Just a few people at Gordon Ramsay's at nine. Have Kutuzov get you vetted. The Prime Minister and a few other cabinet members will be there."

Jerry nodded, "I know. So will our Secretary of Defense. That is going to help with the Joint Committee." Zedadiah had forgotten that was the case. Not entirely. There had been a conscious decision whom to invite to the dinner while the American's fought over the election. The Secretary was invited because ZED Corp now had several billion dollars of defense contracts for the Americans, as well as other nations. The Secretary had a great deal of influence on the awarding of future contracts. For the kind of money they were making, Zedadiah would even have invited the President and stood their shaking his hand and saying pleasant things, even if he didn't believe a one of them.

"Yes, of course. Let's get through this little shindig and then we can talk. See Kutuzov, Michael…" Zedadiah called the assistant who was close. He motioned to Piedmont and knew that the two would take care of scheduling time later in the afternoon.

Penelope Vruder came over. His most able lieutenant of all of them. Originally he had hired her when Carter Investments started. One reason was because he liked how she looked, and she had used that to her advantage. She still worked out every day to keep her figure very trim. She had a beautician and makeup artist at her beck and call, and the top designers in London and Paris kept her clothed in only the best dresses. Zedadiah had never seen her in a pant suit, and the few times over the last twenty years that they had maintained an affair, he could recall her getting up an hour before he would just to fix her face, as she would say.

"So, trouble in the Colonies?"

He nodded, "Nothing to worry about. Nothing we haven't seen before." Penelope was the mix of a German father and English mother. She had graduated top in her class from Heidelberg. Zedadiah knew how she thought after twenty years. But he also knew where she was blind and used her looks to finish what her other talents could not. That was always the reason they never had fallen in love. Penelope could not be trusted to forget to trade on her looks and just use her very brilliant mind.

But then his ex-wife, who he had married was because of how she looked. Not how she thought. He had learned that was a mistake the hard way. So badly that it had affected his two children.

"Good. That announcement, the water in every village, a television in every hut, are you serious?" she said.

Zedadiah nodded. "So far we haven't ever seen any fall off in sales of water. Why not be altruistic. It is good publicity. It will guilt everyone who buys a bottle of water to buy one of ours. They will be drinking clean, fresh water, and we'll play on that. Clean, fresh water for all the world. And it will make our employees feel that they are part of something productive. There are a lot of studies that show employees like to feel good about their company."

She trilled a laugh, "Employees just want bigger paychecks each year."

He shook his head, "We are coming off the worst recessions so they know that bigger paychecks each year are hard to come by. Besides this is going to be a great tax write-off and we need those all the time."

"Ah. I knew there was another reason," she said.

He smiled, "There is always more than one reason for a plan. I thought I taught you that. And it all goes to the purpose." Zedadiah had made that up. The purpose. When the media noticed that Carter Investments had been not only trading securities and all the other instruments on the world's stock exchanges, but buying companies as well, he had said it was 'to the purpose.' They had believed him, that he had a purpose. So too did those in the company believe about 'the purpose.'

After the water company, they had bought a gold mine, and gold was in the doldrums. Then cattle ranches in Brazil. The truth was, there was no 'purpose.' Or rhyme or reason. Some companies were undervalued greatly. Those were the ones he purchased. Warren Buffett did the same when he was starting his Berkshire Hathaway. Buffett had a great deal of money, and managed a large conglomerate of companies, though Zedadiah actually did manage the men and women who ran his companies, while Buffett had a more hands off approach.

That was what the purpose had become, everyone believing that Zedadiah had a plan and that he was executing it. Sometimes he believed he was doing so like a Japanese Keiretsu, or a Korean Chaebol. Anytime there was synergy between companies Zedadiah had to ensure the companies worked together. Sometimes bashing heads together to get what he wanted. Other times chopping them off and finding new underlings who would implement his ill defined vision.

"Yes, the purpose," Penelope said. Then she added, "Water again though. I do not like this. We are too far reliant on water."

One of their companies was heavily involved in trading on water rights in Chile and other parts of the world. "We were reliant on water at one time. Not so much anymore. Less than a tenth of our income comes from water now. Not like when all we owned was the one bottling company and had the income from the investment portfolio."

It was two years from the purchase of the bottling company before there had been enough capital to purchase the gold mine. When he had turned thirty, with much less fanfare then turning forty involved, Zedadiah had set his sights on E4As assets. He knew that the market undervalued the company greatly, and that E4A had access to a great deal more of the world's resources then they even realized.

The ownership of resources were the true key. If one looked to Russia and the former Petro Czars, he could see how one could manipulate the system. The key was to own resources where the law protected you from the vagaries of heavy handed politicians like Vladimir Putin. Zedadiah snorted one of his laughs. Putin was the true Vlad the Impaler. Looked like it as well, and Kutuzov had nothing good to say about his former KGB colleague.

No, own the resources, or if you were on tentative ground with some dictator, ensure the cards that you held, were greater than he did. Even Putin would be wary of reneging on a deal between ZED Corp and Russia now. He might think to cut off oil to the country of Georgia, but should the Prime Minister of Russia think to spar with Zedadiah he would find he didn't have enough grain for winter. Millions would die of starvation.

Such recognition of what ZED Corp could do caused even the modern Vlad the Impaler to respect or fear Zedadiah. So much so that several dozen cases of the best vodka had arrived that day from the Russian Embassy, a birthday gift. Shame, Zedadiah wondered if Putin knew he hated the stuff. Made great gifts to others, but vodka was not his drink at all.

Knowing the kind of man the Russian was, he expected that the Prime Minister did in fact, send him vodka knowing he hated it. The Russian was not of much concern. None of the world leaders he interacted with were. He had them over a barrel more often then they had him on a leash. That was the purpose if he would let himself admit it. That he had power. It hadn't been at first. But it was now.

Power was not just intoxicating, it was freedom. Penelope had turned to look about the room as he too surveyed it. The people in it combined to earn over three billion pounds a year. Penelope alone made over two hundred million in salary and bonuses the year before. And Piedmont was compensated nearly as well. Even Kutuzov made close to sixty million pounds, while the heads of various operations could command well over a hundred million. And they all thought that they had freedom.

They were wrong.

Money was not the true way to freedom.

The ability to look at another man in the face. A man who wanted to do nothing more than spit at you and break you with his bare hands. A man who could do none of those things because he knew that you could do that to him, and much, much worse. That was the true way to freedom.

And that was what Zedadiah had done.

Forty years old, and he had accomplishments. He was rich, he had built up the company. He had two children. He even had his own plane and a very large yacht. (It was more like a mini-cruise ship with forty staterooms should he want to entertain that many guests. Saudi Oil Princes always seemed to tire of their excessive extravaganza and then sell them for a tenth of the cost to build.)

Zedadiah's true and only important accomplishment, he had power. He was free.

He laughed again, "This must have been what it was like to have an audience chamber where all came to pay homage."

"Yes, that is what we are all here for, to recognize you. Your greatness," Penelope said. She of those gathered, had been with him the longest. But he could see something that perhaps she did not. She had fought against age and time for years. A battle that she would lose. That everyone lost. Already her hair coloring was lost to the artificial. And having a stylist to attend her when she needed could not always keep a grey root from showing. Penelope would not be with the company when it came time for the fiftieth birthday.

"Sarcasm is more my skill, not yours. I think it has to do with your German half," Zedadiah replied. "I am going to have Kutuzov's division dig the wells. I am sure that there are ways to work that to our advantage as well. When you dig a well, and place some filtering equipment, why not a few pieces that will collect important information as well. Where is Van De Laar? He'll take care of that."

Once Pieter Van De Laar was a senior engineer of Phillips N.V. He wanted to be more. Zedadiah cultivated him, bought the division the man worked in, and promoted him to manage it, adding more pieces until the labs of ZED Corp could rival the research and design facilities of the best technology companies. But where other companies sold to the consumer, or to the world market, ZED Digital only worked on projects for other companies within the ZED conglomerate. There were inventions that others outside of the company had no idea had been made. There was a flash drive, less than half an inch square that could hold a terabyte of information. When the marketplace thought that the largest drive was twice as big in size and could hold less than a tenth of what a ZED Corp device could.

They could easily perfect a solar powered information sensor the size of a stick of gum. Put one on every well, and the ability to collect knowledge would increase. It would work hand in hand with the same type of device that had been built and hidden in every cell tower that was built on the planet.

"Are you picking me up for the party tonight?" Penelope asked before he turned to find his electronics genius.

Zedadiah looked at her, "I think I best go alone tonight. Yes, that is what I must do. I shall see you at the restaurant." No, Penelope might not even be a part of ZED Corp when he turned forty-five.

-Chapter 3-

"Dr. Phillips-Lee, Dr. Lee, this way please."

"Dr. Lee, what is your opinion about the situation on the mainland?"

"Dr. Lee, tell us how it feels to be back in Hong Kong." There were more questions after that as well. All shouted at him. But that was to be expected. Or, he thought sadly, it was what he had come to see as part and parcel of his life.

Daniel raised a hand to the reporters, and squinted at the bright lights from the video cameras filming him. "Come my friends, I shall have you up to my rooms later for interviews. I am sure my staff has arranged such, and if you do not have an interview scheduled, then you can see my assistant. I will answer one question, the one I think is most important to me this week. It is with great happiness that I return to Hong Kong, for my cousins wedding. These are always great occasions in my family and the banquet shall be a great feast. Now I shall rest a few hours from my travels, then we shall meet and you can ask all of your questions. Thank you," he waved and smiled and then walked into the elevator that was being held for him.

The Peninsula hotel had not changed since he was last there, but he came to Hong Kong for one family function or another, at least twice a year. In 2011, he had been four times. Travel home was always the same, now that he had become rather rich. Even before that, he had stayed at the hotel, but not in a suite. Not until he had sold his second company.

"Doesn't that tire you out, boss?" Moshe Ben-Levi asked. He headed the 12 man team that was Daniel's security team, as well as monitored the other security teams that worked in one capacity or another for him. Even though Daniel had sold his third company, which had made him very wealthy, it did not mean he hadn't a few other irons in the fire. Seven other companies that would be considered small. None more than thirty people, except for the Academy. That was an entirely different beast, though, and it wasn't quite his in regards to ownership. The Academy had partners.

"A little. But it is the price I have to pay now."

"That and having all this muscle." Moshe always mocked what he did. Except when he needed to be serious.

"Yes, all the muscle. There is some point in how much you are worth when you have to have muscle as you put it. I hear that Warren Buffet, who is much richer than I, used to be able to drive himself in an old Lincoln."

"Well, he's giving all his shekels to charity, so maybe he won't need as much muscle as you." Moshe said. But it was clear the man didn't believe it.

The Peninsula Hotel had many rich visitors, and things were set up so that Dr. Phillips-Lee could have privacy, but also be safe as well. When his second company had sold, and the drug trials had succeeded for medicine to combat blood clotting post surgery, then he had become noticed by all and sundry. He no longer even owned the company when the drug came to market, but because he had sold out and made a great deal of money, the media getting it wrong how much he received, he had become famous. Or even infamous as his drug, Reloosapen was sure to help many.

"I give a lot of shekels to charity as well. But that's enough for now. I need to rest for a few hours, and then let the vultures in. Where is Patricia? Still downstairs with the press. Very well, could you tell her I've gone to lie down?"

"Sure boss. She's young, she doesn't need to rest anyway." Patricia, who was in her mid twenties had been one of the first graduates of the Academy. She then asked to be on his team, and though a brilliant chemist, her organizational skills were even better. She did a great deal of work on the first few hours of the flight from Los Angeles, and then went and slept after they had refueled in Hawaii.

Daniel had never been able to sleep on a plane. Even in the corporate jet with all it's comforts. And it had a great many. He did nurse a couple drinks, and knowing when they were an hour out of Chek Lap Kok airport, he took the first sleeping pill, for he knew that it would make him drowsy.

Removing his shoes, jacket and tie, he fell onto the bed in the hotel room. It no time, he drifted off to sleep, remembering what it was like to be a child in Hong Kong, fifty years before.

It had not been good then. His father had been a successful trader, and owned a few electronics factories. The mainland had not yet become the powerhouse that it would later be. Hong Kong was the place that the western world trusted to make their items cheap.

What had been difficult for Daniel is that his Chinese father had married a British woman. It was a relationship that lasted for some years and produced Daniel. But only he.

With mixed parentage, he didn't fit in, and his father spent far too much time working, then remembering to value his mother. She left the man.

It happens, Daniel had told himself. Mother had been born in Hong Kong, but when she divorced his father, she moved to England where she had family. It was clear that when the colony reverted back to China, she had little desire to remain, especially as the ex-wife of a man who had begun to see the writing on the wall and spout communist dogma.

Not that Daniel's father believed it, as most in Hong Kong did not. But China could prove to be a hard taskmaster and freedoms were soon to be forgotten memories. Daniel, a gift from his mother, held dual citizenship. She did love him enough to pull him from the colony and to an education at Oxford. But when he had finished, after staying for graduate studies, he returned to Hong Kong and began his first venture.

He had seed money from his father, who now had a few factories in mainland China and was navigating very difficult waters as China learned how better to serve, and then master, Western Capitalism.

As an employer, then, setting up his first laboratory, his mixed heritage was not a problem any longer. It was a bonus. He had ties to the United Kingdom. He had ties to the Western World. People who came to work for him, only hated him as they hated any other boss. He was never taunted about his English mother again.

When his research, which had cost money for three years,

started to show promise, and then results, his father negotiated a sale of the patents and research.

At first Daniel was beyond angered. He could not believe the betrayal, and soon came to realize that the company was bought to keep his research from the market. His father had made thirty million Hong Kong dollars from the sale, and Daniel had made ten.

His father pointed out that they had the one offer. The company that had offered would just as easily have used the money to quash them. And that it was to be at least ten more years of his pouring money into Daniel's company with no sure end in sight before they might make any money. His father only had so many dollars that he could afford to give Daniel.

Daniel had left Hong Kong again, but had not gone all the way back to his mother in England. Instead, he had stopped approximately half way in California. Sunny Southern California.

He could afford a beach house with his money and spent the next few months living in Malibu. That was where the second idea came and he started another company, this time seeding it with the money that his father had given him from the first venture.

Again they had not stuck with the research all the way to completion, but at stage two trials sold Reloosapen to E4A and this time made a great deal more money. The media noted the company sold for well north of three billion US dollars. But Daniel had taken on partners. His stake was worth just over half a billion. That was more than the money his father made from all his factories.

It gave Daniel enough wealth that he could do whatever he wished. But a nagging desire to stay in science and work with bright people had him start his third company weeks after he had left his second.

And what a bidding war that became.

Monsanto, Dow, ZED Corp, Cargill, ContiGroup, all came forth and offered more money then the last. He had to admit that the presentation that Penelope Vruder had given had sealed the deal. Not because they offered the most money, but because she had enticed him like none of the other teams. And this time, he had no partners. It was his decision alone to sell, and he received all the rewards.

Ms. Vruder had promised him the chance to still run the division, but Zedadiah Carter and he did not get along when they met. It was not even six months after he sold that he was asked to leave. Mr. Carter made it quite clear that the several billion dollars Daniel had received should not cause any hard feelings.

It did though.

Daniel had thought that what he had to do to keep governments from taking a great deal of that money in tax had been extreme when he had sold a company and got half a billion. Now, he had to come up with a solution that would not dilute his money all over the world. Creative accounting people and a desire to keep finding solutions helped him.

That was the birth of ECO Academy. *Ecological Conservation Organization's Academy of Higher Learning and Scientific Achievement* was really a very large mouthful. Shortening it to ECO Academy was much easier on all who had to say it.

Daniel had been getting older. He knew a great deal more than he had when he was young. Three great scientific advances, was two more than many scientists often came up with. It was a young person's game, and the older scientists he knew were good at mentoring. Daniel saw a need.

One that he had enough money to fulfill.

And even more when he negotiated with government agencies to make the idea a reality.

Daniel had been drifting when there was a knock at the door to the bedroom. A voice called, "Boss, twenty minutes before the vultures want their meal. Better get up and get ready. Boss?"

"Yes, thank you Moshe. I'm awake. I'll be out soon." He did not have to get up and be on time. He was rich. It was the media that wanted his time, which he would give them. But they needed to come to the mountain. He was not the one seeking something.

He changed out of his shirt and found a new pressed set of slacks. The luggage had been brought into the room while he dozed and a very efficient member of his entourage had hung his clothes up for him. When he had first become rich, he was told that this was the way things happened. Daniel was not going to complain. He felt a little guilty, but he also put to work several people who otherwise would not have had a job. And after the double dip recession, jobs were wanted.

And Daniel paid very well.

He did not keep the first reporter long at all. This one was from the local news and she wanted to speak Chinese. "Ni how…"

When the interview was over, ten minutes later and five or so questions answered for a sound bite, the next reporter came in.

"English if you don't mind, Dr. Lee," the reporter said.

"That will be fine. I prefer it these days."

Chinese, and being thought of from China was actually a burden. The government of the People's Republic was not helping either. With hand and a smiling face, they were telling the world how they wanted to be a part and really aid. Then in reality and with the other hand, they were as corrupt and acquisitive as always.

More than twenty five hundred years of history and breeding ensured that the Chinese considered themselves the greatest race on earth, and they would eventually prove it to all the other races of the world. They might not have done it by militaristic warfare, but economic and information warfare was leveling the playing field in their favor.

"I thought we might talk about your current projects, and ECO Academy as it is the tenth anniversary this year."

"Well, twelfth if you add all the time I spent lobbying the various world governments, and then building our campus."

The reporter nodded. She was very pretty, and young. Most of the time they were young, and pretty. Then in a few years they would move on to more substantive journalism, or move out. People who watched these reporters were fickle enough that they wanted to see youth. There was a lot to be said for youth.

"Yes, twelfth, but this year you will graduate the tenth class, is that right?"

He smiled, "Yes. Commencement is in a month and we are very proud of our twenty graduates. We look forward to great things from these men and women."

She shook her head, "Though some of the young people are

not even eighteen?"

He nodded, "I hope your viewers are familiar with our school."

The reporter looked to her camera man, and after he nodded she replied, "I am, but we should let our viewers know, the ECO Academy gives the highest education on a par with the best universities in the world. Students can enroll at the age of fourteen and four years later have a masters or doctorate degree, where they then can go do additional work at the world's leading universities, or if they have a good idea, see if they can build upon it. You invest in some of the students that have graduated your Academy. Some say that you train these young people so you can exploit them."

"I would argue that was not the case. I do employ some of our graduates. I fund the research of others. But a great many others in the international community do so as well. Companies, governments, private individuals. I am not the largest employer of our former students. There are at least three others who employ more."

"Yet your critics still contend that you started the ECO Academy for your own gains, and continue to gain from it."

Daniel laughed, "Well those critics are wrong, and if they should care to look at our finances, which are made public, they will see that ECO Academy costs me more each year, then I am paid from it."

That stumped the woman. She obviously had not got all her notes correct.

Daniel continued, "The ECO Academy was started for many reasons, but predominantly because we are hurting the Earth more every year. We thus need to heal what we have wounded."

The girl shook her hair. Black, like almost every other Chinese girl. "We have tens of thousands of scientists who say that is wrong."

"China has become the leading gross polluter in the world. Of course they feel that we are not hurting the world. But even within the community of scientists who live in the People's Republic, more recognize that it is impossible to cover this up. The graduates of the ECO Academy will find solutions to help heal the world. They come to us as children from every country on earth, and they leave ready to solve the worlds problems, or at least they are on the path to solve those problems."

She laughed now. "You say they come from every country on Earth. How many have been Chinese?"

He had to shake his head. Three had been of Chinese extraction, but not born in China. Two had been Taiwanese. "We have only had 260 students to date. Just twenty a year come to us. China, has never allowed any of their sons or daughters to test to be admitted. We even have come to the People's Republic several times with offers to have a particular student join us. Two of our faculty are from China, and we have had three students from Taiwan."

"Yes, they are very progressive in Taiwan," that was an insult the way she said that.

"They are. It is a shame that those of the People's Republic don't recognize that. We are now looking for applicants, not for next year, but the year after. I would hope that you will aid me in seeing if we can find an applicant from China."

"Oh, of course Dr. Lee. That is surely what I shall do." She let a pause of a few moments play out then snapped her fingers and the cameraman stopped. "Thank you Dr. Lee. This was a terrific interview. My producer is going to love it!" The reporter was now full of smiles.

China. He understood.

"Yes, I am sure he will. Makes me look bad though."

She said, "Ha, you live in the west and are quite rich. What do you expect?"

The reporter and her cameraman bustled out. The next was shown in, another pretty girl, but this one was for a newspaper. She just wrote down what he had to say, or rather held up her iPhone to record what he said in response to her questions.

"Can we talk more about those who come to ECO Academy? Why? What makes ECO Academy so special. Don't prodigies want to go to other schools. Harvard, Oxford, MIT?"

He nodded, but then remembered to speak as well, "Yes, of course. And in a sense they do get to. Not only do we employ thirty of the brightest minds we have found at our campus in Malibu, we also video conference with the best professors in the world. Our students, I sometimes think, pack six or seven years of study with the best teachers in the world, into what other students only have four years to study."

"You wanted to focus on Ecological Conservation. You are basically a learning institute for the Green movement." The reporter stated. It wasn't a question.

He said, "True and I make no apologies. My research has not always been focused to Green initiatives, but now they are. Global Warming is playing havoc with our ecology and pollution as well. We often ignore these problems in the press, unless they become topical, but we are killing the earth. Not the next generation, or the one after that. But our children's grandchildren and great-grandchildren will have terrible challenges that if we do not work to solve now, will very likely be unsolvable, or solutions would be found too late."

"Your critics say that is alarmist. Global Warming may indeed be happening, but it has not been as bad as the American Vice President Gore said it would be."

"True, but it is much worse than those who said it was not happening when Vice President Gore started to speak about the issue. Even if the community can not agree to the severity of the issue, all can agree that it is occurring. That it is having a significant effect on our world. Ice packs are melting. If the seas rise just 8, 12, or 15 inches then how much of the coast lines of the world will disappear?"

She said, "I am no scientist…"

Daniel interrupted her. "I am. I can tell you that were this to happen suddenly and not gradually, millions would die. Even gradually we will be forced to retreat from the coasts and loose all the development that has taken place there. We will lose cropland, which will lead to starvation, not to mention the disease we will have from having to develop new centers of habitation for those that are displaced from the coasts."

"We have heard this alarmist bluster before." The reporter said.

"Check your facts. It is not bluster. That is why we have the ECO Academy. We know we have to train bright minds to think how to solve these problems, and make up an army of scientists who will be able to aid in the solutions we are going to need. And not only I feel this way, but clearly the sixty-three other governments who helped me to fund the Academy as well."

The reporter was not completely antagonistic, "And the international group of professors who make up your faculty, both in Malibu and via Skype, all over the world."

Daniel said, "We actually use another computer program we developed to communicate, but yes, essentially like Skype."

"Let's talk about something else then. The United States, why settle the Academy there? Why always defer to the United States? Don't you feel any loyalty to Hong Kong?"

That was always a hard question to answer. There was a great deal of antagonism to the United States. "I do feel loyalty to Hong Kong, but I will admit that this is a little selfishness on my part. My mother lives in Bournemouth, and father lived here. Los Angeles was between the two and that is where I settled and have been living ever since. I founded the Academy so I wanted it to be where I called home. My children live near me, though they are attending USC and UCLA."

He didn't talk about his family often. His wife had died when he was in the middle of starting the Academy. His children remembered that as rich as they had become, it had not saved his wife from death. Nor had he been home very often when she had gotten sick. She had complained of a cold, and said she was fine. Though the cold lasted three weeks and the doctor did not think of it as bothersome either.

"Still, most of your students come from other nations?"

"Yes, yes they do. Less than one in ten has been an American since we started. About half of our students are brilliant minds from disadvantaged countries who do not have the resources for such a university level education in any of the sciences. I am very proud of that. That we have offered such education to so many, even if we are just approaching our 200th graduate."

She smiled, and Daniel recognized that it meant the reporter was ready with their big question, "And how much would you say it costs to educate each of your graduates? Do you know?" He did, and so it seemed did she. It was not a figure that they talked about often.

"It costs about six million dollars, US."

"Each?" she asked. Again the smile that said she had been the cat who had drank all the milk from the bowl and was going to convince her owner for more.

"Each year. About twenty-five million for each of our students by the time they are finished."

"And you charge the world governments, to help fund you? Is that a good use of money. I am sure I can get a college degree even here in Hong Kong for a great deal less."

Daniel had to agree with that. This is what his public relations team called spin. "Yes, I know that my education here in Hong Kong was a great deal less, and then even my college at Oxford was much less. The Academy costs about half a billion each year to operate. The results though are what is important. Our mission is to produce the best minds that we can. And their challenge is to heal the wounds that the Earth has been taking."

"And you can tell us about your results?"

He shook his head. What could he say to that. The first class, which had only experienced one year at the Academy, had been in the real world for less then ten years. Most had gone on to higher degrees, some were still attaining them. Young people not even thirty years of age.

Daniel may have had a success at an earlier age than that, but only just that age. How could he explain that science research came slow and steady. Not something that you could do in a few weeks. Not like in the movies. Though, he supposed sometimes research was thrown out the door to rush to a needed conclusion. The Manhattan Project certainly finished quickly enough.

Something that in this century would probably have taken six times as long.

"There has been very little in the way of tangible results from those who have matriculated from ECO Academy. I believe we have had four of our students finish projects that are beneficial for the world. We have a new adhesive that is used to reinforce the concrete of dams for instance. Too often fifty year old, one hundred year old dams are found to be unstable, and this adhesive, when governments have chosen to adopt and apply, should provide the dams with an inexpensive solution for another hundred years or more."

Little Mykala Ambosure had come up with that. And it did work. It was certainly a lot cheaper then any other solution, but coating a 25 square foot surface still cost three or four hundred dollars. The material and time to concoct the adhesive was expensive. And it was needed to be applied every ten years as well. That was something certain countries looked at as too expensive. It could cost them a great deal to re-coat a dam each decade.

There was just not enough talking points to show that ECO Academy was doing what it was supposed to do. Produce minds that would help the world. One day he knew that his graduates would be something that others, besides himself, would have great pride in. That his alumni would be doing great good across the planet.

The Scientific Peace Corps.

But the press was not ready to let him off the hook.

"So you have been spending about five billion dollars on this little experiment and have some glue to show for it. That is a lot of money when some countries barely have that to spend on themselves."

He could only agree, "True, but not everyone pays the same amount, or even uses cash. Bangladesh produces promotional material and subsidizes advertising to attract students for the Academy. And a great deal of our operating budget is paid by myself, and goes to preparing candidates for the Academy. For every student we accept, we turn away many. But some of those who can not attend the Academy, we ensure they study at local universities or colleges in the sciences. Their tuition is then paid by the ECO Academy."

She nodded and had little more to ask, it was time for the next interviewer.

An old British expatriate came in with his a cameraman. "How do you do Dr. Phillips-Lee. So glad that you gave us this time to chat."

"My pleasure," Daniel said. The region was filled with Anglos making the world commerce go round. There was always going to be a commentator who supplied them news.

"I hope you will allow me to ask some questions about what

the great Dr. Phillips-Lee is involved in now? Not your work as Chancellor of ECO Academy, though I should imagine you have a great deal more free time with only 80 students at your college, then say, the Chancellor of your alma mater, Oxford. I believe you were at University College at University, weren't you?"

"Yes. The Master and Fellows of the College of the Great Hall of the University of Oxford, 1980. Fond memories. I do have free time as you were saying. Time for instance to come to a cousin's wedding, or to meet with various ministers of state to discuss the Academy. I meet with the Chief Executive of the city-state of Hong Kong here the day after the wedding for instance. Business and pleasure or two birds as it were."

The reporter laughed a little, "Quite. Good use of time management. Always trying to do two things myself as well. For instance my daughter, whippersnapper of a kid. Don't suppose I could get an admissions application, do you?" Then he laughed at this. "No, seriously, she's twelve but I was told to start the process early."

"Of course, Patricia will make sure that you get an application." Daniel was pleasant. He had a list of fifteen children that were potential candidates for the Academy here in Hong Kong, and he was sure one was a twelve year old girl, daughter of a British expatriate.

"Now let me get down to the meat of things. It's been reported, elsewhere, that you invested about half of your wealth in your academy, and I am sure you spent some of your money on yourself, but what about those other investments. I understand you still are doing some research."

Daniel laughed, "Thank you. Most don't ask me about that. I don't do as much as I would like. I have ideas, and I work on them, but I do not have the time to bring them to fruition, so I have started a few companies where I have others working hard on my ideas. And then I have also backed some of the graduates of the academy on their research. Sometimes I have little more to do than write a check, but a few of these ventures, I am like the senior researcher there as well, reviewing their findings, guiding them to the next breakthrough. At least we hope there is a breakthrough."

The man nodded, "Tell me, be honest, ten years from now, will the world be a better place, or worse? Based on what you and your students at the ECO Academy are doing?"

Daniel took a deep breath, "Better I hope, but unless more of the world gets behind this project, probably worse. Over the next ten years we have to increase the size of the academy by a hundred-fold. Not twenty graduates a year, but 2000 graduates a year, and they need to make brilliant things. I wish we could do that, but I know we can't. I should be heartened if we have four hundred graduates each year, in a decade." That was the truth, but Daniel was going to do his best to beat that number. To beat that number, and start really healing the Earth, instead of just putting band-aids on it.

-Chapter 4-

Priyanka Zadari was a junior at the ECO Academy and very happy to be so. There were not a lot of girls her age at the school, but of the close to forty girls that were attending the college like campus, she was friends with most, and those who she did not get along with, she did not think of as enemies. Her friends, and even those who weren't, called her Priya. The *y* was silent.

Boys were also friends, but her upbringing, had made it hard for her to get close to any. Boys were mostly acquaintances. At lease when she was around them. Now if she were IMing, texting, vidding, anything that put the computer and her fingers flying over the keyboard (or her thumbs) then she easily found she could speak to them. Four older protective brothers, no sisters and very restrictive parents had made her this way.

She was smart enough to know the cause of her shyness. She was intelligent enough to know that she should seek a solution to the problem. She also was to scared to address it.

Boys, were… Boys.

And she thought about them a lot.

Enough that she knew it was interfering with her potential as a student. But still she was in the top five of her class. If she did not think about boys all the time, perhaps she could have been the lead student of the class.

And she didn't think about boys all the time. It was that when they were around her, she had a hard time thinking. Not that she thought about anything in particular about most boys. About dating, or anything silly like that. No, she thought about that with only one boy. But she did think about how to talk to them. About how to be around them without being awkward.

She knew that they looked at her in a way that a few years ago they had not. And her brothers had not been any help. None of them had gone to ECO Academy, as the academy was called by its students. They might have now, but they were all too old, and it had not been around when they had been able to be admitted, or were already at colleges elsewhere. Her oldest brother was twice her age, in his thirties and married with his own children now.

Priya liked being Auntiepee. When she lived with Maheshwaran who was a lecturer at Stanford, he had only just had his first child and Nirmayi needed some help. That was when Priya had moved to America. She had been eight. Her parents had thought her bright enough to enter the Indian Institutes of Technology the year before. But she was too young to live away from home then. Maheshwaran though found that he could home school her in American and have her audit lectures at Stanford.

By the time Priya was eleven she had learned enough to test for a degree as a computer engineer. Just like Maheshwaran. But she was not done then with her education. Chandan was on the faculty of MIT and he saw to it that she also could take courses there. She was off to Boston and found that she did not like the cold and snow at all. At Stanford, it rained, but there was no snow. Boston there was snow. It was cold. Really cold.

She needed to only stay two years, but she was older and was able to go to more classes. She was still the youngest person in the class and when it came time to apply to ECO Academy, she realized that she had not had any friends her own age since she had left the home of her parents, when she was eight.

Entering ECO Academy she was fourteen and placed in a group house with eight other girls her age. At first she had little idea how to interact with others her age. It had been so long. But slowly she remembered and soon she had friends. Some moments she suspected that it was the way she spoke. Her clipped diction, a motley of her growing up in India, then the west coast and east coast influences, caused her to sound exotic, but with English accented from all over the world, it was not so easy to determine if that were the case.

"Priya. Priya!" yelled Shelley Botha. From South Africa and maybe her closest friend came up to her as she looked out over the Pacific Ocean. There was a molded concrete bench under a big sycamore tree that had a great vantage point. And as most days were sunny and warm, studying outside was encouraged.

The beautiful vistas were a reminder of the ultimate goal of ECO Academy. To produce scientists who would solve the problems that faced earth to preserve those views.

Shelley was slim, blonde, athletic. She looked like a young version of Charlize Theron, and everyone teased Shelley about that. Especially since Charlize was from South Africa as well. All the others as school said they had to be cousins.

"Hi Shelley."

"What are you studying? Not more of those computer languages."

Priya shook her head, "Not quite. I am linking Drupal, Ruby on Rails, and Linux to run optimized through an iPhone and these Android phones. I think that I can have a secure and free communications device, with video linking over LTE and capture by next week. About ten thousand lines of code, but I may shave that to eight thousand."

Shelley shook her head. "That is all geek to me. Now you should really think about the hard sciences…" she laughed. Shelley was a marine biologist, with a heavy study on Cetaceans. Shelley had grown up inland with no coast for 100 miles, and was now a whale head. She had her masters, and when she finished her course studies at ECO Academy, she would have her doctorate. Each summer she spent in the Pacific Ocean, mostly up in Alaska, following the great mammals.

Shelley was working on discerning which frequencies employed by naval sonar might be acceptable for both the navies and the whales to get along with each other. Losing the whales because the world's navies wanted to send their sound waves into the ocean had already disrupted the ecological balance, and until this was solved, things were going to get worse.

"Believe me, when you are out there on the high seas and you want to talk to someone in Ceylon, or even your mother back in Johannesburg, then you will thank me for my little program. The only lag will be from the satellite bounce," Priya said.

Shelley responded, "The last thing I will ever want is to talk to my mother. She'll just want me to give up my job and go back home and make babies."

Priya winced. Often that was what her own mother wanted.

Mothers seemed to want their daughters to make babies quite often. "What has you so excited?"

"Oh, I nearly forgot. I was talking to JCubed and he said Parker Thornton was asking about you. Which I think is a little strange. He's a senior, and you're not." JCubed was the nickname of Jackson James Jefferson. Three Jays. He joked that his mother wanted to name him Davis, or Stonewall after the heroes of the Confederacy, but his father had said absolutely not. It would have been strange for a boy of color growing up in Atlanta to be named that. Could cause trouble still, even if the South was more accepting now.

Parker was the one boy that made her think of things other than just how to talk to boys. It made Priya wonder what a kiss would be like. What holding hands with a boy would be like. Talking to a boy and him listening to you. Most seemed to want to talk and never listen. She understood that. Most liked to look, or stare at girls. Especially ones who were pretty like she and Shelley. Not all the girls at the school were pretty, but they could be.

Her own mother had spent hours making sure that she had good saris to wear and how to make up her face correctly so that she would look pretty. For the two weeks a year that they saw each other, her mother cried the entire first day because of all the time they had missed being together, and then all of the last two days as well, before Priya either flew back to the States, or her parents flew back to India.

"I don't believe it."

"It's true. JCubed said that it was really boring. JCubed said he was thinking that he would go to Russia when he graduated and work on the hacking situation and he was telling Parker all about it. JCubed has an internship this summer with the FBI, but then Parker asked if JCubed saw a lot of you in his study groups," Shelley said.

She was hardware and programming, so they did overlap, while JCubed studied software and user interfacing over the internet. If there was information on the internet, and almost all information was, he could get at it. If a machine needed to be designed to get at it, then that was Priya's skill set. Together, she and JCubed often joked, they could set up a two person company and break into any computer in the world, and then break out, no one the wiser.

But ethics was something that was very heavily reinforced in the schools curriculum. Not that ECO Academy had a very structured curriculum. Thirty professors had been recruited from the best colleges of the world. Each student worked with one mentor, following the British tutor system. And then with a second mentor in their discipline in a group which had a student from each grade. A team of four students with a professor to lead them throughout their course work.

It was in the group teams that true learning was made, while in the individual sessions that breakthroughs were found. Then there were two structured classes each quarter as well. One that was made up of students from just their year in a 12-week lecture cycle. The second, another 12-week lecture that was a pet project of the professor, was open to all years. And it was encouraged that during the freshman to junior years, each student at the academy take one of the courses. Most students though took two.

Not that students were spending all their time on their education. The beach was a short climb away, or for those who had privileges, they could use golf carts to drive down the hill. There was a very active surfing club and beach volleyball team at the school. Then each quarter, those who wanted to, could go on a group outing to local Los Angeles travel spots such as Disneyland, Universal Studio, other places.

The rumor was that the first year, Dr. Phillips-Lee had made it mandatory that the students had a 4.0 or better average to attend. A perfect record.

Before the end of the year Dr. Phillips-Lee realized that those students who had made it into the program always had perfect records. Such a requirement was funny. Twice, two students had fallen behind in the history of the institute but it was quickly found that they had become sick and needed time in the hospital to get better. And when they did, the students quickly made up for lost time.

But living on campus in a collegiate atmosphere that was nurturing of study, and not of partying, had made the ECO Academics think of themselves of brainiacs. Most came to the academy at the age of 14 with collegiate level work. All had finished their secondary education by that time. Over the four years at the Academy, all students were to earn a masters and/or doctorate degree.

Shelley had her undergraduate degree when she applied, Priya had a masters. But all Priyanka's four brothers had been ahead of their age at school. A family of prodigies that usually made her parents smile with pride. A family of prodigies where more than half now lived in America and Rajeesh, the youngest son, was thinking of moving to England for a position at the London School of Economics.

Priya thought then of Parker Kenneth Thornton. He was an Earth Science major and was very much concerned with the effects that global warming was having on the ice cap in Antarctica as well as the receding glaciers in the Arctic.

He was everything that spoke to Americas dominance in the last century. He was from the heartland. Kansas City, Missouri where his father was the president of a small regional bank. It meant that Parker had money. All the money he had ever needed.

Priya might say she had that type of life as well, for by the time she was born, Maheshwaran and Chandan had been seen as prodigies and were going to get large salaries when they had finished ITT. Kal, the third brother also was proven to be brilliant. Her parents though, had been lucky to see fish in their soup every third day when they had been children. At least they said so. Priya's father's father had sold textiles, starting with a cart, and then a shop, and then, as big shops came to India, he opened one that tourists found to buy their Sari fabrics. Priya suspected her own father's tales about fish every third day was a fabrication. That they were better off than that.

She would never admit it, but she had been introduced to hamburgers in Boston by Chandan. Bartley's Burger Cottage was famous and all the other students had hung out there. She wanted to try a steak as well, but had not worked up the courage to do so. Far too many of those at ECO Academy were vegetarians, though there was a heavy lobby for livestock proteins amongst the students, everyone respected the decision to become a vegetarian in their many different incarnations. Though the dietician and medical staff ensured that no one over did adopting their beliefs in a way that would become harmful.

The school wanted to promote a better partnership with Earth, but even Dr. Phillips-Lee said he was a carnivore, and that had been the way of evolution.

Parker Thornton ate steaks. She had seen him do so. And he ate hamburgers. He talked a great deal about a place in the city called Tommy's that they had to travel to for a really good hamburger. Priya was sure there was a Tommy's closer then Downtown, Los Angeles. But Parker insisted that the best was where it was originally from. She found all this from texting with him. She could barely say hello when they were actually in the same room.

And he was in her current class on chemical regression amongst inhabitants of the African Continent. Priya saw him three times a week and she was supposed to talk to him. She had found it difficult to breath when he was there sometimes. Especially when she had noticed him looking at her.

Like some of the other boys would at times. Not the ones who just thought about having sex with her. There were a couple of those, especially once she started to grow and had to wear bras. That seemed to get almost every boys attention.

But some looked like they had as much trouble talking to girls like she had talking to boys. And they wanted to talk to her. Those gave her a different look, than those others she had gotten. That was the type of look that Parker Thornton gave her.

"What else did JCubed say?" JCubed was in his second year at the school. He came from both Atlanta and New York City, and was one of the few other Americans at the school. Any student who came from other countries in the Western Hemisphere took exception for a week or two that those of the United States were called Americans, but that was the way it was here, and in the rest of the world. It wasn't hubris or arrogance that those from the US thought of themselves as Americans.

Priya had learned when she lived in the country for a year. It was how their vocabulary worked. She supposed they could have learned to call themselves United Staters, but then objectively no other nation in America thought of themselves as American first.

Guillermo Cordovan, he was also a sophomore, said he was Costa Rican, Pedro Montejo was Mexican first and not Central American.

"He asked JCubed if you had anyone special you saw. Parker says he knows that you and JCubed work on a lot of projects together." With eighty students, only eight were involved in the computer sciences.

"Oooh," Priya said in surprise. "But Parker was dating Melanie Daplyn." She was from Australia and was beautiful. And if not rich, closer to being wealthy than anyone else at the school. She also was a senior and an earth scientist as well.

Shelley laughed, "JCubed told me, because I asked as well. Melanie likes Volcanoes. She's all hot and fiery, and Parker likes Ice. They did not mix at all, though you might think they would."

Priya smirked. "Good," she said very quietly.

"Sorry? Anyway, JCubed said Parker told him they only went out twice. Besides, Melanie is a Vegan and Parker eats meat. Didn't you say he wants to go to a hamburger joint and get a group together. I thought we were going to do that at term break."

Priya had been encouraging that they do so. At the end of Professor Lyakhova's class, they were going to celebrate. "Yes, you said you wanted to go too."

Shelley smiled, "Well maybe you and Parker can go and try it out first and then tell us if it is good. He has a car."

Priya and Shelley both had permits to drive, but they could only do so under supervision at the school. In Priya's case, she could not drive by herself until she was eighteen because her parents were not going to give their permission. Shelley was going to be allowed to drive as soon as she met all the training requirements.

"I thought it was all torn apart in the shop lab." Priya said.

Eighty students at the academy, and fifteen of them, took shop. It was considered a prerequisite for those who wanted to have practical engineering backgrounds. There were a lot of moving parts on a car. And it was a good grounding for later in life when a mechanic would tell them what was wrong with their car. Dr. Phillips-Lee had told them on orientation day that many of the classes that were offered at the Academy were designed to help them later in life. That adjusting to being an adult was also part of what they were there at the Academy to learn.

"No. Really? Why would he do that. Isn't it an Outback?" Shelley asked.

"Yes, the dark green one. But he was converting the engine to be a hybrid, and run on rendered cooking oil and electricity." Priya said. "I think someone said it smelled when he ran it after the first rebuild."

"You mean oil already used? How does he get that? Does he go to the dining hall and ask for it?"

"I think he gets some from there, and from the Taco Bell off campus. There is a lot of oil and restaurants pay to have it carted away. Parker texted me…" Priya said.

Shelley laughed, "It is always easier for you to text, then to talk to someone like Parker in person. Come on, we're juniors this year. We need to start dating. You need to start dating."

They had only just finished the first month of the quarter, summer just having ended, but it was still nice and warm in Malibu. But it was true, they were juniors and it was time to expect that they would be asked out. Priya did not think she was the best looking girl in her class, but she knew a lot of the boys looked at her.

There was a dance in two weeks, though they usually had a very poor experience. It was mandatory that all the students of the Academy attend the cultural activities that were arranged. But with such a small number of students, critical mass was never achieved. Dr. Phillips-Lee had taken to inviting the honor students of other local high-schools. They were sure to send students of a similar age, but not as smart as those of the Academy.

It was a good lesson, for they learned that other young people had the same problems they did in fitting in, especially those who were honor students. Often the geeks and nerds of their schools. The misfits. Which most of the students of the ECO Academy had been from the parts of the globe that they had come from.

"And how did your last date turn out?"

"Errr, don't remind me. He was all paws and not nice at all," Shelley had seen a boy surfing, and he had seen Shelley. He was all ripped and had those six pack abs that American Television seemed to be obsessed about. Brad something.

Shelley and she both had new two piece bathing suits, but Priya found it hard to sit on the beach in hers. Priya kept her t-shirt on and had run into the water to get it wet and ran out to sit and then bake in the sun. Not that her dark skin was going to tan much, but she had used a UV 45 lotion to protect her skin just the same.

Shelley though had no qualms about lying out and letting the boys see how she had become even more curvy over the summer. A summer that she had spent at the Academy except for two weeks back to South Africa. Now many of the young students who were in school at Pepperdine University, about a mile away, came to surf at ECO Academy's beach. Brad had hit on Shelley and they had gone out for dinner.

Shelley had come home early and not happy at all that night. "Alright, so I have a poor track record with dating anyone normal. But where do you think we are going to find husbands? And don't tell me that you are going to let your parents arrange a marriage for you. That's just archaic."

"My parents will make a great choice for me," Priya said. She was teasing. She would never let her parents choose for her. They had wanted to for her brothers, but they had lost that chance. Maheshwaran at least married an Indian girl. Chandan had no intention when he married, of marrying an Indian woman.

Priya wanted nothing more than to be Parker's wife. That at least was the dream. She was smart enough to know that once they were all gone from the Academy, that they would most likely see the old classmates infrequently. That Facebook and Twitter was not really going to keep them all bound together.

They would continue to meet in cyberspace, but you could not be married to someone who you only saw through the internet.

Which was why it was alright to fantasize about Parker. For if nothing came of it, then that was alright as well.

"Your parents will find some rich man for you who will want a beautiful brilliant wife he can wear like a watch on his sleeve. You won't get to do any of your own research married to such a man. I am not going to marry until I am thirty and have published at least ten times!" Shelley said. "Now, are you going to talk to

Parker or not?"

Shelley first talked about publishing academically, which was important in the regard that it showed you had used your mind and found something new and different that no one had ever thought of before. Perhaps she would solve the problems about naval sonar and whales in the near future. That would be wonderful and precisely what Dr. Phillips-Lee was looking for to report as a success of the Academy.

"I'll text him. But what do I say? I can't say that I heard that he was asking JCubed about me."

Shelley shook her head, "No of course not. But you text him every few days. Just think of something to send him today. See if he will try out your phone thingy or something."

Priya let out a quick laugh, "It is not a thingie, it is a way to make free video conferencing calls with great resolution and audio, and totally secure. It will have 256 bit encryption, and that would take a few years by a supercomputer to crack."

Shelley probably did not know, but it would take such a long time that Priya could not keep track of how many decimal places the years would take. 128 bit encryption took 149 trillion years to crack. There were 53 decimal places in the number of years 256 bit encryption gave you. It was beyond secure. And she had gotten the code for it in her program in just over 100 lines to securitize the communication channels.

"Whatevs. Just go and text him. Come on. He's only a boy."

Priya knew that she was going to have to do so, or Shelley was going to tease her about it. And Shelley would tease her about it when they weren't alone as well. That would be embarrassing. So far, Priya thought, others did not know how interested she was in Parker.

But how interested in her was Parker?

"Very well. Just let me think what to say." Priya maneuvered her laptop and then set it up so the messaging screen was in front of her. She went to her favorites list and quickly found an image of Parker to click on and began typing.

"R U Busy?"

"That's it? That's how you get his attention?" Shelley said, looking over her shoulder.

"Hey, do you want to talk about Brad some more? Just be quiet."

"No. Not 2 Busy." Parker wrote back a few moments later.

"He's on his phone." Priya said aloud and then typed back, "How's the car? Is it put back together yet?"

"That is what you want to ask?" Shelley was impatient.

"Quiet. What if he switches over to video. And yes, if he is going to drive anywhere, he needs his car. Now where is he…" Priya typed some more. "Oh, Descartes Library."

There were libraries for all the major science disciplines. It was easier to find things and allowed the librarians to be experts of what was in their care. There was one very large library which covered all the humanities.

Priya got her books at the satellite libraries when she needed books, and took them to Socrates Library. A lot of what she needed though was digitized and she could sit at Socrates and just use ECO Academies network to get what she needed.

In computer sciences you found that they led in digitizing their research materials.

"This weekend. Have to get more fat from Taco Bell. Fancy a Taco?"

Shelley giggled. "There. He's asking you out. Say yes."

"I don't like tacos." Priya said. It was honest. She didn't like them.

Shelley said, "That's not the point. They have other things on the menu anyway. Everybody has a salad. You could get a salad."

Priya shook her head. "Alright. When?"

"Late Sunday, after 4."

"I guess that means we are going to Taco Bell on Sunday." Priya said then wrote, "K. See U then."

"Great. I'll pick you up." Parker wrote back.

"Yes. You have a date. Now we have to get you ready for it. We'll have to take the jitney after studies tomorrow to Santa Monica and go shopping. You need a new outfit. I wish there was enough time to have your hair done." Shelley said.

"My hair? My hair is black and straight. You always say its unfair as it needs no help." Priya said.

"But that was before you had a date with Parker Kenneth

Thornton."

"It's not a date. We are going to Taco Bell. He has to get oil to run his car," Priya said.

"That is a date and we are going into town tomorrow and shop. You need to learn to like shopping more too," Shelley said.

"I like shopping. I go on eBay and get things cheap. I have alerts for my favorite auctions…"

Shelley was shaking her head. "Sometimes you need to buy new."

Priya said, "There are a lot of new things on eBay."

"And you never buy them. And I see you shop at Craigslist as well."

Priya laughed nervously, "People don't value things like they should. Especially Americans. They give away a lot of things that are still good. Or they price them too cheap. You could make a fortune just driving around and picking things up that people give away on Craigslist."

Shelley shook her head, "Yeah, but you don't drive yet. And wouldn't that cut into your time to study? I thought the idea was to not only graduate from here with all the degrees that Dr. Phillips-Lee will let us get, but also find jobs after that pay really well. Better than picking up peoples' junk. And how are you really going to know if you can get a good dress on Craigslist. We are going to the Third Street Promenade Mall tomorrow."

"But I have to…" Priya began. She did not want to go shopping.

Shelley said, "Tut. Tut. We are going. Say no more. Look, you can pull up all the shops on your computer and decide which ones we are going to go to first. But we will get you a new dress tomorrow. Or, should I call Nirmayi? She said that I needed to call her if you were ever obstinate about these things."

Maheshwaran's wife was born in America, not India. She had much more progressive attitudes than Priya had. Nirmayi had tried to make Priya learn more about being an American the three years she had lived with her brother and his family. Some of it had worked, and some had not. Priya did after all own a bikini, even if when she wore it, it was always under a dark t-shirt.

Priya knew that when the South African girl got it into her

mind to order anyone about, then it was all over. Shelly's grandfather had been an old time Boer farmer and some of those traits that had ensured that the western Europeans learned how to survive on the veldt, even if they had adopted Apartheid to do so had passed on down to Shelley. Shelly's grandfather, she said, would hate the fact that she was such a good friend with JCubed.

"Very well, tomorrow we go to Santa Monica and shop," Priya said.

"Oh don't sound like it is the end of the world. You have a date with Parker on Sunday."

Priya sighed, "It's not a date..." though she hoped that Parker thought that it was.

-Chapter 5-

"You know we can put a GPS in this heap, don't you? And that isn't anything. I can hook you up to a cross indexing feed that will knock that Apple Siri on your iPhone off its rocker with voice activated search and response through Google, Bing, and every other search program on the planet." Jackson said. Everyone called him JCubed, which he liked. But he thought of himself as Jackson.

Parker was a senior, but he and Jackson had become friends. Parker, Jackson had realized, had an understanding of technology, but did not know how to tweak it to his advantage. The man did research with books for instance. The Professors even thought it a little strange.

Jackson tutored Parker in all things tech. Which was really great since Parker's parents were rich and he passed along that money to the tune of a twenty spot an hour. That added up quick and far faster than Jackson had found ways to spend it.

"I know. You've said so before, but I don't really want to talk at my car," Parker said. It wasn't strange at ECO Academy to have a Sophomore and Senior be friends. What was strange was the reverse tutoring part.

"You know, if you don't take my advice, then why have me as a tutor about all this?" Jackson asked.

Parker took a moment, "Well, up to last year I could go to Yisroel, but he graduated. He, helped me out a lot. Set up my iPhone and my laptop. And, he didn't charge me for it…"

Jackson knew about Yisroel. He had been in a few of his classes when Jackson was a freshmen. They had only talked a few times. Even though the school had only eighty students, you did not have a chance to talk to everyone all the time in a year. Jackson also knew that Parker had arranged for his father to invest in Yisroel's startup. Parker's father and grandfather had invested in quite a few of the graduates of ECO Academy.

Jackson knew that bit about not charging was a dig at him, "I suppose I could teach you for free, but then what value would it be? You have the money, I need the money. You need the knowledge, I have it. Seems like a good mathematical equation."

Parker laughed, "I think you need to study more rhetoric. I think you are a natural."

Jackson laughed too, "Just let me put in the GPS and Priya's HUD display. It won't affect your driving at all. It will enhance the experience for your passenger."

Two other students approached. Jackson knew they were in Parker's study group.

"What HUD display?" the older asked. Guillermo Cordovan was from Costa Rica and studying Botany and Ecology. He was a junior, and the other was his own age. Giulio Andrianò was a chemistry major. Jackson could think of nothing more boring then studying chemistry. And he had to take two courses in chem to round him out, his advisor kept saying.

Things were really only exciting around computers and surfing on the net. But he had gone so far beyond that. He had servers in the cloud that he controlled and that found and indexed new information for him at an exponential rate. He had started on the internet ten years before. Now at fifteen, all the work of the previous years were paying off.

Jackson had made first one server farm, then a second, and then found a way that they could build their own virtual farms. Far too many of the other cloud servers, Dropbox, Amazon, and ISPs gave away free space. Link that together and you could use the hardware that they paid for, free of charge. In a highly scalable way, if you knew what you were about. And Jackson did.

Parker was explaining about the HUD display for the car to the other students. As usual, with technology, he got things wrong.

Jackson said, "No. It is driver safe as it is only controlled from the passenger side window. A night enhancing overlay can be displayed for the driver, but that's it so far. Oh, yeah a small pop up will show and you can position it everywhere but the middle of your window to show the rear view, but only when you are backing up. But for a passenger, it can give you the power of a full computer, and with the voice activation, it is really powerful."

Parker said, "And there are a whole lot of organizations, like the National Transport Safety Board which would want to see it and test it before letting it into a car. You could get into a really big accident if you are distracted by it."

Jackson shook his head. He may not have been driving yet, but he knew that Priya had built precautions into the hardware applications, and he had tweaked the software so a driver could not override things. "Try it. Really. It will make a difference in your Oilhack."

Giulio said, "Oilhack? Instead of Outback. What about Lubearoo?" he laughed and Jackson did as well.

"I like that better," Guillermo said.

Parker said, "You are all just jealous because I have wheels. There is something liberating about being able to drive."

"In Costa Rica, not all that many can afford to have a car. You are fortunate my friend. In more ways than you know. Now JCubed we are to study about the deforestation affects following a hurricane, such as Katrina. Was that not what this hour is to be? Professor Larkman said you were having some difficulty." Guillermo had come to collect him. The truth was that Jackson did not care all that much about the subject. But he knew he had to finish a sixty page report for the end of term. And he had not even thought of a premise yet.

He said, "Very well, later Parker."

"Alright JCubed. And you can install your GPS in my car if you call it an Outback. Not an oilhack."

Jackson nodded. He would do it later that day.

Guillermo often mused about what a different life he and Parker Thornton had. Parker was wealthy by Guillermo's standards. Not that Parker would think so.

Parker admitted that his father made a good income. Parker had never known hunger, and Guillermo had his memories of that. Thankfully, though, as he grew up, Costa Rica had received the bounty of tourists. They gave and spent in ever increasing amounts at home. So much that his parents had found their niche.

His father drove a bus for the tourist companies and most of those who visited Costa Rica liked to tip the driver as they left after an excursion. Usually with American dollars and in denominations they felt were comfortable to America.

Couples would give ten and twenty US dollars to Guillermo's father. With his mother working, they made much more than five times what an average Costa Rican earned. Guillermo and his sisters had started to see the benefits of their parents' good fortune a few years back. Just when he was able to start studying in earnest. After two years of school, his parents had placed him in a techica a few years ahead of when he would normally go, and then at the age of eleven he had his degree in Ciencias. It was off to the Universidad de Santo Tomas. His professors there helped him to excel.

Guillermo's parents worked hard to put him though school and then to be accepted to ECO Academy. It was always a struggle, but they lived better than many others in Costa Rica. Sometimes Guillermo conceded that his life in San Jose was like Parker's life in Kansas City. They were better off than many others. Parker however was a lot better off than Guillermo.

Only when he thought about it, did he envy the other boy. Almost all the rest of the time, he and Parker got along very well. They were in the same study group and saw each other all the time because of it.

"Wow, you look like you've zoned out. Earth to Guillermo. Earth calling Guillermo," A girl said.

"Huh? Oh Jenny. How are you?" Jennifer Smythe-Lytton sat down next to him. She was a sophomore and studying biochemistry. She seemed to be always about. He had once asked her on a date, but she had said no. Guillermo did not have the courage to ever ask again.

"I'm good, but what's wrong with you? You were staring into the wall like Superman with those laser eyes. Can you really see what is on the other side?"

He smiled, they were in Descartes Library so he said, "Books. And then more books."

She giggled. "I knew that too. Hey, did you ever have Professor Dejanu tell you that the research you needed was not in any textbook? I don't get it."

"Ah, she means that you have to do your own work and slice

and dice your own DNA sampling, then let what you create live in a Petri dish for a while. You have to do the work yourself. You will find that whatever you need may indeed already have been done, but Dejanu wants you to do some work yourself," he said. Dejanu made all her sophomore students do that at sometime.

"She wants me to take a sample of my own blood?"

He smiled. If anyone could do it, it would be Jenny. Her father was the head of the university medical facility. For 80 students and 30 senior faculty, and several hundred staff Dr. Smythe-Lytton actually had a very comprehensive team. There were five doctors, and though not listed as professors, they all lectured. Trying to find ways and means to train the next generation of scientists to save the world meant understanding how the human body interacted on the planet now, and in a future that had some of the earth's ills cured.

All the students took a course in medical biology once each year to better understand man's interaction with the planet, and the planet's interaction with man. A few even were also working to add preliminary work for a Medical Degree that they could pursue after they graduated from ECO Academy.

Guillermo suspected that Jenny would do so, if she and her father ever could speak to each other. The two were estranged. It was very curious. Apparently the Doctor and Jenny's mother had divorced, which was not unique. But the Doctor then saw little of his daughter as she grew up. Again, many families had similar circumstances.

When Jennifer was accepted to ECO Academy though, Dr. Phillips-Lee had hired Dr. Smythe-Lytton to head the medical staff. And there was no way that Dr. Phillips-Lee could not have known about Jenny and her father. The two doctors were friends. Which led some to think that Jenny had been accepted because of it.

Those who did not know that Jenny was as smart as all the others at the school, were severely oblivious to the obvious. O2theO. Everyone said O2theO when they wanted to talk about a fool. It was something that was right for the conversation he and Jenny were having.

"O2theO. Any DNA will do, though you can swab your spit instead of taking blood. Blood is so yesterday. The point is to learn how to use PCR machines, gene sequencers, and biotechnology programs to determine how proteins function. Or to compare species data. There is going to be a lot of that in your junior and senior years, as well as in practical application once you leave ECO Academy. In the real world, we are going to be looking at DNA from many different species, including flora. And one day, we'll be able to analyze a person's whole genome in minutes, and we theorize that just by looking at DNA, and using computer testing protocols, we can see how specific biochemical reactions, drug reactions, will proceed in any person, without human trials. Individualized medicine will become a reality. It will save billions, and reduce the cost of medicine."

She laughed, "Oh no. It may save the cost for big Pharma, but nothing will ever reduce the price of medicines. They may cost less to make, but they will still charge the same for it. Even more if they can figure out a way to do so."

He laughed. Medicine did not cost as much in Costa Rica as it did in the United States, or England he imagined. Jenny was from London.

"You are probably right. It does seem that the big companies are always talking about cutting costs, and if they do, the consumers never benefit from it," Guillermo had to agree. When he finished his schooling, he did not know if he was going to go back to San Jose, or pursue work that was more international. He was a Junior so he had some time before he had to really think about it.

One thing about attending ECO Academy was that you really did not have to worry about your future. Every graduate was either gainfully employed, or pursuing additional learning somewhere. The world's richest companies may have often been opposed to doing things Green, but there was such changing sentiment amongst the people that the grassroots movement was sure to swamp the same old same old mentality soon.

Guys like JCubed, plugged into the 'Net and the mathematical sciences that went with it, calculated that there was an upswing happening amongst the world's populations that would make it a reality soon enough. JCubed felt sometime in the next twenty to thirty years. Guillermo hoped he was right.

"Of course I am right. I am always right about stuff like that." She was very self-assured for a sophomore. "So a saliva swab and comparison to other DNA. I did not even know we had DNA sequencers… They must be in the chem lab, but I've been in the chemistry lab and I haven't seen them."

He smiled, "Would you know them if you saw them? You know we have tweaked them a few times since they were first invented. In any case, they are in Medical, not the labs. You could speak to your father…"

She gave him a very dirty look then. "I'll talk to anyone else first, thank you very much. Why does medical have them?"

"We are, after all, children, Jenny. You do remember that. An adult has to supervise all such use of gene sequencing. There are laws in the US about who can know what about each of us. Their is a clause in the admission packets which had to be signed, or initialed by your folks so you could do the test, but the test is supervised so that an adult ensures no one else can see your DNA information."

She nodded. "What about the sampling we take to compare against for our paper? Professor Dejanu wants that from living organisms, right?"

He smiled, "Yes. You can collect the samples from the Ark, or anywhere really. No other human as I remember from last year, though, and then you take the sample back to Medical to get tested. If you take another human sample you would get in trouble."

The Academy had a farming and veterinary project further up the canyons. Most called it the ECOArk. There were a male and female of many of the animal species that were common to earth, and then plans were underway to also include many of the animals that were endangered, and were not too hard to take care of. The deadly species, and not only protecting them, but studying them, might one day be brought to the Ark, but there were not enough people, both students, faculty, and employees to take care of such a menagerie.

There were however, some animals that one would not think to see in Malibu California. Giraffes for instance and Gazelles. Dr. Phillips-Lee wanted to bring over Elephants as well. Mating pairs of every sub-species of the big beasts, but the Ark's neighbors protested and the billionaire founder of the school was slowly buying those who had objected out of their homes with the long-term goal of creating a definitive place of learning for all.

"Hmm, Priya says she likes going out to the Ark. Maybe I can get her to go with me."

"Priyanka Zadari? I didn't know you were friends."

"Yes, she and I have the same class on the History of Technology together. You know, that Connections class."

He nodded, "From Dr. Burke's series, *Connections*. Yes. I have all the videos from the original in the cloud. There are other imitators but it is fascinating to see how one step here, and then another there, and everything connects back."

"We stand upon the shoulders of Giants," she quote Sir Isaac Newton. He was sure that not everyone knew who to attribute that to. Though he was sure all the students at ECO Academy had heard it. If they looked hard enough, they would see that the Physics building, which was actually small, had it inscribed above the entry. There were only three lecture rooms and two labs in the Physics building. But as with all the instruction halls on campus, room to grow up and out from the long quad.

There were 12 buildings clustered around the long quad, and eight at each of the two grass plains that spoked away from a central circular area. Often he thought that a bird might mistake the whole of ECO Academy for an airport terminal. The buildings were where airplanes might park around grass and tree lawns that students sat upon when the weather was nice. Which it quite often was.

"Yes, we do. And you need to think carefully about which animals, or flora you choose to run your sequencing against. A too complex species and you will only make some BWAGs. At least that is what Professor Dejanu thinks. And she is usually right. No one, for instance, has compared Humans to Ostriches."

"Really? We have some Ostriches at the Ark."

He smiled, "I was joking. That is what Dejanu said when we

turned our results in last year." And after he had considered it for a bit, there were probably researchers who had taken the time to compare virtually every species' DNAs to man. To each other might be another story.

Jennifer, Guillermo thought, was someone fettered by her relationship with her father. Dr. Smythe-Lytton was supposed to be pretty smart. Brilliant else he would not be attached to ECO Academy. But Jennifer was poised to eclipse the man. Everyone could see it. She was probably smarter than anyone else on the campus and she was just fifteen. Her father may have been a brilliant doctor but Jennifer was going to be a brilliant doctor and scientist provided she could get rid of the baggage she carried. Mention her father to her and she would get all mad, but she was British. So you could see it in her face, and her words became short one syllable things that all seem to have the ends bit off.

Mention her father and Jennifer would almost always find some reason to leave really quickly.

"So perhaps comparing and cross-comparing exotic species…" Jennifer began to think of the problem.

Guillermo said, "Remember, it is only a quarter course. You have what, eight more weeks to complete the assignment."

"And if I can line up time at the Medical Center next week it will be perfect," she finished her thought with a smile on her face. Guillermo didn't know why and he knew that his own face must have betrayed that.

Jennifer enlightened him, "The chief doctor is away at a medical conference next week. Which means that he won't be around the center at all." Calling Dr. Smythe-Lytton by his title allowed Jennifer to keep even more distance from him.

Guillermo knew that she did this more from reasons other than not wanting anyone to think she had favored treatments But Jennifer acted like that was the reason. She forgot that she was at a school of geniuses. Run by geniuses.

Everyone knew that she had not gotten favored treatment to get in, and anyone who spent time talking to the girl could see she was destined for a great career. Though each year all students had a course on practicality. There were a few scientists so wrapped up in their brilliance that they could think of things that were too far beyond understanding that their research would have no helpful bearing for humanity.

That was a great thing, and the faculty encouraged such intelligent thought. But they also wanted their students to be grounded. Dr. Phillips-Lee said on first day orientation to all new classes, how it would be great to invent Faster Than Light travel, but having an FTL drive would do no good if the other sciences had not advanced to build the starships for it. Or the technologies to aid what to do when they had used the FTL to take them to other worlds. Worlds that probably did not have oxygen.

So Dr. Phillips-Lee encouraged those who might discover such a breakthrough. But he reminded the students that saving the earth might be a more productive use of their time then figuring out how to get off of it.

Guillermo's parents, even starting poor, had provided him with a loving environment with a tremendous amount of support. He could see that, and he could see how Jennifer was troubled by her own family life.

"I don't think that your father is going to disappear from ECO Academy all the times you need to go to the Medical Center. And you are studying Biochemistry. You'll need the gene sequencers again over the next three years. Maybe you should, if not make peace, at least a truce, with your father? Don't run off mad, just think that if you find a way to work with the man there, you might find it easier to live here at ECO Academy, knowing that he lives here as well?"

She shook her head, and clearly was getting angry.

Guillermo shrugged his shoulders.

"Thank you!" she said but he could tell she did not mean it. Jenny walked away. He shrugged his shoulders and then looked down at his iPad. JCubed had jailbroken it and put a whole host of programs on it. Right then, he was using a Windows interface to retrieve documents from the Sorbonne on Water Conservation. There was a lecture upcoming about it, and Dr. Phillips-Lee was going to speak at a conference as well.

The Aral Sea and its disappearance had become critical. If someone, a team of someones could make a breakthrough and refill it, the world would heal a little bit. And that was the goal of ECO Academy. Healing things. Including the bonds between a daughter and her father.

"It is just terrible!" Jennifer said. She was talking to Shelley and Priya in the middle of the Right Spoke oval. There was a garden in the center of the oval. Though all the ovals seemed empty for the grounds had been laid out for thousands of students. Not eighty.

If someone wanted to be alone, there was plenty of space on campus for them to be. But that was also a security issue. All students had locators on them that the security team, headed by the ex Israeli commando, was able to monitor. More importantly heat sensors and other devices matched up the locators and their images to determine if there were intruders on the campus. And on occasion there were that the security team then caught and turned over to the Los Angeles Sheriffs.

"That Guillermo would talk to you about Dr. Smythe-Lytton? But at some time, almost everyone talks to you about the man," Priya said.

"But Guillermo knows that it upset me."

Shelley was trying not to laugh. She was not doing a good job at it. "Come now. You like the boy. I like him too. He's kind of sexy, in that latin way."

Jennifer shook her head. She would never say that Guillermo was sexy to anyone else. Even though she thought it. "No. I don't like people prying into the relationship with my father."

Priya said, "Jennifer, everyone is going to over time. You said that the Dr. Phillips-Lee even mentioned it to you specially."

Jennifer shook her head. She had told the two about it when the head of the ECO Academy had done so earlier in the year, shortly after there had been an incident between Jennifer and the staff at the Medical Center. Jennifer had to go to the center and have a physical. She had requested a female doctor, and though they complied, they thought it strange since Jennifer was not from a culture which put weight on such matters.

The doctor had mentioned she would share the results with Jennifer's father, but Jennifer had told her not to. That he was not her legal guardian and was not to see or be told of anything about her health. Part of the Doctor Patient confidentiality that American Doctors thought sacred.

Jennifer had to take a very strong stance, and used words that a fourteen year old girl was not supposed to use. It had infuriated the woman physician, and later she had gone and told Jennifer's father of the test results. Doctor Biatch, as Jennifer had called her, was fired for breaking the pact of confidentiality and Jennifer's nickname for the Doctor had stuck. But Dr. Phillips-Lee had taken Jennifer into his office to explain a few things.

Dr. Phillips-Lee had seen her father when he had been a student at Oxford. They had known each other for over thirty years. Her father had treated Dr. Phillips-Lee when he had been in private practice. Dr. Phillips-Lee had been at the wedding of her parents, and had even sent her a christening gift when she was a baby. When she had proven smart, he had begun watching her with an interest in bringing her to ECO Academy if she could meet the requirements.

Which she did quite easily.

Dr. Phillips-Lee had only thought to bring her father to the school when he had learned that the two were estranged. That her parents had a falling out and her father had retreated back to Oxford and his original practice, leaving Jennifer and her mother to live in London. Jennifer's mother cashed her father's checks readily enough, but never spoke well of him.

Jennifer was sure that her father had done something so bad that her mother did not even like to date men any longer because of it. Jennifer's mother was always saying how thankful she was that she had girlfriends to support her after all the trouble Jennifer's father had caused her.

Dr. Phillips-Lee had told Jennifer that part of the time at ECO Academy was to help the students build character as well as learn advance studies. Healing the rift with her father might just help Jennifer prepare for being an adult, he said. Jennifer had told the gist of the conversation to Shelly and Priya, knowing that they would keep a secret. Shelly though had to be often reminded that the matter was a secret.

"Dr. Phillips-Lee said that I needed to deal with the matter else it would stick to me as an adult. He has children that he shares custody of with one of his ex-wives. He says he does not see them as much as he should. That no parents ever see their children as much as they should, and that he is sure that children resent that." Jennifer had seen Dr. Phillips-Lee about the matter three times now. He was doing his best to broker an entente.

"He's probably right. Do you resent your father for not seeing you?" Priyanka asked.

Jennifer was shaking her head but she did resent her father for abandoning her.

"Not for not seeing me," was what she said.

"Hell, I hate my father and I saw him all the time. Well, I don't haaattte my father so much as think he is out of touch. He's old, you know," Shelly said.

Priya laughed. "He's older than you. But Old is a very subjective opinion. My father is a little older than yours and I do not think him that old. My father is not yet fifty. My father's father is old."

"My father isn't forty yet. But he is still old." Shelly said.

Jennifer said, "Really? My father is older than fifty. He married my mother just a year before I was born. She was a lab tech at his offices." Jennifer knew that. It was actually seven months before she was born. Jennifer knew enough now to understand that her mother was probably pregnant when her parents had gotten married.

"Well, age does not matter so much now as the relationships with our parents," Priya said. "That is what all the sitcoms are about." Jennifer thought that a little strange. She didn't think that Priya watched a lot of television.

"Urggh. Okay. I'll think about it!" Jennifer said. She had enough of the subject and was sure that sounding angry would get the other two to stop talking about it. She had wanted to talk about Guillermo butting into her life, and instead got her two friends to butt in as well. It seemed that whenever she brought up the subject of her father, or someone else did, everyone wanted her to reconcile with the man.

Changing the subject worked best. "Did you see that Dr. Phillips-Lee is going to take five students with him to the Aral Sea conference? All you have to do is write a great paper, and make a presentation to him about it."

Shelly laughed, "He wants you to do his work for him. He doesn't know much about the situation, but it is obviously a thing that would benefit from Green help. From the help of the Ecological Conservation Organization."

Priya said, "His specialization is in chemistry. It will take more than that discipline to solve. I don't believe my studies can help in any way?"

"Why not? There are a lot of dams that choked off the flow of water to the Sea. Can't you think of some sort of computer program and mechanical system to monitor so all work together in harmony and more water flows back to the old seabed?" Shelly asked.

Jennifer said, "Yes, I bet we all could think of something. It should also be an all academy challenge. Eighty of us having ideas, should create something for the conference."

Shelly said, "Or five somethings. I bet the five lucky students get to present their ideas as well, and that is exposure."

Priya agreed then, "I have never heard that Dr. Phillips-Lee steals the ideas of his students. Very well, I'll work on something. Maybe even the integrated program you suggested Dr. Smythe-Lytton." Priya was smiling.

Jennifer smiled back. "Thank you Dr. Zadari. I shall work on something as well. Dr. Botha, shall we see something from you too?"

"Oh, very well. What, we have two weeks to submit our solutions? Like I have time... And Priya, you were going to tell us about Tacos with Parker..." The clock though was chiming signaling that it was time for class, and Jennifer picked up her laptop bag so she could hurry off, not hearing what Priya was saying to Shelly.

-Chapter 6-

The ZED Corp offices in Santiago were not considered as plum an assignment as being posted to Rio de Janeiro, which was the main office for all the South American presence. But being the head of any national office in the ZED Corp hierarchy had its advantages.

You were like a god amongst the other employees of the company. There were rules in effect to protect the various underlings from being blatantly abused, but only a few. Should you show that you could make them all work towards a greater profit than the Rio office expected, or even better, get the London office to notice your work, you were a God who was going to rise a rank or two in the near term.

That was one thing that Francisco Valdez y Gonzalez knew. He used to be the number two at the Bogota office. No one could point a finger to his showing up his boss there as wrong. No one had the cojones. No one had the guts to point a finger at Francisco.

But then Francisco was very good at covering his tracks. He had learned a few things about the Columbian operations. He had learned that there were certain warehouses you could purchase and then offer to share the space with others who needed warehouses. You could then put very expensive machinery, or other items in the warehouse and no one would think twice about touching. You could cut down on your security costs greatly.

You could do this because the cartels of course were providing security for their product inside the warehouse, gratis. Partnering with the Drug Cartels had other advantages as well. He allowed them space on trucks used for shipping, and they gave him little gifts.

Such gifts as arranging dates with some very beautiful women. Women who liked to live expensive lifestyles and were on the speed dial of cartel members. Francisco did not do enough favors for the Cartels to cause the leaders to trust him entirely though. If they wanted to be seen with a woman that Francisco liked, they got to date her and Francisco would have to go out with another.

One did not assert oneself with even the least member of the illegal organization. That could be deadly. You just kept finding new favors to do for them and you were rewarded.

Francisco was also smart enough to know that one day he might be deleted on a whim.

ZED Corp home office liked some of the numbers that Bogota was producing. But soon enough they were going to ask questions. It took being a little creative, but documents showing the agreements between the Cartels, at least between ZED Corp and the legal operations of the Cartels front companies seemed to all be signed by Francisco's boss. A man with a family. Seven children. He took to heart the instructions of the Bishop and was in church every Sunday.

Then one day a few months before he had gotten a call.

"Is this Francisco Valdez y Gonzalez?" he was asked in English. The video feed on the phone was blocked, with the screen showing Private Feed, on it.

"Si." They were in Columbia. The Americanos thought way too much of themselves, always pushing their language.

"It's a little late here for me, Francisco. I can only give you a few minutes of time, but then I have an engagement. Actually I am being driven to it now. This is Zedadiah Carter." Francisco shook himself. That was the boss. The big Padrone, and it sounded like him as well. No wonder he spoke English.

"Hello Mr. Carter. It is a very real pleasure to talk to you."

"Good. I hope you realize that I usually do not talk to my National presidents, let alone their lieutenants. We have a problem and I think you are the man to help me," Zedadiah Carter said. The company was named after him.

"Of course sir. I shall do anything required," Francisco was having his few minutes of fame.

"Good, good. You've put up some impressive numbers. I like that. And the board likes that. Well they usually like what I like. But we have a problem. Those who are helping you to put up those numbers, they often cause problems. Do you know what I mean?"

Francisco swallowed. What was he to do now? Lie? He thought

quickly, for there had been no evidence that he spoke to the Cartels, or any paperwork about such matters. All such paperwork had his boss there in Columbia's name on them.

And that meant that somehow Mr. Carter and those who worked for him in London knew that he was the one who arranged to work with the Cartels.

"I think I do understand, Mr. Carter."

Francisco heard a chuckle. Still no video, but Francisco saw the indicator light showing he was being watched. He was tempted to click on the button to turn off the video feed, but he stopped a second before doing so. If the boss was watching him and he shut off the video, chances are Mr. Carter would make some remark about it.

"Good. I will be frank. I liked the reports out of Bogota, until I discovered our new unofficial partners were making the numbers turn in our favor. Now I have no problem with partners whose respect for the law differ then my own. As long as I don't get dragged down into their troubles. Do you understand what I am saying?" At the end Mr. Carter spoke with some force.

Francisco agreed, "Si. I do."

"Good. I will speak honestly. I had thought of terminating you, and with ZED Corp that means being fired. Not being fired at. Which I think these partners you have brought us would do. Colonel Kutuzov is going to ask you for the numbers of all your contacts later, and you best give everything you have to him. You see I have to undo some of what you have done."

Francisco knew things were now not so good anymore. He had a date later with one of the beauties that being an associate of the Cartel allowed him. Now it was more than likely he would not be able to keep that date. "I understand Mr. Carter." Francisco knew he was being given orders.

"Now don't you worry. Should the Cartels not be happy, well, I don't think they will go after you. But in any case, I am transferring you to Santiago. You leave tomorrow. You can either arrange someone in the office there to send your things to Santiago, or let HR take care of it. Spend six months learning the ropes and then Chile is yours. I'll give you two years to see if you can beat my expectations like Colombia has done, but after that, if you can't do it, then we'll let you go. You understand, in Chile, I don't want to have to have Colonel Kutuzov and his men make any special arrangements."

Francisco understood. "Yes sir. I will not renew my associations that I have made here in Bogota, in Santiago."

"Precisely. You know that we have a significant portion of the lithium reserves that are in Chile, and that is 75% of the world's deposits. I would like to ensure that we have the majority holdings in Chile in the near term, and boost output there to double what it is now. 7,500 tonnes a year makes a great amount of money, and should we have half or more of that, and we then mined twice as much, well that would make me happy."

Francisco understood again. Get over half of the resources of such a valuable commodity, and double the output. Do it all in two years, or be fired.

"There are other items to see to as well. Water rights in Chile are large. A third of the world's copper. Wine. All these are important to Chile and ZED Corp. Look into that as well." These were orders that Francisco knew he had to follow. Zedadiah Carter was not a person to be disobeyed. Just as Francisco expected those who were ranked below him in the company to follow orders, he had to follow the orders of the company president.

If he wanted to keep his job. And the job not only paid well, it provided opportunities for graft.

He couldn't steal from the company. That would be caught.

Just as they seemed to know about his dealings with the Cartels despite trying to place such transactions on his boss in Bogota. No, cash transactions, satchels and briefcases full of money, that could be transferred from one person to another without the home office ever knowing.

And that money could be taken to banks in the Cayman Islands, which were as good as Swiss Banks for discretion. A numbered account and only his banker knew what he looked like. He could be at a branch and back in a day from Bogota, but Santiago, he would have to stay overnight in the Caribbean.

Francisco was not married yet. Vacations to the Caribbean to play would not be seen as inappropriate. He could mask what he was really doing, and put money into his own accounts. That was something he was sure that Zedadiah Carter would never know about. And if Francisco exceeded the demands and goals that Mr. Carter set, then he would never question Francisco.

That was another thing about Americanos. They were very indignant should they find that they were being cheated. But here in countries where a little money was used to grease a deal to success, they would provide the slush to make such a deal work. They just did not want to hear the details of how it worked. If they did learn of it, they had to act all indignant in their newspapers, and make corrections until no one was looking any longer. Than they could go back to making things work as they should.

And along the way, Francisco was going to line his pockets. At least he could say he did not do it just for himself. The money he earned not only helped to give him a great living, but his mother no longer lived in a two room decrepit apartment. Now she lived in a modern condo with two bedrooms, a kitchen, a living room. A modern bathroom with water that was always running and clean. Electricity that almost always worked, and a great big screen television.

When the phone call was finished with the Russian security chief, Kutuzov, Francisco had to think how to tell his mother he was leaving for Chile, and then decide if he should move her or not. In the end that decision was easy. His mother had no intention of leaving Bogota where she liked to show off the riches her son had bought to their old neighbors and her friends.

He had lived in Santiago a week when he had another phone call, this time the video feed was not obscured. "So Francisco, you have moved away. I hope you are well." The speaker addressed him in Spanish and the whole conversation was spoken in that language.

"I am Señor. It is good to talk to you once more." You addressed a man in the Cartels with humility and as a supplicant. One should never try to have the upper hand with a man who can say a few words and field an army of hundreds prepared to kill, or prepared to die.

"Good. I am disappointed a little that you left Bogota so

quickly and did not say despedida. We are such old friends now, that I do not expect a Russian to understand how close we have become."

Francisco knew that the men of the Cartel needed to think a little more respectfully about men like Colonel Kutuzov. He was sure the Colonel paid the Cartels the respect that they clamored for. "If you will allow me to point out, the Colonel, from what I know, takes his job very seriously and professionally. I hope I have never misled you about the abilities that he and the men he has who work for him can command."

The man chuckled on the screen, "Oh no, you have been a very good friend. In fact you have a reservation tonight at Astrid y Gastón and I believe there is a very fetching woman who shall be your companion at your table. A gesture that you should remember who your friends are. As for the Russian, we will let him think that he has made it clear, is that not what the Americanos say? That he has made it clear on what he and his Corporation will allow."

Francisco had hoped he was to get away from the devils that ran the Cartels. But it was just a hope. He knew when he offered the warehouse space and other favors to them that he would never find it easy to distance himself from them. Now it was proving true. Astrid y Gastón, the restaurant that the man had mentioned was very hard to get into in Santiago. Having lived in the city all of a week, Francisco had learned that.

"I am being watched now by Mr. Carter. If I am to be useful to you, I have to be very discreet about what I do for you."

"Si. We know this. We want you to be circumspect in all that you do, for one day, when you can do us a great deal of good, that is when we shall talk to you. And you know you do not want to disappoint us. I shall make sure you have a phone that you may call me to give me a stock tip perhaps. Or to tell me of a shipment that this billionaire you work for, will find can be taken from him. I do not just sell the coca to make money."

Though Francisco talked to a lieutenant in the Cartel, he was quite sure that the Cartel probably had more financial assets than ZED Corp. The thing about a criminal organization is that they did not report to the SEC. Though they paid a great deal of money to the governments where they operated, none of it was in the form of tax. It was all in the form of graft.

There was no government official that was immune to bribery, or coercion. Even in New Zealand, which had been rated the least corrupt government on the planet. With a reputation as a member of the drug cartels and the measures that they would go to, the mere threat against an honest politician or one of his family members, and they became like clay to be molded any way the gangster wanted.

"Yes, Señor. Of course I shall do this little thing as you say. It is nothing."

It was not nothing, but to say otherwise was only begging for trouble. Trouble was something Francisco had learned to avoid with the Cartels very quickly. He knew that should he ever suggest that he was not a compliant friend to them, his life would be over. They would kill him. They had no compunction about killing policemen, judges, politicians, and innocent bystanders. A man who did not jump when they said to do so was a dead man.

And then they would look at their phone list and call the next man they had bought or corrupted to get to do their bidding. It was as simple as that.

"Of course you will amigo. Of course you will. Now go to your dinner, and not a word of this to our Russian friend. He may have thought to have listened in on this conversation, but some friends took out three bugs from your home yesterday. If the Russian looks at you funny, you will tell me, for I do not want him to think we have not given every consideration to his strong suggestions." Francisco understood that as well.

Colonel Kutuzov was said to be part of the old KGB. A man who knew his way around force. He might even have threatened the man Francisco was talking to. That would have been a mistake. The man he talked to did not like to be threatened. Francisco did not think that any man or woman who had thought to threaten him was still alive.

"Of course I will tell you at once, Señor," Francisco said.

"Good boy, Valdez y Gonzalez. I shall send flowers this week to your mother. I am sure an old widow as she will find that they brighten her home." That was the threat to a loved one.

"Señor, please do not trouble yourself."

"Oh son, it is no trouble. You do not think I have forgotten where she lives, do you? Now go on your date. I think you may like it so much that you can have a table there once each week." A hefty bribe indeed. Especially if it meant he would entertain the beautiful ladies.

"I would agree, Señor, but Mr. Carter does not pay me that well, and the Colonel would surely notice."

That gave the man on the other end of the video call pause, "Hmm, yes you are right."

Francisco, if he was going to be killed at a young age for this connection did not want to lose all the creature comforts he could get. "There are less expensive restaurants that I can escort lovely señoritas to. Perhaps if you allow me to choose the location…"

The man laughed, "Ha! And I find you the girl and pay your bill. Yes you are a smart one. Too bad you are there in Santiago and not still in Bogota. Oh we could use you here still. Well, your Mr. Carter did not totally kill the deal that you had worked with us. There is hope that one day you will even have more power than you have now."

"In six months, Señor. Then I am to be in charge of all of Chile. I must learn from the man already in charge."

The man in his phone screen nodded, "Yes. This next week or so, a man will offer you and your company shares in his copper mine. It should be enough that your Mr. Carter will think that you do well. But I will say no more, and I cannot do such favors often. We do not have as many friends in Chile as I do here in Columbia."

Francisco said, "Gracias Señor. Muchas gracias."

"Do not grovel, Valdez y Gonzalez. Do not grovel. It is a favor. You shall do me one soon, you can rely on it." The video connection cut right after the man said that.

Francisco knew those last words were true prophecy. The Cartel had him and they would never let him go. Or they would kill him first. Not that he looked back on his deciding to work with the Cartel as a mistake. It allowed him to enjoy life on such a scale which he had not before, he had agreed to work with them.

Francisco may have sold his soul to the devil, but the rewards were worth it.

Two years later, he ruled the operations of ZED Corp in Chile as if he were a king. Or at least a prince in the empire of ZED Corp. He had heard from the Cartels three times and had sent them information that they could act on to their interest, perhaps a dozen times since he had moved to Santiago.

He was known as a playboy, and dated a handful of the most glamorous single women of the city. He could not choose to settle and have a family with any of the girls for they were all controlled by the Drug Cartel, just as ultimately his strings were pulled by them. And his account in the Cayman's was very full. Nearly eight figures in US Dollars full.

Sometimes Francisco fantasized that he could take the money and run from his current life. He just was not sure where he could run too. He might succeed in hiding from the Z Men of ZED Corp security, but he would never run far enough to escape the Drug Cartels.

No one was able to run far enough, hide well enough, that they could do so. Even if his money was in a private unidentifiable bank account. He would be found should he try to spend the amounts he had saved.

Today he was reviewing ideas to boost the ZED Corp financials even better than they had reported before. One thing that he had achieved was producing better results than Zedadiah Carter had expected every year. Francisco had even been at the reception at the London Headquarters for the man's fortieth birthday. Francisco thought wryly how the billionaire had joked that he wanted to visit the Chilean offices, especially if Francisco would be able to introduce him to the models and starlets that he knew.

The ladies that Francisco knew would jump at the chance to meet his boss. And then try to keep him. They would hope it would be their way out of the traps they were in, just like he was. The Cartels would even encourage such a match, hoping that one day they could reach out and grasp their former girls to do whatever they wished once more.

That birthday visit to London was more than two months ago

and nothing had come of it. Today, unless he thought of new ways to exploit the wealth of Chile for ZED Corp, they were not going to have another breakout year. And being noticed in London depended on breakout years.

They had more than half the lithium reserves tied up, and they had more than half of Chile's copper output as well. All the low hanging fruit was taken. But Pedro Ramirez had an idea that was worth talking about.

"Pedro, sit, sit. No need to stand at attention. You have not been in the army for much more than a year now. Time to think like a civilian," Francisco smiled, "Or to at least act more like one."

"Yes sir." The man sat, though he did so with precision and stiffness. He perched on the chair opposite Francisco more than he sat in it.

Francisco had come from around his desk to sit in one of the two chairs that were around a low coffee table in the corner of his rather large office. ZED Corp had several floors from the top down of a modern gleaming tower in the Sanhattan area of Santiago.

There also was a couch along the wall, but Pedro was smart in not sitting on the couch. Francisco knew that the rumors at the office were that all the glamorous women that he dated had spent time with him on that couch. Most of the rumors were wrong.

"Now Pedro, your report. We have purchased a great many rights to water. I do not see how cornering the market in these Regions, Aisén, Magallanes and Los Lagos, will make us a power in the world all based on water."

"It is a three fold plan sir. I have done my best to spell it out in my report."

Francisco nodded, "I have read your report, but I wanted you to take me through it anyway."

Francisco had glanced at the report. Others often used hyperbole to claim that they could corner a market from their ideas, and always he knew it to be exaggeration and nonsense. When Pedro wrote of it in the report, Francisco knew he had to find out more.

The report was exhaustive with details. Charts, tables, full extracts of scientific articles and of nonsense that no sane man could understand. Best that he make Pedro put into simple Spanish so he could then tell those in London what they were going to do.

If, that was, Francisco decided it was worthwhile.

"Sir?" Pedro had risen to Captain in the army, but could not see that rising higher was all about politics. That was a legacy of Pinochet. The man had good combat abilities, but no one wanted a war in South America unless it was to kill rebels.

Or to hunt the drug dealers. The one way he could be released from his association from the Cartel were if another rose to power and destroyed those who had his life by a leash.

"Come, Pedro. I have to translate all this to English and tell not only Rio, but London what it is we should do. To purchase a monopoly of water rights in three Regions is going to be expensive. Much more pesos than I have to spend from our normal funds."

Pedro nodded, "I understand Mr. Valdez y Gonzalez. I shall see if I can speak to the important points."

Francisco laughed, then picked up the report from the table. It was over half an inch thick, "It is rather a lot of material."

That was the first Francisco then saw of the man smiling. Far too serious to advance at ZED Corp, but a good tool to use. Francisco prided himself on knowing how to use tools.

"Firstly, just owning water rights in large quantities poises us to control speculation. As many did with the oil markets a few years before. Rising prices to near 150 dollars US for each barrel. Owning enough rights, and we can put pressure to do the same, but with water."

"You do know that were we ever caught manipulating the price of water, or of profiting inordinately we would be subject to legal prosecution." Francisco had been lectured for over three hours once by Colonel Kutuzov that the company did not like to be scrutinized so. At the end of which the Colonel reminded Francisco of how much help he had been with the Cartels and ensuring Francisco could still breath. The Colonel was a fool is what Francisco thought and did not understand South America.

"Yes, I do, but there is little that can be done. We have fought for the right to sell water. We have villages where they no longer get any water because all the rights have been sold, and the government has to buy it for them and disperse it like charity. You are Columbia, but here in Chile, we shall never give up this right, and that is where ZED Corp will make a fortune."

Pedro spoke like a zealot, or a patriot. Many though, Francisco knew, believed as the man did. "Very well. We purchase rights, but that is no guarantee that we can make a monopoly or that we can make a profit."

"It is industry, Señor. Every year, it needs more water, which makes it dear. Now the people need water as well. That causes the value to rise each year, and should we have these Regions, then we have the tail that wags the dog, no?"

There was a part of the report that explained how that was. How three Regions set the tone for the price that water would fetch. Francisco was not sure he understood it. But then he did not have to understand it, if it was true and would work. "Very well. We buy enough of the rights to control the market. That could cost a lot of Pesos"

"Si. Billions. But then we would triple our money in a year, even more than triple." Pedro spoke with confidence. "You see we have other things we can do, we must do to, I do not like to use the words manipulate, but prefer describing it as making the markets respond to our hand upon the tiller."

"Explain more," Francisco said. The man's report showed that he did not exaggerate, but here was a great deal of words that did not say anything.

"There is the new initiative by the Chairman, by Mr. Carter to put wells in every village on the planet in the next ten years. We will need many here for those who no longer have their own water, but what if we need a lot less. Wells, will of course steal the water from those who have purchased the rights to them. Already this news has made the markets for water cheaper than they have been for a decade. And they look to go lower."

"Si, which is why I think your plan has some merit. It does not take as much investment now to corner the market. We like to own markets. ZED Corp likes monopolies. But the wells would be like letting air out of the tires."

"Ah, here is the part of the plan that deals with that. We have a division that has been working on chemicals that reduce hunger in people and animals. That also reduces thirst. If we supply that to the aquifers, and that water comes down to these villages, then they will not need so much water."

Francisco shook his head, "I do not follow you. Explain more, por favor."

"Do you see, the issue of wells has everyone worrying that the amount of water for industries will diminish. It is causing a problem in the equity market as well." Francisco saw that. "The government has had to allow the idea of the wells because starving people is a bad thing."

Francisco laughed, "No politician will allow his constituents to starve. Then there would be no one to vote him back into office."

"Si, of course. And they also like that ZED Corp will pay for the wells. This should have made the water rights skyrocket, since less for industry, but uncertainty has made no one know what will come tomorrow. That is why we must act now."

"Very well, we buy the water and we put in the wells. But then we have less water for Industry and that makes the water we do have more valuable, but not three times as valuable."

Pedro shook his head, "But now we have a monopoly and can charge for how much we sell to the Industries. And we can sell far more than they know because we use the chemicals that have been developed by ZED Corp. Here let me explain some more.

"Say the market thinks that only 100 gallons of water is available because the people will be drinking the other 100 gallons. The government actually likes this because they have been trucking in so much water to so many places for a long time now. This causes the price of a gallon of water to be 100 pesos. But we put the chemicals into the water. And instead of 100 gallons that the people take to drink, they take 20 gallons. That means we can sell 80 more gallons for the 100 pesos. The industries want that water too because they have been using it."

Now Francisco could see it. "Two things, one is that more water is used for washing and cleaning then for drinking, and eventually the industries will see we can meet their demand for water, so the price will return to normal."

Now Pedro had an answer for that, and Francisco remembered

reading about his objections in the report, "First, when you only get so much water rationed to you, you develop a lifestyle around drinking and being sparing of its use in cleaning, or watering your flower garden. Those that are served by wells will not be wasteful of the water. Secondly, we will have made such a profit that when water settles back to normal, we can be selling water futures short on the way down as well. From what I have learned since I left the army, one can make a great deal speculating, and even more when you know which way the market is headed."

Francisco nodded. The idea was sound enough to do. London would appreciate it. And once they gave him the funds to start the program, he knew he would have to call his contact in the Cartels as well. Not telling them of such a scheme to invest in would definitely lead to an unpleasant final outcome for him. The type that involved undertakers and arrangements.

-Chapter 7-

Parker shook himself and the water that was on him and his wet suit went flying in all directions. As he had told his friend Kevin back in Kansas City, he had taken up surfing. Parker knew that there were a great many sports that you could do while you were young, and then later on in life you would not be able to do. You had to choose which ones you would pursue before the body was no longer able to engage in them.

Youth for instance was also a great time to bungie jump. That, however, was an activity Parker had decided not to do. Though he was considering to learn how to skydive. The fear of leaving a perfectly good airplane that had a floor and relying that all the pulls for a parachute would work, held him back.

"Hey! We're working on our tans here!" Shelly shouted at him.

He looked and grinned. They were working on their tans, but she, Priya and their friend Jennifer were doing more than just working on their tans. Jennifer and Shelly had on attractive bathing suits that showed off their curves. And though they were in the midst of a few days of 80 degree temperature, it was near the end of October, and sometimes there was a coolness when the wind blew. Cold enough that the girls had to pretend not to notice.

Priya, though, wore a t-shirt that covered her bathing suit. Most of her legs showed, and she had put sunscreen on them. Parker had offered to help her, as had some of the other boys. Most there knew that he was interested in Priya. That they had gone out for tacos and were planning a trip to downtown LA for hamburgers at the Original Tommy's.

Priya didn't want any help lathering up, but her friends had expressed their need for aid. Parker didn't even have time to reach for the sunscreen before other boys all rushed for it so they could coat Shelly. She was very good looking. And she was pretty damn smart.

Jennifer wasn't forgotten, but she was clearly the second choice. She was younger and not flaunting her sexuality as much as

Shelly. And then her father was nearby. Not down on the beach with the other students. But he was up at the campus. The only parent of any of the students at ECO Academy because he was the head of the Medical Center.

Parker said, "Sorry ladies. I did not mean to get you all wet. Hey, Priya, don't you want to learn how to surf? I'll teach you. You know we are only young once."

She laughed a little at that, "Oh, we are only a great many things once. But I must study. I should not even have come to the beach."

Shelly jumped on those words, "You aren't studying. We have no tests the whole week coming up, and then you are going off to that conference at Aral'sk. Priya's working on a secure computer that the Kazahks won't take. Has to disguise it because it is pretty powerful."

Parker laughed a little. He knew that Priya was capable of doing things like that. "It'll be better than one of those supercomputers, I bet."

Priya smiled, "Well, a little. You do know that the chips today are much better than what the early supercomputers used. My problem is electricity and cooling. Oh and like Shelly said, hiding it from the Kazahks."

Parker shook his head. They did not see the obvious solution. "We are going to be part of Dr. Phillips-Lee's team. No one wants to piss off the Doctor. Especially not soviet era thinking communists, I mean capitalists. No, you tell Dr. Phillips-Lee that you are bringing the computer to support our presentations and he will make sure that no one but you touches it."

"I don't know about that. It is a lot more powerful than anything they will have there. The country is just not that wealthy yet," Priya said.

"Truth is, we need more liberal disciplines around here to do effective research. Solutions for a greener world involve more disciplines than just the sciences we all specialize in. We saw that from our papers and our solutions for the Aral Sea," Parker noted. He had found this flaw in the design of the ECO Academy and had written a supplemental paper to Dr. Phillips-Lee explaining it. "The solutions for the Aral Sea, to bring it back to life are not from just one discipline but from many, which is why five of us are going to go to Asia. Funny, isn't it, but I always think of that part of the world more like Europe, but it isn't."

"I think you are right about more disciplines needing to be studied here at the school." Jennifer said.

"Oh don't say that, he will think that he is a genius." Shelly said.

Another boy came over to join them. JCubed was toweling himself dry from having been in the water with a boogie board. "Parker, think he's a genius? Like that would ever happen," JCubed teased.

The thing was most of those around him had entered the Academy already awarded a bachelor's degree from a university. Parker had come to ECO Academy having mastered college level coursework, and having tested through many university classes. But he did not have a degree. He did not even have a high school diploma until the week before he enrolled in ECO Academy because his home schooling had been all over the place, course wise.

Parker also didn't think he was a genius. That was a problem when he was surrounded by so many smart people. When Priyanka was easily smarter than he. When a girl two years younger than he, Jennifer, was probably the smartest of any of them. And he was certainly in a place where people kept track of how smart you were. Not how much money you had.

The usual way that Americans determined rank. Though, there were only a handful of Americans in the whole student body at ECO Academy.

"I don't think I am a genius but it is clear that we have to have backgrounds also in sociology, history and politics to see how some of our ideas will play out. We may not need music majors, or a drama department, but for instance, if we did not pay attention to the history of a place and just decided to tell everyone to follow these new rules on conservation, do you think they all would? I have a feeling that any country that was once a soviet satellite and has been experimenting with freedom, even on a small limited scale, may not like to be told what to do." He didn't want to sound preachy, but sometimes having an opinion made everything sound preachy.

Guillermo joined them, "It is an observation that others have made about ECO Academy, especially as so much money has been spent, not just on us to attend, but to make the school ready for more students. Already next year we shall have fifty in the new class and a few more professors. Other adults have told Dr. Phillips-Lee that it would be beneficial to have the other disciplines but he has held that science is supremely important. Just because he then got a detailed paper from one of his students might have made him believe that his thinking was short-sighted. Don't any of us say that Parker has done good work for it will go to his head."

Priya spoke up. "But he did good work, whether it swells his ego or not. Did anyone else read Parker's paper? He let me read it, and it was the arguments that he made and then supported that were important. He took all the winning papers that we wrote on solutions for the Aral Sea and then did what most of us hadn't, put a price on the solutions. All our ideas would lead to major undertakings which need funding. A pittance for some of the nations of the West, but for Kazakhstan and Uzbekistan which are poor nations, it would bankrupt them."

Here Parker had to add, "But should your plans work, and mine I suppose, then the reinvigorated Aral Sea would provide a stimulus for the entire region."

"So? These hard-line Soviet cast-offs seldom do what is good for them," JCubed said. "They do what will put money in the Swiss bank accounts of their leaders."

Parker smiled, "That is why we need to be able to study politics. Can we create an international resolution to protect whales if Japan will still allow its fishermen to kill them?"

Shelly rose from her chair, and you could see the plastic hatch pattern in her back. "Leave my whales out of this. You are all going away on vacation for a week and we poor slubs have to stay here at school and study."

Jennifer laughed, "Oh we have to study too. Dr. Phillips-Lee said we will be auditing classes remotely, and have to take our work load with us. We get to go sightseeing and present at the conference, but we have to study. I think we will have a harder week than you. And Aral'sk is no picnic. There are no five star hotels anymore. Not since the Sea shriveled to almost nothing."

Shelly looked at her friend, then said, "You're probably right, and it's going to be cold there too."

Parker said, "A lot colder than here. Though don't know how many more beach days we are going to get here anyway."

Giulio Andrianò said, "Well, I've checked the forecast for while you are away. It is supposed to be nice. And I've already gotten the Proctor's permission to have a beach barbecue. It's going to be daylight standard time in a couple weeks here, which means it'll be dark at night. We want to have the last barbecue of the year, and you'll all miss it."

Parker and Guillermo both kicked sand towards Giulio.

Giulio jogged away laughing and he was joined by Pedro Montejo. Shelly said, "Hey, don't be mad. Even if you have to study while you go to your conference, you get to go in Dr. Phillip-Lee's private jet, and even though there are no five star hotels where you are going, you still are going."

Priya said, "That is true. It is a very special thing that we have been asked to do. And we are very young to present papers to a conference of scientists. There will be experts at the conference who we should be very honored to meet."

Parker really liked Priya, but she hadn't researched enough about the conference. Hence the need to look at things from other disciplines beside their own. It was as if they had those horse blinders on for anything other than what they had become trained to be interested in. Parker had actually used that analogy in his report to Dr. Phillips-Lee and that, he was sure, was why Dr. Phillips-Lee was going to add more courses from other points of view than the scientific soon.

"Experts yes," Parker said. "But there will not be as many leading scientists as we could hope for. The cost of projects to get both the North Aral and the South Aral, which far too many people forget about, is in the billions, and will impact those who have changed their lives to live on the water that was diverted from the Sea. Many others have tried to solve the problem but they let regional and historical politics get in the way. There is a great deal of blame against the Soviets for the predicament that the region is in. Now, there needs to be almost a super authority that can make decisions for all…" Parker realized he was again getting preachy.

His plan and report had targeted that issue, and Dr. Phillips-Lee had said "through the eyes of children…" for more than a few days after. The adults knew that they had to force the right plan on all the nations in the region and were reluctant to do so, but it was like medicine.

Everyone knew they had to take it to get better, and no one really wanted to unless their parents forced them to do so. That was why this conference, even without the greatest environmentalists on the planet, might be successful. The Premier of the Soviet Union and several of his people were going to attend. So to were two American Cabinet secretaries and the Vice President. Parker's father had told him that if the President went, it would make the Premier look a little bit weaker. And a strong Premier probably would mean a greater chance of success for the conference.

His father's commentary had opened up an entire line of thinking, "Did anyone else besides me look into the editorials and commentaries about the conference? There hasn't been a lot of material about it, but there has been some," Parker asked his friends.

"Like what? Were we supposed to watch CNN? I don't watch that kind of television." Guillermo said.

JCubed though had taken a look, "Yeah, I put a spider together and got a bunch of blogs on it. About twenty posts. Not a whole lot, but you are right about it not being earth shattering news. It should be. If it can happen in that area of the world and reduce one of the biggest bodies of water to, well one guy I read said a drop in the bucket, it can happen here. Hell, it is happening here. Over in the Salton Sea, Tulare Lake and Lake Mono, all in California. That can't be good. Water in California is precious enough and losing it is going to be bad in the long run."

"There is always my suggestion," Shelly said. "More desalination plants. We can drink sea water."

Jennifer sniggered, "As long as it has been desalinated. Otherwise it will make you mad. The Israelis have made great strides and have several plants doing just that. But it is energy inefficient.

Making it efficient is the win there."

Parker nodded, "That I think Shelly is why you aren't coming with us. Either that, or Dr. Phillips-Lee thought you really wanted to work more on your tan." That got everyone to laugh. "No, sorry, the solutions we think of have to be viable. And while we have some courses in physics, we don't have a full physics department, which would have addressed the energy issues in our limited education."

Guillermo was his harshest critic, "You can't really say that we have a limited education. You earned your bachelors degree in your freshman year, have finished your masters, and will have gone a long way towards a doctorate when you graduate in June. How can you say that we have any limits here?"

Parker knew that Guillermo saw everything at ECO Academy as nearly perfect, trusting that the adults had done everything correctly. Especially in comparison to the life he had led back in Costa Rica. But the truth was that scientists were imperfect in their quest for perfect solutions. And Dr. Phillips-Lee had set up ECO Academy with his traits of humanity, and not as a scientific experiment. Or rather it was an experiment but had not proved its hypothesis yet.

"If we had some sociologists, or even a course in sociology, you could see. Don't you ever get the feeling that we concentrate so much on our specializations, and connected scientific disciplines that we are becoming just bigger geeks? You know, though budgets have been cut at public schools, other kids our age learn about art and music."

Priya shook her head, smoothing down the T-shirt that covered her bathing suit. "I play the viola. And JCubed plays a keyboard, and I don't mean just a computer keyboard." She giggled. "I like art. There are great museums all around Los Angeles, and I've been to the Getty down the road twice and seen all those antiquities." J. Paul Getty, the billionaire who had a near lock on Saudi Arabian oil in the fifties and became the richest man in the world of his generation, had two museums in Los Angeles and one was nearby in Pacific Palisades, the city next to Malibu where ECO Academy was.

"But we have to study all things not scientific on our own.

Think about it. Even a lot of the sciences we don't study yet," Parker said but knew he was being redundant. In any case, Dr. Phillips-Lee and a few of the administrators had started a blog to show what actions they were taking to expand the school and add those disciplines. It would all start the following year though, and Parker would have graduated by then.

JCubed said, "The contractors are building the Music hall. And we'll get some artists in residence next quarter. Jerry Simons has been making albums for years and is a great Jazz act. We get his whole band and he, teaching and performing next quarter."

Parker had a rueful smile. He did not like Jazz all that much, but he knew such an artist was popular with the older professors on campus. And it was the beginning of an experiment to see if weekly concerts by the group, lessons in music, and the history of Jazz would add to their education. He knew that the idea for an artist in residence as part of an established music program was something he had suggested in his paper to Dr. Phillips-Lee, and the Dr. Phillips-Lee had recognized him on the blog for the idea. Parker just wished it was an artist that he was a fan of.

The whole school had downloaded music of the J. Simons Experience and he had listened to most of it. Parker just could not seem to like it. But it did mean things were changing in the right direction.

"Who cares about some old people and old people music. We should have got Lady Gaga, or the most recent winner from the The Voice. I am so addicted to that show," Shelly said.

She had several people in her dorm room watch every episode. They made a party, though Parker was sure some of the boys who went did so because they wanted to be friends with Shelly more than they went to watch the show.

Jennifer cleared her throat and then said, "Shouldn't we talk more about next week? Aren't any of you a little scared of going to Kazakhstan?"

Giulio said, "Not all of us are going. It gets a little boring to hear you talk about this big trip of yours."

Priya shook her head, "No, don't think of it that way. I know I am going too, but don't be jealous. Or at least hold onto your jealousy. One day we will all be away from ECO Academy. We will have graduated and be out in the real world. We will be pursuing our research and trying out things. Some of us are going to be successful before others, and some will be stuck in research for years and years. Some will become really rich, like Dr. Phillips-Lee. Then what? Are we going to resent each other for being successful? Don't we all want the same thing?"

Parker knew, even without having taken a sociology course that they all didn't want the same thing. "We want similar things, but not the same thing. I've learned that in my years here." He was sounding like the old man, but there were no other seniors down at the beach just then. Food services were holding dinner at the beach though and all those on meal plans, which were all the students and some of the faculty, would eventually have to wander down to eat.

JCubed snorted, "What different things? We get recruited because we all fit the profile. We all have the minds that the next generation of science needs."

Guillermo looked at the internet wunderkind. "I get what Parker is saying. Broadly JCubed is right, we want a greener world and have shown we are good scientists before they even gave us an application for admission. But say that I just want to make sure Costa Rica is better. That I don't care about any Nobel Prize, or a lot of money, isn't that different then some of you?"

Shelly let out a big exhalation of air that was somewhere between a gasp and a laugh, "You don't care about a lot of money. Everyone cares about a lot of money."

Parker knew that Shelly did. She wanted to be rich enough to buy the diamond mines of her homeland, or at least buy a lot of diamonds and live where there was no racial tension at all. She was friends with JCubed here at ECO Academy, but being so friendly with a person of color back in South Africa could be difficult.

As for Guillermo, Parker wished he could remember the quote and who said it about protesting too much. A broader education and he would know. Instead he was going to have to Google that later. Guillermo played all altruistic because he was from a poor country, but he was not poor himself. He talked about having been very poor as a small child, but that was a long time ago, and

Parker knew he had very little memory of being that young.

"I don't know that many of us will be as lucky as Dr. Phillips-Lee. Some scientists make tremendous discoveries, but do not get rich from it. Dr. Phillips-Lee had a rich father to help him get started," Parker pointed out.

"Like you do too?" Shelly said, but it was Guillermo who was nodding vigorously when she did say it.

"I do not know if my father really cares about the sea rising and causing an impact to the coasts of the world. He is very happy to be an ever bigger fish in Kansas City. That's pretty far from the coast," Parker said.

Guillermo then spoke, "But a change in the coastlines of the world, anything that would cause the dislocation of populations would have an impact even in Kansas City."

"I know that." Everyone at the beach knew that. But no matter how many times Parker had told his father about what was certainly going to happen, his father had said that he was sure it would be corrected before it became too late.

Far too many people had that attitude. That the government would take care of things. That the government would hire people like he and the other students to be the scientists that came up with solutions to stop the coastal cities from sinking under the rising ocean.

"You're father is a fool!" Guillermo said. Not that he meant it personally, but that the other boy meant it in the way that all those who wanted to ignore the facts they uncovered in science were fools.

"Take that back. You do not know my father!" Whatever his father was, he was not going to let Guillermo call his father a fool. The man had taken Grandpa's small bank and made it worth millions. Tens of millions. Probably more.

"What? Come on, you are dedicating your life to the problem of the oceans rising and the icecaps shrinking, and your father doesn't trust you or your research? He is a fool."

"Take it back Guillermo. I won't tell you again," Parker was not being preachy then.

JCubed was moving to stand between the two of them, and motioning for help from the other boys, "Hey you two. Enough of this big testosterone battle. Are you trying to be big bad bulls and show the very pretty breeders that you are fit to lead the pack? Enough of this."

"Don't push me JCubed. You know as well as I that those who don't want to listen to scientific truths are like ostriches with their heads in the sand," Guillermo said. He was not apologizing and Parker was getting much more angry.

"Get out of the way JCubed. I'm going to show Cordovan just how far his mouth can take him," Guillermo had a way of saying stupid things that he held as truth and not caring for what others felt. The ECO Academy students needed a class on etiquette as well. Or at least Proctors who could help them transition from children to adults with an eye to proper rearing, and the integration into society. They should not be ostracized as geeks all their lives.

"Stop it! Both of you stop it!" Jennifer said.

Priya also added, "No, Parker!"

Shelly started to laugh. It only made Parker more angry at Guillermo. He had a lot to learn about what you said, where you said it, and to whom you said something. Even if the boy thought such a thing about Parker's father he shouldn't say it. Parker may have had a prejudicial thought about his fellow students at ECO Academy. He may have been handicapped to have such thoughts right on the tip of his tongue that anger should have loosened and made him spew out. But he was focusing on dealing with the insulting Costa Rican.

"Apologize, Guillermo. Do it now, or I swear I will cram those words down your throat. Do any of us talk about your family here?" he demanded. "Does anyone at school here talk about their parents like that? Only Jennifer's dad because he is here. It is one reason we all have been separated from our parents, because Dr. Phillips-Lee knows that the environments they created influenced academic achievement and learning. It is why we only see our families so seldom. Now apologize!"

Guillermo took a step back and held up his hands. "Okay. Okay. No reason to get so angry about things. I did not mean anything by it."

Parker was pretty sure that the apology was insincere, but Guillermo had said it. It wasn't male pride that had made Parker pursue the matter. Even if there was a bit of truth about his father not understanding the science involved in Global Warming, and how the loss of coastline could affect land locked Kansas City. The point was to get Guillermo to shut his mouth. To make the younger boy think first before saying something hurtful.

Parker could let the boy speak things that were controversial all day long, but personal attacks were not to be allowed. What was next, criticizing Priya for being from India. Parker wouldn't even let the boy retract such a slight. He would just pound him.

Guillermo was twenty to thirty pounds heavier and a couple inches taller than Parker, even though Parker was a year older. But Parker was more athletic than Guillermo. That might be telling. Guillermo did play futbol, and might have a strong kick, but Parker was sure the boy did not know how to throw a good punch.

Parker knew how to do that. There was more than three hours a week of gym at the ECO Academy and Parker had spent a lot of time with his home-schooled classmates back in Kansas City. One semester they learned boxing and wrestling.

Parker knew that he was angry and took a few steps to a cooler that had sodas and water chilling on ice. He grabbed a water and walked off a few paces twisting the cap so he could drink. He thought that maybe he should take another dunk in the ocean and catch a few more waves. He would be alone with his thoughts. Which he found all scientists needed.

In order to think through to a solution, all scientists needed someplace they could really let their mind concentrate on the problems that they were working on. Was Guillermo a problem? They were nominally friends.

Parker did not think that the boy was a problem, but almost punching him might be considered a problem. The lord knew that Guillermo was not selective against Parker. The boy had made disparaging remarks against the parents of many students. Guillermo was choosing the wrong people to do it to, though. Next time, Parker was going to give the boy a fat lip.

"Hey." He turned to see Priya had walked up to him and was

standing next to him as he looked at the ocean. Her arm touched his and he felt her hand reaching for his. They had touched hands before, and at the end of their last date, he had kissed her on the cheek. She was his girlfriend he guessed and this certainly made it so.

"Sorry. I may have got out of line just then."

She shrugged and he could feel it as her left arm rose up and down on his right. "No, Guillermo was wrong. He does that far too often, and against you he does it more because, well because your family is rich."

"We do alright. You know your older brother makes more money than my dad."

She laughed, "Shh. Don't tell Guillermo. And Maheshwaran was lucky with the IPO from his research. He's not rich like Dr. Phillips-Lee." Priya had told him about the company her brother had founded with some of his research. And after investigating, he had sent word to his Grandpa who had a lot of money these days. When the company went public, Grandpa had been very happy and told Parker to keep giving him ideas like that. He said he was making more money then he ever did when he had run the bank.

"Guillermo has a chip on his shoulder and he better get rid of it, or he'll need to move back to Costa Rica to pursue his research. Everywhere you go, unless you're like Bill Gates, you meet someone who has more money than you. And amongst us, scientists, no matter who you are, there will always be someone smarter than you. If not today, then in five years when the next group comes up having not only everything you learned to study from, but all the advances that have come in those five years. Guillermo wants us all to bow down to him and say he is the smartest."

She laughed a little then, "Maybe amongst you boys, but you know that Jennifer is the smartest of all of us."

"Believe me, I never forget that. It is a blessing that she is, because if Guillermo was the smartest I do not think we would ever hear the end of it," he said.

"Hmm, well you had better find a way to make peace with Guillermo, because you have to share a room with him and

JCubed when we go to Aral'sk. I'm just saying, if you two are still fighting, it isn't going to be pretty, and Dr. Phillips-Lee will be there as well."

He breathed out a little laugh, "No, you're right. I'll apologize as well. He's right of course. Guillermo, about my father. Dad just doesn't realize how bad things would be should the seas rise and take away the coastlines of the world. He just doesn't understand."

-Chapter 8-

"Shelly wasn't kidding when she said that the hotel was going to be a dog. I don't think the heater works in our room, and the desk guy's English seems to stop the minute I complain about it. I bet Dr. Phillips-Lee doesn't have these problems, or your father." JCubed said. Jennifer wrinkled her nose. At the last minute her father came on the trip with them for he was being consulted as an expert on the diseases that had invaded the area once the sea had shrunk.

Even with the efforts to restore the north Aral Sea, which was going so slowly, there was still a great health risk. "And yesterday when we got off the plane you said how exciting it was and that the brisk air was sure going to keep you on your toes," Jennifer said.

JCubed paused then said, "Well that was in the afternoon. It gets a lot colder at night, and in a room with no heat, it gets colder still."

Priya laughed, "Our room was too warm if anything. I had to kick the covers off of the bed."

Jennifer and Priya shared a room with two twin beds. It was one floor above the floor the boys were on. Dr. Phillips-Lee explained that he and Dr. Dejanu were officially their chaperones, but Jennifer had her father along, and Colonel Ben-Levi and his security team were really going to ensure that there was not going to be any fooling around. The students were going to be watched even closer than they were in Malibu.

Not that Jennifer thought that Priya was doing anything serious yet with Parker, and she certainly had no desire to do anything with JCubed or Guillermo. Guillermo was such a snob, and JCubed was far too hyper. She could only think that if she and JCubed had sex it would be over in about three seconds and what fun would that be?

It was a shame that Parker was really interested in Priya and not her, but there were other boys back at school she could date. A romance with Parker while they were away on this vacation, though, especially with her father right there, would have been fun. At least fun in making her father feel uncomfortable.

"Isn't the thermostat electronic? Why don't you see if you and Priya can hack the system. If our room was hot and yours cold, it must be something you can correct," Jennifer said.

"Hello young scholars," a voice from a distance called. They all turned to see that Dr. Phillips-Lee was walking towards them. "I hope you all got enough sleep last night and are rested. Did you follow the procedures to fight your jet-lag?"

Their chorus of yesses gave the man a smile. "Where are Mr. Thornton and Mr. Cordovan? We need to go to the conference hall and check in," he asked and then turned his head and looked to Colonel Ben-Levi. The Israeli pulled out his smartphone and tapped a few buttons, then held up two fingers and pointed towards the elevator.

JCubed was saying, "They were right behind me."

Dr. Phillips-Lee said, "Yes, well it is not yet ten and we agreed on ten. I shall not hold it against them if they do not arrive before me, only if they do not arrive on time. Punctuality is so important, and by punctual, when a meeting is called for a certain time, it is not just important to arrive at that time, but be prepared to start at that time. Ms. Smythe-Lytton, I have made a distinction, can you elaborate."

Jennifer could, "I think the simplest way to express that is to have your coffee in hand, and your notes out and ready for when the meeting starts, instead of after."

"Precisely, very good." Jennifer was reminded that the founder of ECO Academy did not teach any courses, or mentor any of the students personally. He liked acting as ubermentor. He liked being seen to be above the day-to-day coursework, but step in to mold the students with little tweaks and jabs.

Guillermo and Parker exited the elevator and Dr. Phillips-Lee waved them over. "Good, now we can go over the schedule. Dr. Dejanu is already over at the hall and she has been talking to several of our colleagues. What they are saying is that they think you all have put together a viable solution and are being given the penultimate slot for tomorrow's presentations. The selling point was linking your five solutions together as one, and then providing a real cost and financing solution for it. Mr. Thornton, that seems to be what made the difference here."

Parker swelled up, getting much bigger. Now Jennifer knew she could picture what swelling up with pride meant. "Thank you sir. It seemed what has been needed for all the Aral Sea solutions. Someone to link them all together, choose the best and then go for it." Parker said.

Dr. Phillips-Lee was nodding. "I could not agree more. And the Premier also has found that so. He and the Vice President of the United States have both requested to meet you, but I have turned this into a little bit of public relations for the Academy. You will get an hour with both men later today, before dinner, and they have their science advisors so be ready. If you don't know something that they ask you, do not worry. They know you only had a few weeks on the project. Just answer the questions, after which… Well I sent the jet back to Dubai to fetch dinner. There are a lot of great restaurants around here, I am sure, and we shall be dining on food from them, but tonight, there is a chef named Nobu Matsuhisa. He even has a restaurant in Los Angeles. Started in Los Angeles. I think the Vice President and the Premier will like it, and you might also. No sake for any of you though. Dr. Smythe-Lytton says only drink bottled water as well." Dr. Phillips-Lee looked a little upset and following his gaze, she saw a ZED Corps vending machine that was just off to one side. ZED Corps water was as good as any other. They were the number two selling water on the planet. But Dr. Phillips-Lee seemed to look like he had dirt in his mouth when he saw the machine.

"Dr. Phillips-Lee, we are not really ready to present to the Premier. You said our collective presentation was not going to be any more than a half hour in front of everyone and so we have been working towards that." Parker said. It was good that he stepped up and spoke. He really was the team leader, though he kept trying to make it a joint decision. One that Guillermo would fight him on if he insisted on putting it to a vote instead of acting like he should.

Parker had asked around while everyone was finishing their projects to see if there was uniformity in them, and then asked about economic impact, about energy, about political considerations. Which almost all the students at ECO Academy had not taken into account. He then had more than half of his own report linking the others together for a uniform decision, as well as citing the need for an extra political endeavor, like the ECU, or the UN. But with power, and economic resources. Otherwise he cited that the will of the governments to support the endeavor would fray, as it had before.

For a seventeen year-old to tell these powerful adults that they were as naked as the Emperor in his new clothes, because they did not want to face that reality, had earned him respect from all the professors at ECO Academy. Everyone knew that such an authority needed to be created, but none of the grownups seemed to care to do it.

"If there were another way to get the Premier to consider this, I would do it. Here is the truth, as I see it. The Premier can force all the countries of the region to allow the solutions of the symposium to be implemented. Until now, the Premier has been reluctant to get involved, but you have shown that for relatively little effort, just pushing his weight around and a few rubles, he can get this matter finished. He can even push responsibility onto the super authority you say should be created. One that will need the United States as well."

Priya said, "And China. They have little to do with the nations this far west, but they will not allow any superagency to be created without meddling. It is in their nature." Jennifer knew Priya well enough to know she raised a valid point. Others who heard a young girl that was Indian say such a thing would quickly discount it as national prejudice.

No one should have realized that more than Dr. Phillips-Lee who had lived under the Chinese government. "Yes, I know that they will try, and that too is a reason the Premier will back this. He will show some defiance against the Chinese. It really is not a matter for their concern."

Parker spoke, "I think most in the world would understand that. But the Chinese seem to have a very singular view of what is their concern and what isn't. Anything that will set off a reaction that would affect them is now their concern and they throw their weight around. It is, I am sad to say, the way the United States often acted as well."

Jennifer felt she had to do so as well, "Let us not take all the national blame on one self. When we English ruled the waves, we were quite guilty of poking our noses into many places we shouldn't have."

Parker continued though, "There now might be some justification for the Chinese to want to speak up, though if you look at their delegation to this conference, there is only one scientist and three security team members. Do the other delegations break down the functions of their teams so well, or is that part of Colonel Ben-Levi's contributions."

The Colonel smiled from behind Dr. Phillips-Lee and said, "Actually, that was Mr. Jefferson's analysis. Though my team was very quick to want a copy. Well done by the way son."

JCubed smiled back. He got great grades like the rest of the students did, but a verbal pat on the back from the Israeli Commando counted for something.

Parker said, "Before we go on, the point I want to make about the Chinese is this. They are like the Americans of the twentieth century not only in their acquisitive nature, or protectionist nature, but also with their need for mineral wealth. China of course has a tremendous amount of natural resources, but there are many commodities that China does not have and they have been purchasing these for the last few years, driving the price up of all such minerals and other items. Several aspects of the plans we will present, and I am sure that other scientists have thought of, to return the Aral Sea to viability will need those items. A super national organization, that I proposed in my solution, would have the right to preempt the Chinese purchase of materials. They have shown no reason or desire to be vested in helping the world. Only helping themselves." It was impassioned. It was the difference in the year of age between him and Guillermo. It was this self-assurance that Dr. Phillips-Lee liked so much.

Jennifer had known the Chancellor of ECO Academy all her life, since Dr. Phillips-Lee had been friends with her father back in the Oxford days. Dr. Phillips-Lee had even been a guest at her parent's wedding. He was a brilliant man, but speaking with passion about an issue was not his style. He used jokes and stories to get his point across, while Parker had facts, and then seemed to her to have the ability to cast his gaze ten, twenty, 40 years into the future and see what answers were needed to get there.

Now, in a collegiate setting, she was exposed to professors of many different demeanors. Many different styles. That was a good thing. That Dr. Phillips-Lee had stocked ECO Academy with international professors in many different teaching and mentoring styles, meant that the students were not all going to turn out the same. Though all were going to have the same accented English, most likely. Perhaps a carry over of the Oxford phenomena. Something that the fictional Shaw character, Professor Higgins would notice.

Most of the time though, the professors of ECO Academy did not get to lecture the students of the Academy. Classes were more like workshops as they were too small a student body to fill any large amphitheater-like room that older centers of study had. And often the professors of ECO Academy conducted lectures through modern video conferencing technology, back to their former campuses or even to other campuses across the world. Then the professors were in lecture mode and that was when Jennifer had a chance to see how they spoke to hundreds, or now, even thousands of students.

Parker could hold an audience, she was sure. And as he was becoming the leader for the five students, she was going to push him into that role. "I think that we can all speak to the Premier of course, but it is Parker's plan that unified our ideas, and his idea that we need a coalition to make the adoption of our solutions a reality. Don't you think it would be best if he is the lead in our presentation, Dr. Phillips-Lee? Even today he's adding more depth to our efforts by citing the Chinese and the probability that they will be opposed to this."

JCubed was holding a tablet and doing some quick research. You could hear the sounds of email being sent off. She knew that JCubed often found research articles he had a program translate into a more readable format, then automatically index the nouns as keywords to a formula he and Priya had made. It then sent the document off to the cloud for later retrieval, and sometimes copied out emails to others that the program automatically thought would benefit from reading, or JCubed manually chose people to get the information. A tingling in her hip pocket on her phone and she connected that JCubed had copied her on one of his articles.

Seeing Guillermo make a crossed face too, Jennifer suspected that he too had received a message from JCubed. Guillermo certainly did not like that Parker was a leader. But then Parker was destined to be one. Jennifer saw that Parker was right about needing more disciplines at the school. There were other traits that showed that Parker's background and upbringing contributed to his becoming a leader and speaking in front of large groups of people.

Parker did not talk about it, but JCubed, along with the many other things he manipulated the Internet to provide, developed dossiers on all the students. Everyone knew that Parker's father was a very successful businessman. Owned a bank, and his grandfather was even richer. His mother was a beauty queen.

Parker would have been raised in an environment where his parents would have exposed him to the lifestyle of a public person. Guillermo was a junior, and the son of a working class family from a third world country. He would have a great deal of catching up before he could hope to emulate the ease which Parker seemed to mix amongst those who were older and who had more authority.

"I don't think this is the best idea. We should all take our time to present our solutions. The Premier and his science advisors surely will see the merit of each concept," Guillermo said. Jennifer could see that he was trying to be diplomatic about undermining Parker. The two had pretended to make up after their argument on the beach, but it did not look like they had.

"No, my thoughts had already paralleled that of Ms. Smythe-Lytton. I shall introduce the entire team and then quickly hand off the presentation to Parker. You, Mr. Thornton should be prepared to weave in all your companions' ideas. Then, leave Dr. Dejanu and me a few minutes at the end so we can present our thoughts. Though I shall give more time to Dr. Dejanu. My solutions are more in line with Dr. Smythe-Lytton and seeking medical solutions, advanced drugs, to treat the side effects that have come from the reduction of the Sea."

Guillermo cleared his throat to say more but Dr. Phillips-Lee spoke, "Now Mr. Cordovan, surely you can see that a logical argument is the key to success? Passionate irrationality will not carry the weight one needs to convince some of the most powerful men on the planet. I can speak to this from experience. Now we are all gathered, let us go register at the conference center. And Mr. Jefferson, I do hope I can convince you to put away your tablet as we walk. I fear sometimes that you are so engrossed in the device that you might walk into an oncoming car."

"Fat chance of that, Dr. Phillips-Lee. There are very few cars in Aral'sk," JCubed said.

Colonel Ben-Levi's hand came down quickly on JCubed's shoulder. "Best to put the tablet away and watch where you walk. When you have graduated the Academy, then by all means do something foolish and get yourself hit by a car. For now, let us keep you alive."

JCubed swallowed hard, and nodded. He put away his tablet. The rest all got up and they walked over to the conference hall. It was an old soviet era building. It looked like it had a new coat of paint for the conference, but it had been haphazardly done. Jennifer had heard often when out of the way places were chosen for international conferences, that was what was done. Try to make it look new and inviting, when the truth was, the hotels had problems with the heat and air conditioning. She bet that the Premier and Vice President did not have such problems in their rooms.

Parker had given the group's presentation and had done exceptionally well, at least in Jennifer's opinion. At least he had done his best, though Guillermo still acted as if he should have been given time for his presentation. "Now, if the Premier or Vice President should like to ask the students questions, or my colleague and myself, we are quite ready to answer them."

The Premier cleared his throat and then passed a note to his science advisor, who thought for a second, then nodded vigorously. While that was going on the Vice President stood. "Children, or should I say young scholars. I am very impressed. Very impressed. I had no idea that ECO Academy was doing so well. If you will permit me, Premier and Dr. Phillips-Lee, it is an honor that we can host such a center of learning, but Dr. Lee, I think you need to consider a European Satellite to enlarge upon your excellent work."

Jennifer knew that the Vice President was sucking up to the Premier. So too did the Premier, apparently. "At a later date, perhaps. Around St. Petersburg we shall find land when you are ready Dr. Phillips-Lee. Now, it is Mr. Thornton, yes. You touched on something. I wrote this down to be sure I understood correctly. You said that if I did not support the endeavors here, then in ten years, fifteen years, we would be back at the table discussing it all again. More people sick, billions spent all to no avail. You said I and not Russia. Why is that?"

"In post Soviet era politics, from what I have been able to research from primary and secondary sources in the last week, sir, it is clear that when you wish for a project to be completed, when you put your mandate behind anything in Russia, then it gets done. Were a proposal to go to the Duma and not have your backing, then that measure would lapse. Nothing these last years that has not had your backing has succeeded. Surely that is obvious to the world, even if many do not comment on it. Not that you are king of Russia, sir, but in the future, when histories are written after we are all gone from the planet, that is probably the comparison that will be made."

The Premier's face clouded. "This is what you have found in two weeks?"

Parker nodded, "If you would like, I will share with you the research."

"You are not much of a diplomat, are you?" the Premier asked.

"Sir, we are scientists and the stereotype is that we should not care about diplomacy so much. That is why the Vice President is here apparently. But you know what the World thinks of your rule in Russia. You are intelligent. Everyone in this room is very bright. Taking the lead on an altruistic project that only has an ancillary benefit to Russia will enhance your status as a world leader. It should also lead to confrontation with some of the other world powers, but as America so often points to having right on their side, you will have that in this instance."

The Premier nodded. "Let us talk about something that you may not realize. I think the term you uses is brinksmanship."

Parker took his hand and rubbed at his forehead. Jennifer could see that he was sweating a little.

She had heard the term before also, but was not sure what it meant. JCubed was looking it up on his tablet so he did not know either. She looked across his chest to see his result.

Dr. Phillips-Lee though said, "I am sorry Premier, but the students are still young. Mr. Thornton is only just seventeen and has never had a political science course at ECO Academy where such would be discussed and taught. Though we shall plan to have such a course in the coming year, for it seems our future scientists will be participating with world leaders and need to understand more about politics."

"It is a lesson that is always changing and evolving, is that not so, Mr. Vice President." True to form, the American Vice President chuckled and agreed with the Premier.

"Dr. Lee, when you have such a course finished, I should be happy to come to your Malibu, or better, your St. Petersburg campus which I am sure shall make them envious in California, and give a lecture. Perhaps on how a simple man such as I can bend a whole nation to adopting his vision, eh Mr. Thornton? Let me tell the children this, about Brinksmanship, for it will be a concern if we create a coalition to deal with this mess."

Guillermo said quietly, "Your mess." But the Premier heard that as well.

The Premier gave Guillermo a look and then said, "What? Well yes, our mess. Though you should know I was younger than you when those who headed the State started the actions that have led to this disaster of the Aral Sea. But we will correct it. Brinksmanship means that I know how far I will go to, what do children say all the time, 'Piss Off' the other nations. Will I start a war over this? No. I have had enough of fighting and mourning over dead babies like the Chechens have caused me. I do not know if you can appreciate that for you are young. Parents grieve more over such little children then anything I have ever known.

"No, the Chinese, as you say Mr. Thornton, will try and force their way in. Because they want to be recognized as important as we, or the Americans. We allowed these people to take a place on the world stage, you Mr. Vice President have to take credit for that more than I. You have given them too much economic power. They hold that sword over your head, which makes it even smarter that Russia take the lead in any coalition of nations to save and restore the Aral.

"The other part of Brinksmanship is knowing before you go to a meeting of your 'peers' what you are going to discuss and agree to before the conference begins. I had thought I had done so, for we thought to pledge one billion of your dollars a year, for five years to these efforts. We thought that we would only need to sway some others to giving money, but you are right, without an oversight, that money would be poorly spent. None of us had considered a superagency that was above all governments as far as this objective was concerned. You have stood us on our head," The premier smiled which Jennifer was sure meant that he was considering what more he could do to gain an advantage.

"If I may, Mr. Premier, it has shown in the post cold war era that cooperation amongst the superpowers is a key to success. Coalitions for matters such as the liberation of Kuwait, the Libyan and Bosnian no-fly zones, have shown that working together, even just the agreement to work together and these programs achieve victory, but when either of the superpowers continue to balk at such an agreement, then the goal is doomed to failure, or delaying such an agreement only results in exponential increases in suffering. More dead babies, to use a matter you touched on, sir."

The Premier squinted for a moment, and then shaking his head smiled, "It is good that I already agreed to this. You do know Stalin, a predecessor of mine, would have taken you outside and had you shot."

The Vice President forced a laugh, "He's joking children. He's joking." The Premier did not look like he was joking. "Come Mr. Premier, let us not scare these young people who quite likely will be giving us all sorts of help in the next few decades, on how to make the Earth a better place for all of us."

The Premier nodded, "No, of course. The conference shall be

very interesting, and there are some good Russian ideas that the Aral Sea Superagency shall want to adopt."

JCubed sniggered and Jennifer felt she had to speak, "Ah Mr. Premier, I think you had better choose another name for the coalition."

The Premier looked at her for a moment, then realized what she must have meant and said the name quietly to himself again, "Aral Sea Superagency…" He then laughed and others also joined in.

"Very well," he said when he got his voice under control, "Perhaps the Superagency of the Aral Sea, or SAS for short. That is quite British, is it not Ms. Smythe-Lytton. An agency known for great success."

Jennifer nodded. The SAS, Special Air Service was well regarded all over the world. Not Scandinavian Airlines.

She nodded. She did not really want to say anything else in front of the world leaders. Jennifer did look around the room very quickly, and saw that her father was staring at her. She did not really like that he did so, but there was little she could do to stop him. What was so infuriating about being at the Academy with him was that her mother was not at all upset by it. But then once she had her girlfriends surrounding her, her mother did not seem to care much about any of her prior life.

And with Jennifer now living in Malibu it seemed that when she talked to her mother, her mother was living a life of perpetual partying. Jennifer was even worried that she might endanger herself by getting carried away. Jennifer had to lecture her mother on just saying no, but she was not sure it was doing much good. Jennifer knew that when her mother was out with her friends, which now seemed almost every night, she did drink too much. But living in London, her mother did not drive, which was good.

Over the next three days, others at the conference gave their presentations, and the scientists and politicians gathered there asked questions and identified procedures that really warranted further study. What was funny was that the day after Jennifer and the rest of the ECO Academy students spoke to the entire conference, a larger delegation from China and several of their satellite allies arrived.

Guillermo and JCubed found that Parker's idea for a super national coalition had already made it's way to the press, and the President of the United States immediately answered a question from the press supporting the idea, and of the Premier taking the lead. It was obvious that the politicians and their government machines had begun to work the idea, and the Chinese were playing catch up. But as Parker had said, they wanted to be an obstructionist to a plan that did not include them.

"It just seems too predictable, about the Chinese," Jennifer said.

"Don't look to me for confirmation. I'm Indian. You know they think that the only good Indian is a slave to them. Look at Tibet," Priya said. "The Dalai Lama is a holy man and still in exile. The Chinese are really not a nice government."

Parker said, "I saw a report once, that after the Tiananmen Square incidents, when they executed those they arrested, they sent a bill for the bullets to the families of those they had killed. They want to pretend that they are part of the current world structure, but they have some catching up to do. And then they clamp down on the Internet and employ millions of hackers. The world should stand up and say J'Accuse!"

Jennifer saw the confused look on JCubed's face, "J'Accuse was the anti-semitic court-martial of Dreyfuss in France. It was very famous. All the French Generals were anti-semites and framed the man."

Parker said, "Right, and then a few men stood up and said the right thing for justice. Justice demands that the world tell China that we don't want them to play in our sandbox any longer. They have terrible treatments of workers, they are gross polluters, they are doing their best to hack our top-secret computers. What more do we need to do to tell them to act like the rest of us and get better, instead of breaking every law that every other nation puts into place. And Priya is right, they really do not like the Indians."

Guillermo spoke, "We do need that political class. I can see that. I don't disagree with anything you say, but they have the world economy by the, uh you know. That has to be balanced with any discussion about China. How the world has made them their manufacturing center. Could society even survive if they took all their marbles and decided to stop playing?"

Parker smiled, "Yeah, I don't have an answer for that. Good point though."

Guillermo smiled, "Thanks."

The Colonel was near and he looked at his phone then walked two paces to wear Jennifer sat with her friends. "Alright, time for a little sightseeing before we go home. Grab your stuff. The van's pulling up and we'll go take a look at what remains of the Sea that you all just saved."

Jennifer smiled. If everything worked out, then the Colonel was right. They had just saved a Sea. That was a good feeling.

-Chapter 9-

Zedadiah relished taking time off every few days from his phone. Managing his calls was a job for three people. And then himself too. He did not want a lot of people to have his private number, but invariably those who had it let it out one way or another and he had to change it. Those who had his public number were in the thousands, and then, once it was public, a great many of the world wanted to get in touch with him.

Each day, trying to run a mega-billion dollar sized company meant he had a call list of well over 100 people he had to talk to. It was craziness. If in his youth he had been told that he would talk to so many people each day, he would have told that person they were nuts.

You had to discipline yourself to run such a large company, and you had to put in a lot of hours. It was why he was having such a difficult time with any close relationship. Such things took time. So when the cliché of being married to the job was bandied about, Zedadiah knew exactly what it meant. He thought, now that he was in his forties, it was perhaps time for a trophy wife. One that would jump when he thought it was time to jump. One that would like that she had as much money as she could think to spend, and then provide him with the home life that he needed. One that did not make any demands on his time.

Were there any couples that had two people who had jobs so demanding? Someone had to suffer in a relationship where one was in a position of a power. You never heard of a First Lady, the wife of the President, that was busier than the President. Or the wife of the Prime Minister having an important life. Though you did hear about the French Prime Minister's wife, the model.

Zedadiah shrugged his shoulders. Why not have a wife who was a former model? One that would not divorce him, and stay with him until the end of days? That was a concept that young people seldom thought about, but now in his forties, Zedadiah was giving some thought to it.

That morning though, he and his assistants had set aside time for him to relax his mind. Every few days he had to do it. Nearly every minute of his day was scheduled. He woke at a quarter to five each day, and by five, was dressed in his work out sweats and exercising. News from all over the world displayed across the wall from his treadmill and stationary bike. His voice searching and surfing through the information and getting the displays he needed. He also dictated emails to subordinates all over the globe as he exercised.

By six he had showered and most days had shaved, unless he was seeing his barber. By six thirty he was finished with breakfast and in the car, where he began making phone calls and seeing to the running of ZED Corp. At his desk before seven, he had two hours of communications to catch up on, and scan the agenda for the nine o'clock meeting. A few of his executives were in the office before seven, before he had arrived. None of them arrived after nine unless they were deathly ill. A little ill and they all came to work, despite Zedadiah admonishing them, and having HR send them messages telling them to take their colds and flus home.

Once, one of the lieutenants had given Zedadiah the flu. Now the man was a department head in Zambia. Big loss of pay, and the man's wife had left him because she did not want to live in Zambia. Well, Zedadiah thought that was the rumor anyway. Frank had a tough project in Zambia and was paid adequately for it. Zedadiah did not think the man's wife had left him because he had been transferred to Zambia.

For an hour, or longer, five days a week, and nearly five hours on Mondays, he and his top lieutenants reviewed projects throughout the world. There were so many that they needed to meet each and every day, while on Monday they discussed and worked through the most crucial ones. Then, after the meeting, more phone calls. Between which Zedadiah read reports, dictated a little, and even typed some of his own emails.

Every once in a while he needed time to himself. Time to watch the silly YouTube videos his children sent him. Time to remember he had a great library filled with classics to read, and that he needed to read one, else his mind, so consumed with business, was not taking pleasure in any of the great wealth he had amassed. Which led back to dating and taking vacations with a super model, or two.

But as with most things of pleasure, he had to put that time aside also, and return to work.

His assistant Michael handed him an actual file folder when he stepped out of his office. He was going to request his lunch, an American style sandwich of Roast beef, with lettuce, tomato, cole slaw, on Jewish rye bread and spicy mustard. Cucumber salad, potato chips, and a Dr. Brown. He had been reading *Ab Urbe Condita* by Livy, the History of Rome. One of the many classics he owned and felt the need to read.

"I think you need to look at this right away sir. I picked up chatter about this out of Rio this morning and they are trying to handle it locally in South America, but it seems too have escalated. You may need Colonel Kutuzov."

"When you say that, it means that I do need the Colonel. Have you read him in on this?" Zedadiah hefted the folder.

"I have copied him what is in the folder about a half hour ago. He should be ready for your call. You will remember that he is in Copenhagen today," Michael said.

Zedadiah remembered that Kutuzov was not in London. He did not keep track of where all the subordinates were at any time. Kutuzov was often on the continent. He had a great many contacts that were on the Continent. Men and women who had once worked for the same organizations that the Colonel had worked for and who had information that proved to be very valuable to ZED Corp.

In business it had proved very profitable to cultivate such people. In fact, Zedadiah might be generous enough to say that half of the corporation's profits came from the knowledge that Kutuzov's contacts supplied. Not half the sales, but half the profits they made each year. Secrets were very valuable and when you knew them, knew that others still thought them secret, you had the Midas touch.

Zedadiah had Michael order the food, which was sure to be prepared immediately by the experienced chefs that the company had in the executive restaurant. The building boasted several restaurants so employees could eat without leaving the tower. ZED

Corp invested in some of them, and also had several dining rooms for its employees. The ones that catered to Zedadiah had chefs that had only worked in two and three star Michelin restaurants.

Meals were very good at ZED Corp headquarters.

Opening the folder he saw that the matter was not about all of South America, but centered on Chile, which meant the fool, Valdez y Gonzalez. That would explain the need for Kutuzov. The Colonel hoped that Gonzalez had become free of the Drug Cartels, but he had also said that they might fail turning the lemon into lemonade. The Cartels never liked to let go, but then Zedadiah did not like to lose either. Especially to criminals.

Zedadiah read more and saw that Chile had become the biggest purchaser of several of the water filtration units and of the cleaning enzymes that had been developed to help with water usage. One of which was ZPakCad-1328. An enzyme that had been developed in Pakistan, hence the Pak part of the coding, but he was not sure what Cad stood for.

Reading on he found out. And then he double-checked the quantities that had been ordered. He texted Michael who stuck his head in, "Call the labs in Pakistan. I don't remember whom the lead scientists are, but they are probably going to be needed here. Anti-thirst? Really? We developed something to cut down on thirst. We make a fortune selling water. Why the hell would I ever want to do this? And why has Ling not mentioned it before?"

Pakistan was part of the Asian Continental Region and Sung Ling Chou, more often called Ling by Zedadiah and the others in the senior management team, headed up the office, based in Beijing. Ling was at the Monday meeting every third week in person, and telecommuted the other two Mondays. Zedadiah had never heard of an anti-thirst enzyme in any of their meetings, yet they were manufacturing one, and selling a great deal of it to their Chilean division.

There was a note in the file folder. The enzyme had been worked on at the request of the United States Department of Defense. Some bright general thought that in field, he could have his troops supplement their water needs with the chemical and during the blazingly hot months, they could survive better. Since the troops were functioning still along the Pakistani-Afgahn border, the labs in Pakistan had taken the lead on securing a contract to develop the enzyme.

Something that had gone into production for Chile before the testing phase was completed. A testing phase that had the Americans refuse the product. The enzyme had the ability to confuse the mind to not only think that it was not thirsty, but that if taken incorrectly, that the user had no need for water at all. Which was a fallacy – and extremely dangerous.

The body needed water, though perhaps not as much as the mind normally desired. The ZPakCad-1328 enzyme did not address the balance correctly and several animals died in testing of the drug. For it had that effect, of a drug. Looking at the notations, Zedadiah saw that the Pakistani labs had not gone to human trials which could have been a disaster. Actually people dying of thirst and thinking that they were hydrated.

No. That was a good thing. But what fool thought to release the enzyme widely elsewhere. Every other nation may not have thought to have or follow stringent guidelines like the United States, but they should have thought to check for potentially harmful repercussions of using such an enzyme. Especially when ZED Corp advertised and sold its water as pure. People dying of thirst was fatally harmful.

He reached over to his computer, and with a few swipes he had the number for the Chilean office in front of him. He also had the number for Francisco Valdez y Gonzalez as well. He noted that it was very early in the morning or late depending on your perspective in Santiago. A time when he would waken someone up.

The thing about the national offices of most ZED Corp divisions was that someone was always awake and working.

"Uh, hola?"

"Good morning, this is Zedadiah Carter, I hope you speak English." Zedadiah spoke a good deal of Spanish now. He had to learn as the years went by and he had a great many employees in Spanish speaking countries, but he wanted to set a tone.

"Si. Of course Mr. Carter. This is no joke, but the Zedadiah

Carter who is Chairman of our illustrious company?"

"Yes. Who is this?"

The man he was looking at on the screen was young. Clean cut. He could not see Zedadiah in his screen because Zedadiah had turned off the video feed. "I am Pedro Ramirez sir."

The name was familiar, from one of the reports he had just read through.

"Good, Mr. Ramirez. I want to speak to Mr. Valdez y Gonzalez. Is he there?"

The man shook his head, "Sorry Señor, but he has left for the evening. There are not many of us here at this time of night. Most are at home asleep."

Carter flipped on his video camera then, "I want to speak to Gonzalez now. This call will be put through at once. I don't care if he is asleep. Wake him!" That was the tone he wanted. If a report had made its way to Zedadiah's desk there was no way that his people in Chile did not know what was occurring. They had to know that anyone reporting suspicious deaths after they had begun to use the ZPakCad-1328 enzyme was bound to get a call. Someone with courage would actually have made a call to headquarters and explained things first.

Carter cut the line and then flipped back through the papers in the folder once more. It did not take him long to see that the plan that they had implemented in Chile had Ramirez involved in it. Profits for the operation had been very good. Astronomically good in terms of return. Zedadiah recalled a discussion from the Rio office to authorize money to manipulate water rights since the announcement of wells for all villages across the planet was playing havoc in the water markets of Chile. They had heavy analysis that the markets were primed for manipulation, and the analysis had been looked at by his financial experts at Carter Investments.

In fact the amount was large enough that he was informed of the matter, but small enough that Carter Investments approved the use of funds. It was all well documented. They had made so much money, that he had been informed earlier that year and had called Francisco with a congratulatory compliment. The boy deserved that. But every time he talked to the man, he felt like he had to check to see that all his fingers were still on his hand.

The stink of the Cartels were still on the underling after the years since Kutuzov had rescued him from that mess. Zedadiah had visited South America, and the Chilean operation in Sanhattan, even dated one of the women that Francisco introduced him to, but Colonel Kutuzov had separated them quickly. She had her expenses paid for by criminal money and though Zedadiah had been fond of the girl, she was a liability. There were a great many other women who were beautiful and were not connected to felons.

It took about seven minutes for Francisco to return his call. By then there was a secure conference set up. "Hold Francisco, I am making sure your communications are secure. 128 key encryption…" Colonel Kutuzov said from his link in Copenhagen.

"What, we are not alone?"

Zedadiah said, "No, and you will remain quiet. You must realize that you are to speak when you are spoken to. You have been very foolish. Are we set Stefan?" There was the sounds of high speed modulation in the background, and then the Colonel held up a green blinking electronic device.

"Now we are."

"Right, Penelope, you are here because you have to get the spin out." Recently, while she still had her beauty, Zedadiah had moved Penelope to the role of Vice President of Public Relations.

"Whoa," Jerry Piedmont said. "There is no spin. From what I am reading here, only we know that there is some causal connection between ZPak whatever and these deaths in a few backwater regions of Chile."

Kutuzov was a realist, "ZPakCad-1328. It is important Mr. Piedmont that we speak with accuracy. If we start now, then later, we will not have to fumble around looking for such information. Memorize the enzyme name."

Zedadiah knew his head of security was correct, and also had a lot of experience with this type of matter. With death. "Right, Jerry please do as Stefan says. What I want to know is to what extent we are liable."

"None!" Francisco said quickly.

"What extent? There are eight documented deaths here, and these reports are a few weeks old. How many have died since then? I have been pulling up some news clippings from these Regions. Let me get this right, Los Lagos," he looked down at his papers, "Aisen and Magallanes. There have been unexplained deaths amongst the livestock of the area, and I assume that the water that has been treated with this enzyme has watered crops? Next year you may find that more death will come out of the ground. I should think that the liability, without any analysis, is going to be very heavy. You may have crippled a good portion of an entire nation."

Zedadiah could see that Francisco was trembling. "I think Mr. Valdez y Gonzalez we have a very credible problem on our hands. I do not know what the legal punishment would be, but if this gets out, you can be sure that your days with our company are over. You are fortunate that I do not have to inform a Board of Directors about your indiscretion, and that right now we need a man on the ground in Chile. Otherwise we would throw you to the wolves right away."

Kutuzov spoke, "I am sending a team to do what must be done. 'Cisco, how many more deaths since these reports were generated?"

"What, I don't know."

" 'Cisco, you best tell me now what you do know. A dead body with a suicide note often ends an investigation. Don't let this come to that. I have arranged far too many of those conveniences," Zedadiah felt the chill even in London from Kutuzov's Copenhagen room.

"There are now 31 deaths. And five or six times that many ill. No one knows what is causing the deaths, but the weak, children and aged are hit first. They have a tough time of surviving if they are past a certain point, as I understand. As if the enzyme has gotten a hold of them and won't let go."

"I thought you wanted to bring the Pakistani into this, Zed," Penelope mentioned.

He nodded and said, "We still haven't located them. Sung Link Chou is doing his best to find anyone on the team."

Cisco cleared his throat, "I sent an email a couple days ago asking for help. They said they would look into things."

"Forward those emails to me!" Kutuzov said. "If the Pakistani researchers got wind that this is causing people to die, and they have no solution, they may have disappeared."

Zedadiah nodded. He looked at Penelope's screen when he spoke, "When we just managed investments, it was not like this." It was she who had urged him to take full equity positions and own the companies. Like Warren Buffett had done. Now it seemed doing such may have been a mistake. Even though he had no knowledge of what had transpired, people at his level usually would spend the rest of their lives at club Fed, should this come to light. People dead, and more to follow.

"Is there an upside to going public with these details at present? Jerry, what do you say?" Zedadiah asked.

"If this was a disaster that was not caused by man, say a part failing on a jet and it crashed, then sure you go forward right away. Here though, an untested chemical, willingly administered in the pursuit of manipulating a resource. Water. Did you really manipulate water? Oil I can understand. But people need water to live. You, Mr. Valdez y Gonzalez are a real piece of work."

Zedadiah said, "Jerry, please. Right now we are united. Let us not cause us to be divided."

The lawyer snorted, "What do you want me to do, quote Benjamin Franklin, 'We must all hang together, or assuredly we shall all hang separately?' I have no intention of hanging."

"Of course not. You are a lawyer. Lawyer's get disbarred. They don't hang. Jerry, pull it together. You get paid a great deal of money and until now, things have been rather undemanding. Now they are a little involved." Zedadiah said. He also sent a text to Kutuzov. Their lawyer was going to have to be watched. It was men like Jerry Piedmont who would give the best advice to Zedadiah and the Corporation while cutting a separate deal for himself.

"I do not want to make light of the situation. We can't even offer any public charitable contribution, but I think Francisco you can call for the organization of some such organization and put in a sum of what, 100,000 pounds for each victim?"

"No!" Kutuzov said. "That would make us known to care. And

that is way too much. 31 deaths, soon they will not think this is just natural causes, but something else. That is when we step forward, when the tragedy is recognized. Then 'Cisco will go forward and Penelope can have plans drawn up for this. I will take care of making sure those that have died, and those that will die, stay away from being linked to us and to ZPakCad-1328."

"Yes, 100,000 is far too much. 10,000 dollars US is a fortune to these people, well most of them. The areas that are hardest hit are where water is trucked in, and the new wells have been dug and treated with ZPakCad-1328. Here the people are still adjusting to abundant water, that they have little wish for." Francisco said.

Zedadiah said, "Little wish for because you have spiked the supply with the enzyme. We must find what the long-term effects are, and if they will effect next year's crop. Obviously Francisco you are to stop administering the enzyme at once. I want all traces of the enzyme removed from your offices. Every piece of paper destroyed. Every hard drive erased and reformatted."

Kutuzov smiled, "You have been listening to my security briefings. In any case that is my job. My team will take care of that. And we will gather up all remaining shipments and send them back to Pakistan. They will be labeled Lithium of course. That is one of things that is shipped regularly from Chile."

Zedadiah wanted to keep charge of the meeting. That was one thing he had learned how to do well as he matured in business. There was no course taught on running meetings. No one took you aside and said this is how it is done. It had no recipe like making an omelette, though the adage there, you had to break some eggs, held true. You had to get people to speak and commit.

Kutuzov had done so, but then he readily stepped up to take care of the messy end of things. "Right, Stefan is going to send a team to Santiago."

"I actually will go as soon as I finish here in Copenhagen as well."

Zedadiah turned his mind to Penelope. He said, "We need ideas and plans for all sorts of scenarios. Hopefully no one ever connects the dots. But if they do, we need to be able to speak to this.

Perhaps the enzyme, ZPakCad-1328, was a solvent from a bad batch in the Chilean distribution of the wells? Could we work that up? I know it is a cover-up, but we don't want to be found to have manufactured this on purpose without it having been tested or even passed by the FDA. We could lose a lot of licensing elsewhere for such a violation."

Jerry cleared his throat, "Actually on that score you are protected. First I will have to double check, but the regulations in Chile are a lot laxer than those of the United States, and Pakistan, it is of course the reason that the lab and manufacturing are located in Asia. No rules whatsoever that we need to worry about. Now as for the US, well, the enzyme has no legal connection to the United States. And though ZED Corp has a great presence in the US, the corporate protections apply. This enzyme, Z Pak Cad 1 3 2 8," Jerry said very clearly, "was never used in the US, money from its sale never came to the US. There is no US jurisdiction for what another part of the Corporation has done. You are in the clear here. There are no repercussions except perhaps one of image. Or what Chile might come at us for the deaths of so many."

It took a moment for Zedadiah to process that, "So we need to be prepared for looking like killers. That old Tylenol scare, or when meat packing plants all of sudden ship out bad hamburgers to McDonalds and people die."

The lawyer said, "We have a very well funded and defined indemnity insurance plan. Rates will go up of course if you are forced to use it, but should you be linked to these deaths in any way, and by that I mean ZED Corp, not you personally, then the insurance companies will pay millions to the survivors."

"We own some of the shares in our carriers. Perhaps we need to pull out, not only for conflict of interest reasons, but should they have to payout, then their stock will take a hit. I think I'll make some calls and collar a price point," Zedadiah said, making a quick note for his team at Carter Investments to get on that, slowly and unobtrusively. A good reporter might sense that there was collusion involved and with some date checking, might even determine when they discovered the matter.

Penelope was thinking the same, "Then shouldn't we get out in front of this now and go with the story that there was a bad batch of sealant at these wells? If we are in front of the story, then we will look a lot better when all is done. Even though we will look terrible."

Kutuzov held up his hand to the video monitor, "Wait one moment. Before you all start thinking that you know what is the right thing to do. There is no right thing to do. Even the courts will debate what the right thing is, won't they Mr. Piedmont. There will be many jurisdictions involved, as we are registered in many countries. And in Chile, well there we may have to cause the government to fall to ensure our safety, for right now they are a little too liberal, would you not say 'Cisco? You are there at the moment. I may want you to relocate elsewhere when I get there after I assess things on the ground."

The head of the Chilean operations said, "Si, the government is very liberal. It is why they were so glad that we would dig the wells though, since they want water to all, but are reluctant to repeal water rights ownership."

The Russian said, "A conservative government would thank us even more for they would not want the expense of carting water to these peasants. If you amortize the cost we are saving them, and these few deaths, then it is a small price to have paid." Kutuzov was very cut and dry about it. Zedadiah knew that those who had lost a family member would never forget that price. And no amount of money that ZED Corp paid would suffice.

Zedadiah said, "I have to trust the expert on this, and Stefan has had significant experience, as has members on his team. Stefan, I want you to ask those others you have brought into the organization if they agree with you. And do it subjectively. Don't lead them to answer because you want them to agree with you. It is not why we pay you all very greatly. If a cover-up, and that is what we are talking about, is what is necessary, then that is what we should do. Penelope, I want you, and only people you trust to keep their mouth shut, to develop plans for this. And Jerry, you need to double and triple check the legal downsides. Even if it means closing and selling out all our holdings in Chile, which I would not like to do, then we will do so. Francisco, you need to bring all your people in from the field and do likewise at all our operations involved with water. I think Copper, Lithium, the wineries, will be alright. They need to be available to Colonel Kutuzov and his people. I think that's it for now."

"There is a couple more things," Kutuzov said. "Penelope, your people are prone to talk. I will have some of my people join your team, actually, we will even make one of our office areas available to you in the security floors. That way we can watch, and they will get the sense how secret this is. Send me the names of who you want on your task force. Then I will also call Sung Ling Chou and find out why we still have no contact with the Pakistani team. My people will be mobilizing there, and will find them. If those scientists have gone into hiding, my people will find them."

Zedadiah felt a chill run up his spine and shivered. Kutuzov had shown Zedadiah at three different times the location of Osama Bin Ladin in the years he was being hunted. Kutuzov was very good at finding people.

Zedadiah had given the information to various United States Administration officials. Though they clearly had not chosen to use it until the last time. But giving the information meant the United States owed him a few favors. Favors he had not collected on as yet.

The conference was over but Kutuzov called him back a few moments later, "Cisco is becoming a problem." Zedadiah knew that was what was on the security chief's mind.

"Again."

"I am going to call a few people, his Cartel contacts. He thinks that we don't know he is still tied to them. If I find they have had anything to do with this, or have been manipulating this for their own ends, it won't be pretty. We may lose a few people."

"I don't think we want to piss off the Cartels…" Zedadiah said. He had a bad feeling that should you start down that path, they didn't rest until they more than evened the score.

"Don't worry. I'll convince them that I am worse when angered then they are. But Francisco Valdez y Gonzalez has dabbled where he shouldn't one time too many."

Zedadiah nodded, but knew, he was the one who had to agree. It could mean a death sentence for the man they were talking about. A man who was foolish enough to have murdered a great many others. "Yes, but exercise discretion. We may need his body and his confession to tie up loose ends later. You may want to put him on ice and see how this resolves."

"Ha, I had already thought of that. Don't worry, Francisco is going to have a lot of fun these last days of his, but then, when I need him, that's it." Kutuzov nodded and then closed the connection. Zedadiah thought for a few moments about nothing, for he had just agreed to killing an employee of his. He was surprised that it did not bother him more. In one respect, he was slightly relieved. One problem taken care of. Then he turned back to his screens and began to conduct more business. He had Michael bring in his call list and see whom was most important to speak to about the other matters that needed his attention. It was time to return to less volatile work.

-Chapter 10-

The newscaster was speaking about Chile when Parker walked in. Guillermo seemed to be totally wrapped up in the matter. Yesterday the death toll had grown to well over 100, and the World Health Organization were sending experts now to study the problem. People dying of thirst and not at all showing a desire to drink. Some even refusing water when offered because they said they felt like they were drowning in it already.

"You really should look at this. It could be very important," Guillermo noticed him. Something had changed again with the younger boys attitude towards him. Three weeks since they had returned from the conference at Aral'sk and there were finals in a few weeks. But now Guillermo was being, if not nice, then at least pleasant.

Parker said, "JCubed has been sending me a great deal of news. I have scanned it, but haven't had time to read it all."

"I think that you should. Something is wrong, seriously wrong with the aquifers in southern Chile and that is quite close to your beloved Antarctica."

Guillermo did not say that in a hostile way, so Parker tried not to get upset. "It's pretty far really. Not as far as Costa Rica is, but still a distance."

There was a knock at the front door to their house, and then Jennifer entered, "I told you, you don't have to knock. I am with you." JCubed followed and behind him came Priya.

The boys' houses were off limits at certain times from girls unless there was an adult around. Which usually there was. It was Friday afternoon, though, and the girls could come in unannounced then.

"Good, you two are here. We were at the Oval when my father texted me. He's going to go down to Chile as part of the WHO investigation and wondered if we wanted to go as well. He said we could take our finals from Santiago and then really spend the quarter break in the field. My father said that the five ECOAgents had done so well in Kazakhstan that perhaps another real world test was something we might want to work on."

Guillermo asked, "Is that kosher? I mean will Dr. Phillips-Lee let us go off campus again." Guillermo wasn't Jewish, but he had taken to saying such things. He was also spending a lot of time with Colonel Ben-Levi.

"We should ask him," Priya said. "Not that I don't trust what your father says Jennifer, but I don't want to be expelled."

Parker said, "I don't think that Dr. Smythe-Lytton would suggest something that would get us expelled. But what are the ECOAgents? Was he teasing you?"

Jennifer shook her head and Parker had to wonder if she and her father had called a truce. Or at least she had called a truce. Dr. Smythe-Lytton wanted to make up with his daughter as far as Parker could tell. "I think that is what everyone is calling us now. JCubed copied me something from the UN Security Council about what we did in Aral'sk. That the Security Council was adopting a broad plan with the Premier of Russia as the lead chairman, based upon work of the students of the ECO Academy, or ECOAgents."

JCubed looked over with a grin, "I may have been sending press releases out to the delegations at the UN, and all the members on the Security Council, that sort of referenced the word ECOAgents. I think it has quite the ring to it."

With JCubed's skills and an addiction to watching any spy show that he could see either through streaming, or NetFlix, it was clear that the boy wanted to eventually go work at a government agency that let him say something like, 'Jack Jefferson, special agent-in-charge.'

"I'll text him," Parker said pulling out his phone. But even as he tapped to the right app, the phone rang and he saw that it was the Chancellor calling. "It's Dr. Phillips-Lee," he told everyone.

Parker turned his head a little and tapped to answer, "Hi Dr. Phillips-Lee?" The image of the Chancellor appeared in his video screen of the phone.

"Mr. Thornton, good, I wanted to start with you. I am taking the jet down to Chile with Dr. Smythe-Lytton and wanted to know if you would like to go as well. You and a few of your friends. The last trip we went on proved to be very educational I think, and you young people had an insight that we older ones forget sometimes. I think that some things don't get done because of the stubbornness of adults. The help and leadership of you children, I mean young people, has shown to be very promising."

"Uh, I think I know who you want to go. Jennifer Smythe-Lytton says she already talked to her father. Something about the ECOAgents," Parker said. Then he found that Dr. Phillips-Lee began to laugh.

Dr. Phillips-Lee said, "Well, I learned that Mr. Jefferson was promulgating that term, and I think it fits. It is good advertising for the Academy as well. We have secured the land that the Premier talked of outside of St. Petersburg. You'll have graduated, but in two years we will have a second campus there. Now, if you and the others are willing to travel to Chile, it is not a quarantine area, but should it appear to be dangerous, the plane will fly you out immediately."

Parker responded, "I'll have to ask the others. Just those of us who went to Kazakhstan?"

"For now. It does seem like a reward, I suppose, but there are some things that remain secret and you five know what I am talking of," Dr. Phillips-Lee said. That was the meeting with the Premier and Vice-President. No one who had not been in the room knew that the students had made a presentation and were so frank about it. That they had convinced the Premier to push, as he had after the conference, for the coalition of nations to deal with the Aral Sea.

The news since had attributed much that was accomplished to the team from the ECO Academy. This included the presentations by the adults, and the findings by Dr. Smythe-Lytton. Those who had been the dinner guests of Dr. Phillips-Lee the evening before the conference began, knew that the coalition that was now being formed came from the dialogue of the private presentation.

Parker said his goodbye to Dr. Phillips-Lee and then looked about the room. It was just he and the other four, "Well, it does seem true. If we want to go down to Chile and see if we can help, Dr. Phillips-Lee has said that we can. But it is just us five.

The ECOAgents, and if we contribute we may have to keep it on the QT."

"What?" Guillermo had only been in America for a few years.

"On the quiet. Apparently ECOAgents seem to be a bit secretive. No one knows how much we talked to the Premier and Vice President to get them to start working on the coalition. I think Dr. Phillips-Lee wants us to be as discreet if we go to South America," Parker said.

Guillermo said, "There is another consideration. We could become targets. No really. I have been talking to Colonel Ben-Levi and he says that the Chinese are not pleased at all with what we started at Aral'sk. Priya, you tell them."

Parker looked to his girlfriend. That was how he was thinking of Priya now. He was a little angered that Guillermo had some sort of conversation with Priya that he didn't know about. Guillermo was so often an ass, and he had to count to ten, figuratively, to keep his cool. So much of the time he wanted to smack the other boy.

Priya nodded, "We get about 500 to 1,000 hacking attempts a day on the school computers, and as you know, all of our computers that we have are tied to the school's network for security. That's why, JCubed, when you go up to Santa Monica and buy a new toy, we want to put some of our software on it. We really want to put hardware in it, but most things, we can't really add a part to. Though the Department of Defense and NSA have certain parts of the firmware reserved for various things, we know of a few and kind of piggyback onto them. Actually my brother Chandan…" Jennifer nudged Priya and gave her a look.

Priya said, "Right. Sorry." She had a grin on her face and Parker realized how much he liked her when she smiled like that. She was really beautiful, and she liked him back. Way cool!

Priya continued, "Well we get attacked each day, and we beat them back with lots of security algorithms that we keep working on. But two days after we got back from Kazakhstan the attacks increased from under a thousand to well over 10,000 a day. And over ninety percent from China."

Parker grasped the situation immediately. "You think that the Chinese would try and harm us?"

Guillermo now spoke, "If we continue to threaten their plans, then yes. You know the Japanese companies in the seventies and eighties had big ideas about 100 year plans. Those of course were kind of foolish because we see how quickly new discoveries change such things. But China, they have plans, not at all defined, but in a general sense that go out much further. Their plans are for dominance everywhere at some time. That is their plan and it is pretty clear they always act with such goals. Not the good of mankind, but the good of China."

Parker thought about that for a second, then said, "Not the good of China, but what you said before, the dominance of China. We need a history course. I looked this up when we got back from Aral'sk. Before 200 BC, the Chinese were many countries, not one big country. These were the size of what countries are now. Then at about 220 BC, they unified into the very large kingdom they have been for over 2200 years. They still want to get bigger and bigger. I think that the ECU was designed to make Europe economically as strong as the United States, though they haven't succeeded yet. But really it is to be strong enough to fend off China."

JCubed said, "Forget the world history lecture, what about us being targets. I've got my personal data pretty well encrypted, but the Chinese have armies and stuff. Would they try and kidnap us?"

Guillermo laughed, "Let them try. Do you know how many ex-Seals and Green Berets Colonel Ben-Levi has working for him? And a few from the CIA and Mossad as well."

"Let's not get ahead of ourselves." Parker said. Some of the professors said that as well when the students would jump ahead a few steps, or chapters, or experiments. Sometimes you could, for a lot of the work was not apropos for the research, but if you did jump too far, you might miss something very important in the grounding that you needed later. Einstein did not wake up and know that E was equal to MC squared without having done a significant amount of work before that.

"First we all have to want to go to Chile, and then there is a lot of research to get ready and prepare for the trip. It is also a very long plane ride, I bet. Chile is, after all, at the bottom of the world."

Guillermo who had been studying a little of the situation said, "About fourteen hours to Santiago, and then four or five more hours to get to where the area has been hardest hit by the problem."

Parker nodded, "JCubed, target us primary research from all credible sources. Jennifer, you may want to talk some more to your father and get us the medical data we need. That seems to be the indicator that something has gone wonky there. And your father will have stuff that is classified. I know that JCubed, you can get that too, but it would be good to compare what you can get to what they have given to Dr. Smythe-Lytton, and see if Chile or the WHO are holding anything back." Parker innately assumed the role of team leader. ECOAgent-in-charge.

Soon enough they broke apart to do research and get ready for the trip to South America. They all had to go to the Medical Center before dinner and get various inoculations. Parker received a text message to go to the basement of the Admin building. He knew that there was work being done on the Admin building, for he had seen earth movers and other construction machines parked behind it. The only way to the basement level that he knew of was a stairwell at the far end of the main hall. At the bottom of the stairs were three men who sat in front of a security scanning machine, like at an airport, and they seemed to be expecting him. For some reason this area had heightened security. Parker was a little hesistant.

"We don't get many visitors, so we mostly know who is going to come. Your name is on the list. The Colonel is expecting you, but someone will meet you to show you the way. Just walk through the scanner, slowly please, and we'll scan your computer sack." One of the guards said good-naturedly. He was fit, and looked strong. Parker's first thought was that the man was an ex-seal like Guillermo had said. And the other two guards as well.

He couldn't see any guns, but Parker would not be surprised if there were weapons close by. As he entered the secure area, Parker was met by Major Walter Wilson, the Colonel's right-hand man, who just happened to have a gun in a holster at his hip. Noticing that Parker looked to it, the man said, "This is operations, and we are changing our mission profile. We are no longer just concerned with Dr. Phillips-Lee, which was our first priority, or the academy, but it seems due to your efforts, we are looking to be a leading force in protecting and saving the planet. Something the Colonel thinks may involve muscle some of the time."

"Saving the planet," Parker thought to himself. He was not sure what to make of that. Could a security force be all that necessary to saving the planet? Parker was sure that the only way to reverse the damage humanity was doing to the Earth was to do so by scientific methods.

By finding solutions for sustainable living. By curbing and then eradicating pollution. By living through better means, and not putting horrid chemicals into your body. He knew that it was going to be a long haul, with no quick solutions that he and his fellow students were going to find the path to guide over seven billion people.

Parker was sure that some of the work they had done at Aral'sk, about the Aral Sea was very good, but that other scientists who had been in the field had even better remedies. Some had presented at the conference and the coalition led by the Premier was sure to adopt those ideas. Parker was equally sure that though the other scientists appreciated what the students of ECO Academy had said, their ideas would be built upon and changed greatly. If indeed any of them were really going to be used in the end.

The man guided Parker to a small office, three walls filled with scenes as if there were television sets, but these were video feeds played right on the wall. The covering was clearly one of the new glass constraints that had been recently developed to serve as video screens.

Behind a desk, totally clean of any item but a piece of paper and a pen, was Colonel Ben-Levi. "Sit Mr. Thornton. Relax. You are not in trouble. Yet." The Colonel smiled.

"I don't know why I am here." Parker said.

"Well, because you are nearly a man. In my religion of course you would be thought to be a man, but the religious back home, sometime they are not really cognizant of the world. You are in good shape, this surfing you do, and you jog each day. I am going to want you to follow an even stricter routine. You, it appears, are the leader of your fellow students, and a leader has to be ready for many dangers."

"ECOAgent-in-charge," Parker thought to himself again and slightly smiled. "Ah, Colonel, I still don't understand." Parker was beginning to, but this was one of those situations in life that he knew things needed to be spelled out. Adults liked to talk a lot and make a lot of rules. Men with guns, he decided, he would defer to. He did not know how to use a gun, well beyond the point and pull the trigger approach that he had often seen on television and movies. But if he were to do that, would the bullets hit a target, or would they go and fly to some other part of the planet?

The Colonel said, "Right. And you of course really don't know about the many other issues that surround us on a daily basis. You might think that JCubed has hacked the computer network so we don't know what he gets and then sends to his friends, or what you just requested to be delivered to your reader. You do know that Google Reader isn't really a secure way to get news and blogs, but rather easily hacked itself for us to follow? In any case, Mr. Thornton, security here has always taken an interest in what the students bring into the school's network. The first week that we were operational we had over thirteen thousand viruses, but I will be fair. Most of that was from the faculty, not the students, then." Colonel Ben-Levi smiled.

Parker was shaking his head, "I can understand your concern, but I haven't asked JCubed to get me any particular news…" He wasn't allowed to finish.

"Mr. Thornton, I am trying to teach you something that you probably never thought would come your way. You began to touch on it, with the insight you had, and some students have talked about it before in prior years. Now Dr. Phillips-Lee understands the wisdom of it. You students need a great deal more to prepare yourselves for when you leave here. Something that very few scientists ever understand, but we are training a new type of scientist, and now we need to add the next course to round you out. In Israel, this would have been done when you joined the Israel Defense Force, as all do at eighteen. Many of you from

ECO Academy can go to a nice job somewhere and think of the solutions the world needs. But you know that those will not be as effective as getting your hands dirty in Kazakhstan as you did. Or Chile, where we go tomorrow," the Colonel said.

"But the Academy security team was with us in Kazakhstan," Parker said.

"And when you have graduated, and you go to someplace dangerous. To save the planet going to dangerous places will be necessary. And Kazakhstan is very much dangerous, then what? Are you and the rest ready for that? Chile could be dangerous as well. There is an issue not only about people dying of thirst even when they have enough to drink, but the water itself can be very valuable. Valuable enough that it might be worth killing over to get. And this connection between water and dying of thirst suggests to me that there is an issue there. A fatally deadly issue, and one that is more about a bullet, then a well." The Colonel reached over to his desk and handed Parker a gun in a holster. At Dr. Phillips-Lee's request.

"That's a Glock, and you'll find no better weapon. These are the bullets." The Colonel held up those in his other hand. "We'll teach you how to use the gun and keep the safety on before we let you put any bullets in it. For now though, you are to start wearing it. Know where it is at all times. After this mission, I may have these other ECOAgents of yours get guns, or not. But you are the oldest, a senior here, and from now on all seniors are going to learn how to be gun friendly." Again, as ordered by Dr. Phillips-Lee.

"We leave tomorrow, I don't know if that is enough time to learn how to use a weapon," Parker said.

The Colonel smiled, "It isn't, but we are going to make do. I want an hour today, and then an hour tomorrow before we go to the airport. Also, there is a lot of time while we fly, so I'll take you aside for a few hours and brief you. I'm also putting a couple of my people with you at all times. Two men, and a women, and they will rotate every few hours. Where we are going, no one wanders off this time. JCubed is not too old to be spanked…"

Parker snorted a laugh. At the airport when they left Kazakhstan, JCubed wandered away looking for some kuirdak one more time. He had really taken a liking to the dish of roasted sheep, served with onions. Though at the airport, it was not made with sheep, but other items. JCubed was not only in trouble on the flight back, but his stomach was upset as they returned home as well.

"I think JCubed learned his lesson, but I understand," Parker said.

The Colonel nodded, "Good, then you will have to brief your team. I brief you and my lieutenants on operational matters regarding security, you brief your team. Do you understand? You'll tell them that there is some danger here, and we are still determining from where. The State Department, which means the CIA, says there are Columbian Drug Cartels operating in Chile. It seems they like to launder their money there. We've been told they also may be involved with the water issues. So we have that to deal with as well, and you children are just the type to be taken for hostages also."

Parker said, "If it is so dangerous, then why take us?"

"It could be dangerous, and so we take precautions. If we knew for a fact that you were a target to be kidnapped, you wouldn't be leaving the campus. Not even to go up to Tommy's for a hamburger. And normally, I don't like prying, but as I have dietary restrictions that I don't step over the line on, you do know that to Ms. Zadari, in her culture, the cow is sacred and therefore they don't eat meat?"

Parker shook his head. That was his private life, and though he knew that the security team spied on the students to some extent, he felt some things were his alone. Privacy was an issue.

"We talked about it. She says her brother used to take her to a burger joint near Harvard," Priya had told him that if her brother Chandan hadn't told her it was alright to eat a hamburger, she never would have.

The Colonel shook his head, "One of my ex-wives ate shrimp, and I did so on occasion as well. But some of what they teach us as children makes doing something such as bending a food rule the cause of guilt. And guilt haunts us. Especially when we are led to break these rules of our own by peer pressure. I'm an old man, at least compared to you, and I've had a few relationships. Free advice so you don't have to take it, but I would let the lady pick the restaurants for your dates for a while. Then you really will know what she wants to eat."

Parker bit his lip. He hadn't thought about that. Of course he would let Priya pick where she wanted to eat. That was only fair. There were Indian restaurants in Malibu and in Santa Monica. They could eat at any of those. Or whatever else she picked.

One of the security officers, a different one took Parker to an indoor firing range, another two levels down. The second level, he saw as they walked down the steps, had one whole side and the end shrouded off by plastic tarps and blue tape. There was the sound of the heavy machinery that he had seen outside. Parker figured that they were adding to the security offices as well as building a bigger foundation for the expansion of the Administration offices.

The firing range took up a good portion of the floor. Opposite it, there were locked vaults, and other rooms that he saw doors to, but they were closed. The three locked vaults were closed, but one opened and a man came out, palming the security door closed, speaking a phrase and standing in place for a fraction as a laser came out and scanned the man's face.

Parker's guide said, "One of the armories, and if the Colonel gives you his blessing, you'll gain access to one or two of them. Makes sense to have a scientist that is able to defend himself. Kind of like Indiana Jones, or who is that new one that they have a game for Drake something…"

Parker knew, "Nathan Drake. It's Uncharted. JCubed is pretty good. I only played it a little when I was younger." Parker snorted a bit. His father Prescott tried to play it in his man cave but was pretty slow.

When the officer started showing him how to handle a weapon, though, Parker knew his father never had such instruction. His father never had a Glock, and here Parker now was supposed to wear it until they returned from Chile, the Colonel had said.

The officer went over stance first, and said if he didn't have time to get into the proper stance, it was more important to shoot off some rounds and stay alive, then add to one's chance of a perfect shot with the right stance. But if there was time, the odds increased that he would hit something he was shooting at.

The lesson went on forever, it seemed until finally the man put one round in the gun magazine, and then let Parker shoot.

"Ouch," he said surprised at the noise and recoil that the gun made when he squeezed the trigger. He had not expected it to jump in his hand so much.

"There is more to becoming a good shot, then just pointing and pulling the trigger. We don't have a lot of time to get you ready, but we will get you ready to carry the weapon, and use it to help protect you. Now here's another bullet, you remember how to eject the magazine so you can put the bullet in it?"

They went through that routine several times. One bullet only, until Parker was placing the gun on safe after he used it. Then the officer let him put three bullets in and shoot, and finally he was able to add a full magazine twice, before the man said it was time to stop for the day.

"Wow, that was more than an hour, and I have a lot to do still," Parker noted.

"Yes, and you have a lot to learn as well. I'm on the Chile detail and I will work with you tomorrow. Until then, this is your gun, and you will place it in your holster. The one we shot with, I'll clean that and take it back to the armory. I'll teach you how to clean a gun after you shoot with it at another lesson," the security man said.

Parker nodded and then was shown the way out of the Security offices. He felt a little weird that he had such a lesson, but it was like an affirmation. Like passing a test for a class and advancing to the next class in the series. He had achieved a level he had never thought to exceed.

With a gun on his hip, he raised eyebrows, but the school scuttlebutt worked quickly. Most knew that he and others were going to Chile the next day. There also was a text to all seniors that over the next few weeks they had appointments in security to take a new class about defensive combat techniques. Parker believed the Colonel was very deliberate about labeling the new course, Combat Techniques.

"I don't believe it. A gun?" Guillermo said when Parker walked into the dining hall with his tray of food. Breakfasts were accommodated from the house kitchens at their dormitories. Lunch and Dinner was always in the cafeteria facility, where often faculty and staff joined the students.

"Yes, a gun. All seniors who go abroad on Academy business will wear a gun. I am sure you got an email about it. But don't worry, Colonel Ben-Levi is evaluating whether to allow juniors to be issued them as well," Parker responded.

"You do not know how much violence there is in South America. Wearing a gun is like a magnet," Guillermo said. "Don't you need your parents' permission to carry a gun?"

JCubed was there as well as Priya and Jennifer. JCubed said, "Nah, I looked it up already. It is part of the admission package documents that our parents signed. It is part of the security arrangements where there are a couple lines of legal mumbo-jumbo about teaching students to fend for themselves. They could give us all tanks and our parents have already agreed to it, sort of."

Parker shook his head, "Why worry about it. I'm not going to shoot you."

Guillermo snorted, and the other three laughed a little.

"I don't like it either," Priya said.

"Oh, I think it makes Parker look like some hero. You need a hat, or something," Jennifer said.

"When we get to Chile, we all will need hats. It is late spring there, not almost winter like here." Though in Malibu, it rained and the nights were a little cold. Winters were really mild in Southern California.

Priya said, "Well maybe with a hat, you'll look alright. But you're not going to use it, are you?"

"What the gun?" Parker said. Shaking his head, "The Colonel said that it is going to be part of all of our training. He was worried when we were in Kazakhstan because it is not the friendliest part of the world. And so he wants us to all be able to take care of ourselves better once we leave the Academy. He thinks that we will all be doing a lot of work in places that are not always so nice to scientists."

Guillermo snorted, "Especially ones who have been living like gods in Malibu for a few years."

Parker nodded, "That too. They're teaching me how to use the gun as a last line of defense. We'll have lots of security with us, so I probably won't have to use the gun," he said. He hoped he sounded convincing. Priya was across the table from him so he couldn't reach out to her, or talk to her so quietly that no one else could hear. He hoped what he told to her was true also. That he wouldn't have to use the weapon. If he did, it would mean that they were in danger. It was one thing to shoot at someone who was not shooting back. But what would it be like if someone was shooting at them? Bullets could kill.

-Chapter 11-

Boarding the plane the next day was not as exciting as the first time they had done it, but it was still pretty fantastic to travel in a private jet. As they pulled up to the charter terminal where they were to embark, Parker noticed that the plane was much larger than the last plane. Everyone noticed.

"Yah, modified C-17," Colonel Ben-Levi stood up in the center aisle of the bus and spoke to everyone. I was able to pick it up a few weeks back in a horse trade, isn't that the way it's said here in America? And we've been outfitting it so it is more useful. You'll see. The back has a cargo space so we can transport certain vehicles, mobile labs for you to do your experiments, and the forward compartment allows you all to travel in comfort and for us to maintain a very robust communication and command center once we are on the ground wherever we go. Mr. Jackson has been somewhat helpful with our project."

"What? What did I do?" The boy spoke up.

The Colonel laughed, "And Ms. Zadari as well. Both were given a few surprise quizzes and submitted reports that helped us decide what we needed to install in the plane. Though we hid our true needs just a little. It is about 85 percent operational now, and we'll finish it up when we get back from Chile. Also, we have two of the three mobile laboratories we commissioned on board. So we'll just have to make do."

Dr. Phillips-Lee stood then, "Children, one thing I can afford are some really great toys. Though this may not be as comfortable a flight as we had to Kazakhstan, it still should prove to be very relaxing. The Colonel has promised that the seats are the best, and we will have the same flight team as before. I did not really want to get rid of my Bombardier, but this does seem very practical for what we are going to do. I have not done as much lab work these last ten years as I should have. But we will need the labs where we go and it is better we take our tools with us then hope that the Chilean government has the ones we need when we need them."

Parker thought that Dr. Phillips-Lee was more upset about trading in his fancy Jet for the gigantic cargo plane. The other plane had been sleek and something Parker's father would have been envious of. The Thornton's were not rich enough to afford their own jet, and in any case, all the branches of the family bank were all around Kansas City, and only on the Missouri side at that. Even if the bank went statewide, Parker did not think his father could justify his own jet, though his parents did fly first class everywhere.

"Come on everyone, ECO1 awaits." The Colonel said as the door of the bus opened. He turned and led the way to the plane. There were other security persons from the Academy already outside and they were overseeing the transfer of luggage from the bus to the plane. Parker had not expected such a big plane, not after Dr. Phillips-Lee's old plane, this was really immense.

There was a cordon that the security officers had set up, that led away from the bus towards the plane. Once under the wings of the C17, it was expanded and he could walk a little ways to get a better view. There was new paint on the fuselage, but there were markings that had been missed. Parker was able to see that the plane had been in service to another country. It had bourn the Maple Leaf of Canada.

Parker took a quick picture with his phone's camera of a serial number he found and sent it to JCubed knowing that his friend could double check that very quickly. At the moment there were no students at ECO Academy from Canada. One had graduated the year before. Not every country had yet sent students to the Academy. And Parker was going to graduate so he would not interact with any of the new students who would come next year.

Parker knew it was right about the time of year that the Academy started to send out applications for the next class. Parker wondered if his ideas about additional courses would be adopted in the following year. A music curriculum with the Jerry Simons Jazz Quintet next quarter was a step in the right direction, but a whole lot of other classes were really going to be needed.

"Big plane," he said. Someone had come up next to him, and when he turned he saw that it was Guillermo.

"I'll say. This may be more serious then I thought."

Parker's face quirked in disappointment. "You were the one who told me I needed to look into this more. Over a hundred people are dead, and maybe even more because it took some time to see that this was systematic. You didn't think that was serious?" Parker asked.

Guillermo did not look happy, "Oh, for South America it is serious. But you norte americanos don't ever really care about how many of us are dying."

Parker could see that the others were too far to really hear them. He leaned over and said slowly, "You have a really big problem, don't you Guillermo. Anyone who did not suffer as much as you when you were little is to be hated and is the enemy. And yet you claim to be a scientist. Perhaps you should think how that hatred you carry inside of you can balance with the scientific study of other people. We are not all greedy capitalist pigs as you think we are. Dr. Phillips-Lee is worth more money than I can even imagine and you don't feel that way about him, do you? Because he pays for about half of your education. You, Guillermo are a hypocrite."

Parker heard the other boy trying to say something in retaliation, but he was already walking away from Guillermo. He feared that the only way they would ever resolve matters was going to be to allow Guillermo to take a swipe at him, and then Parker would have to pound him.

Which might stop Guillermo from picking any more fights with him, but not end the hatred.

Parker walked up the gangway and then heard the Colonel calling to Guillermo to hurry up. He said they wanted to leave on time. Glancing to see how the loading of the luggage was going, Parker saw that three carts were being rolled up the back ramp of the plane. They wouldn't be ready to leave for some time, he was sure.

The Colonel must have been reared on Hurry up and Wait. Parker's reading showed that most militaries functioned that way. Get everything ready and then sit around and wait for a long time. Though, to be fair, the pilot was cranking on the engines and they were making start-up noises. Good thing that he had started for the fuselage. If he were still outside, it wasn't likely, but it was possible to be sucked into a jet engine. And once inside, be cut up into a lot of little tiny pieces.

It happened to birds, and in comics, quite often.

Parker had found a seat and was getting comfortable when Guillermo tromped onto the plane and stomped his way down the aisle to find the last free seat towards the back he could possibly take. The adults, there were some security officers as well as Dr. Phillips-Lee and Dr. Smythe-Lytton already seated, looked at Guillermo quizzically. There were three other professors from ECO Academy on the trip, and with the five students and a dozen-person security detail, there were plenty of extra seats in the cabin.

One thing hadn't changed and that was the cabin crew. It had only been a few weeks since the flight to Western Asia, and Parker remembered what all three of the very pretty flight attendants looked like. He hadn't flown much in his life, a few times back and forth to Kansas City, but the ladies who worked American and United were not as pretty, or young.

Parker hadn't thought about it much but the ladies who would work a private jet were probably more model or actress pretty then planning to be full time stewardesses. A pecking order for the very pretty. They served the very rich. His mother was a beauty queen. That he understood.

"Hey, are you and Guillermo fighting again?" Priya asked. Parker had sat in the seat next to her. She had saved it for him while he was outside looking at the plane.

"No matter what I do or say, he wants to fight, so I am just going to have to let him. I keep my temper, but that's me. One day, someone isn't and he is going to get a well deserved fat lip."

She nodded, "He will, and then he'll probably get another and another. The funny thing is he will probably end up being richer than Dr. Phillips-Lee, pay to get his family out of Costa Rica and live some place where the super wealthy live, and still hate all people who are rich."

He said, "I wish we could just bottle up all his anger and make it a cologne. Well it is pretty rotten tomato. Now, I'm going to try and sleep through take-off and then I have to meet with the

Colonel and get some training."

She shivered, "Is it really that dangerous? Last time I didn't think we were in any danger."

"The Vice President of the United States and all his secret service were around, and the Premier of Russia who was quite willing, I am sure, to invade Kazakhstan was around. This time we don't have those kind of people with us. Security is going to be up to the Colonel and whoever the Chilean government assigns to us. I don't know about you, but I don't have a lot of faith in third world militaries."

She punched him lightly. "Watch what you say."

Parker rubbed at his shoulder, "Hey. Don't do that. And you tell me, who do you trust more, a Navy Seal, the Colonel, or one of India's elite commandos. You do have commandos, don't you?"

"Yes, we do. The Para-Commandos. I'm sure they are very good."

He smiled, "Come on, Priya, except for some visits, you have been here in America more than you ever lived in India. Are you really loyal to India?"

She did not look happy at that, "Of course I am. If you moved to some other country, and when you graduate, you might do that, will you still be loyal to America?"

He nodded. He could understand when put that way. "Okay I'm sorry I made a crack about third world countries but you have to admit, wouldn't you rather be protected by ex-seals, or the Colonel who was a paratrooper in the IDF. His unit were the paratroopers that rescued the hostages at Entebbe on the bicentennial of America in '76."

She looked at him blankly. It was well before he was born, but there was a great military movie he had seen a few times. And Parker's mother, even she knew about it. How a plane had been hijacked by terrorists and parked at Entebbe in Uganda. Where Idi Amin was the dictator. Then the Israelis sent their commandos to free the prisoners on the Fourth of July. The only commando to die in the rescue was the older brother of the man who had been Prime Minister of Israel a few times. When one started putting all those little facts together, it was something that he could remember.

He told her about it, and Priya looked to where the Colonel sat, and then to a few others of the ex-soldiers who made up their security force. More than one was also a former member of the IDF. Probably Paratroopers like the Colonel. Priya shivered again and he reached out to rub her arm. "Don't worry," he said.

He then felt the weight at his hip. The gun he had there. He looked about the cabin and noticed that they had a lot of guns out in the open. He had never been on a plane where you carried a gun out in the open like that. It, of course, was a private flight. Still though, Parker had never thought he would see weapons on a plane except in the movies.

"I wasn't worried before. Now I'm worried. Is Chile really this dangerous?" Priya asked.

"I think we are taking precautions because of the issues about water rights. It seems that you can own water and since it becomes scarce, people might become a little aggressive about it. We don't have to worry about that, but we might be caught in the cross fire," Parker said.

"Not helping. And you claim to speak English? You need to think a little bit better about your metaphors. Now I agree with you and know we need an English department just to work on the proper use of language." Priya tried to smile. Her joke was a little bit funny.

Parker shook his head. Priya would be around to see how the school was going to grow. Right then, however, he needed to change the subject so they did not talk of something that frightened her. "I wonder what movies we can get?"

"Pretty much anything, and a lot of the stuff is stored on the hard drives. If the Colonel wasn't lying, I pretty much spec'ed the entire command and communications center as well as a great deal of the labs. There should be every episode of the top 300 TV shows of all time, as well as episodes of everything that has aired in the last three years. And then with movies, the top five thousand movies of all time, every movie that has been nominated for an Academy Award and releases for the last five years. Probably fifty or so terabytes of data. As for music, well a small selection but still a couple hundred thousand songs. The top

1,000 or so albums in every genre, and then add to that the complete works of the many of the artists you would think should be included."

Parker was sure he looked impressed. He felt impressed. It was a great entertainment library. There would be no way not to find something you would want to see or hear during the long flight. "Reading material?"

"Another several terabytes. We know we needed to have the servers burn up to the minute journal articles and blogs before takeoff, so there is a time marker. The databases have all the science data we could think to load, at least that is how I specified it. Then once the plane lands again, it will go back to the time marker and add new data since take-off. For non-scientific or education material, the ten thousand greatest books in seven languages, and then a large selection of magazines. I let JCubed decide which gaming magazines to have in the database. He plays like three times as much as I do."

Parker laughed, "I used to play a lot more before I came to ECO Academy. I would sneak into my father's man cave and boot up CoD on his big screen. He has an 80-inch television. I would get my clan and we would have a great day. But my father hardly ever let me play when he was home. I had to be extra careful to set the room back the way I found it, and log out all traces of my use from his accounts. Call of Duty is a lot better on a really big screen."

Priya smiled, the smile he really liked. "JCubed said that there should be some game consoles included on the plane, but I don't know if they are here. Not only would we want to play, but I bet the soldiers would as well."

Suddenly the Colonel was there. He cleared his throat, "You'll find Ms. Zadari that everything you and Mr. Jefferson specified is here, including all the latest in console games, though we have a few extra for military training as well. There is a modified shooting range, one deck below, Mr. Thornton, that after take-off I should like you to join me at." He was worried about the South American cartels, though he would never express those thoughts. "We have a few gun controllers that would appear to be guns except they shoot light at a screen to see if you are on target or not.

You don't want to shoot a real gun in an airplane at thirty thousand feet. Bad things happen when a pressurized space becomes unpressurized quickly." Colonel Ben-Levi spoke as if he had actually been through the experience.

Parker and Priya both nodded to that. That was often shown in movies and it never did look good. He could not imagine falling to the ground from so high. Would you die before you hit the ground? Was there anything that could make that a soft landing? How long would it take before you impacted? How hard would it be to clean up a body that did hit the Earth like a meteor? Parker thought it best to stop thinking about it, and not even look it up.

He had many other questions regarding what was occurring in Chile that he needed to research. Were the doctors doing enough research on the people who had died? They came from all over Chile, though most were from the three southern Regions. That suggested that whatever the problem was, it came from those Regions in the south. Which was where the WHO also believed they should look first. It was why they were headed south of Santiago once they reached the country.

Takeoff was rather smooth, though much noisier in the C17 then it had been in the Bombardier that Dr. Phillips-Lee used to own. "Don't worry, when we finish remodeling, you won't hear a thing. Still some more adjustments to make to bring this bird up to speed." Parker heard the Colonel tell Dr. Phillips-Lee.

He looked down the aisle at the two, and saw Dr. Smythe-Lytton take a drink from a glass of cut crystal he held in his hand. Maybe the man didn't like flying and needed something to help him fly. Liquid fortification.

As they climbed to cruising speed, before he had to go to the gun range, Parker lined up a selection of material he had to read. He used his tablet and found that there was a very extensive database on the airplane's network, and every few minutes he was sidetracked by one thing or another. He noted that the other students, and the professors, were all busy over their tablets as well. Even Dr. Smythe-Lytton, though he seemed to have a stewardess already prepared to fill his glass once more. When Parker thought about it, the same stewardess had been filling the doctor's glass on the flight to and from Kazakhstan as well.

"Come, Mr. Thornton, it's time to get some more training in." The man who had helped him at the shooting range the day before was at his side.

"Can I come?" Priya asked.

The man thought for a second, then nodded. 'Yes. It is not a real range, of course. There is no room for that, and we would never shoot live ammunition in a plane." He led them to a circular staircase that led up and down.

"What's upstairs?" Parker asked.

"The same as here, in the rear part, and then right above is command and control, all the communications gear. Ahead of that is the flight deck. The pilot and his team," the security officer said.

They went down the stairs though. Here, in the cabin as large as the main cabin, were computer banks. Blades stacked in racks of well over 100, so Parker knew that there was a lot of money invested in the six racks he saw. Infinitely more power than his tablet had, and probably more computing power than he would ever need. There were so many computers in the racks that even if the plane was filled completely with scientists and the command center was maxed out, there would probably be ten times the computing power that these machines were capable of to spare.

Priya said, "They took me too literally. I only said we needed the new 256 racks as joke. They're like 10 million each. That's like 1500 very powerful computers all tied together."

The soldier said, "Not my department. I wouldn't know. I do know that the installers wanted to know if the plane was insured. Then another cracked with the hardware we have aboard, it had to be a government job and they don't take out insurance." The man laughed.

Parker began to realize that this was becoming bigger than just the Academy. Something more was at stake here. Five students from the academy did not need so much power. Even as they approached an area about ten by fifteen feet with one wall clearly a giant screen. "When we don't use this for gun practice, maybe Ms. Zadari you could reprogram this to play some of those movies and TV Shows. It is the biggest screen on the plane."

"There are no seats, won't that be uncomfortable?"

"We can improvise. I expect that the flights we are going to take in this old beast are going to often be long and boring. If you are not sleeping or eating, it can get pretty dull," the man continued as he opened a locker and pulled out some guns. He then went to a very small box console that had a few buttons, a number pad and a digital display.

"Here, feel the weight. It's a fake gun, works on lasers, but it should feel just like your weapon. When you shoot, there are compensators to make it seem like you have discharged a bullet, so it should jerk back the same."

The firing range, was all of ten feet or so. Not at all like the range in the bottom of the Administration building. But this was like a video game and it was on a plane, and the electronics compensated for not having the adequate distance that a true range had.

The next hour the security officer took Parker through another round of weapons training. Then, near the end, they let Priya have a try. She had been paying attention. Three of her nine shots were on target. "Looks like we need to get you a gun and some training as well, Ms. Zadari. I'll speak to the Colonel about that. Of course, you'll get such training in your senior year now, for sure."

Parker was not wholly convinced that this was the wisest course for the future scientists that the ECO Academy was training. But he was a senior, and Dr. Phillips-Lee and the Colonel both told him he was in charge of the other students, so as a leader, he had to toe the company line. Grandpa Thornton had taught him that lesson a long time ago. Parker couldn't help but wonder where all this was leading. The guns, a big plane, more computating equipment then possible to imagine, a flying laboratory. It was definitely bigger than just the Academy.

'You follow orders, but if you think they are wrong, build your case before making your case.' Parker didn't understand that at first, but then Grandpa told Parker what he had meant. The American Revolution didn't start with some rebels firing at Lexington and Concord. There had been years of protest and thought that had built up to militias being formed so that there could be a shot heard round the world. Again, the need for the ECO Academy to offer courses other than the sciences.

The class that started next year would make for much better rounded individuals when they became seniors. Parker had two letters the last week from world-renown university scientists for his next round of education. They of course were looking for research fellows, and not to have him be a student. But should he take a post anywhere, he would have to audit some of the courses that freshmen took so he could work on the gaps in his own education.

When the three returned to the main cabin where the rest of the passengers were, they found that dinner was being served.

The soldier said, "Good timing. And I'll tell the Colonel you did pretty well for our second session. Different than a video game, huh?" The man did not expect an answer and he went his way to the latter half of the cabin, where the security team seemed to have clustered. In fact there was a clear grouping of the faculty from the ECO Academy in the middle, the students up front, and the security team in the rear.

Priya and Parker had the seats that were near the professors. Jennifer, Parker saw, was in the seat furthest from them. She still had not resolved matters with her father. Though Parker knew that they spoke more now since the time in Kazakhstan, than before.

"Hey, where have you two been?" JCubed asked. "We get fish or steak for dinner, or both if you really want it."

"Fish," Priya said. And Parker took notice.

Parker wanted a steak. But since his girlfriend was going to have the fish, he asked for that as well.

Parker and Priya filled JCubed and the others about what they saw when they went to the lower deck, and that led to a discussion about how much computing power the airplane had. JCubed, being the kind of guy he was, started to fiddle on his tablet to see if he could find answers from it.

"This is way over the top," Guillermo said.

"There is a lot of power at our disposal. If you think about how many professors and how many there are of us, we each have the power of a supercomputer at our disposal. Not one of the current ones, but something that we could play chess against at the top level." Priya said. Parker knew she had been talking to several of the scientists on the IBM Deep Blue project. She corresponded to others also. But Parker was fairly sure that she contributed to the next round in the artificial intelligence breakthroughs.

"Why so much strength?" Guillermo mused.

Parker shook his head. Then he said, "JCubed, can you check to see what proposals the Premier and his coalition are adopting to restore the Aral Sea? How many of them come from ECO Academy? Perhaps we have out proportioned the rest of the scientific community. I don't just mean the students, but the professors. At the campus we have 30 of the most brilliant minds who are concentrating on solutions to save the world, and teaching us how to do so. And then you know we have 100 other professors from all over the world who are affiliated to advise and do lectures as well."

Jennifer added to what he said when he stopped, "That could well be it. Dr. Phillips-Lee has made a concentration of the most dedicated people to heal the Earth's ills. You may be right that we were a majority of the sciences that will help at the Aral Sea, but why have a plane that is as powerful as the CDC or NIH."

JCubed, whose hands were moving fast over his tablet, said without looking up. "You mean NIS, don't you Jenny? Most of us are not really involved in the health aspect like you. That is second to healing the world. Healing the world's inhabitants."

"If we don't tend to those who are sick, like this epidemic in Chile, then we might not have anyone on the world to appreciate that we need to save it," Jennifer said. This was a circular argument.

"O2theO," Parker said, as Guillermo and Priya also uttered it a second behind him. "We don't need to argue chicken or egg. Funny, that would be a logic problem and it is one of the things we did talk about in our freshmen year. Dr. Hatcher spent at least an hour on it during Introduction to Biology, Advanced."

Priya nodded, "It seemed longer than that. And Dr. Hatcher

was very full of himself when he spoke. He also plugged his book on the subject."

"I have it here in my tablet…" JCubed said, still not raising his head. "I never read it though. Did any of you read it?"

Parker had scanned the Table of Contents online at the Amazon Bookstore, but hadn't bought it. He shook his head. No one else had admitted to reading it, either.

"Am I the only one who bought it?" The other students all nodded their heads, showing that JCubed was. It cost about thirty dollars. That was a lot of money for a student to have to spend. Though Parker got a nice allowance from his parents each week, more than he could spend. Or at least he got it from his mother. He did not think his father felt he should have an allowance while living at school.

"That just sucks. See if I trust any of you any more." JCubed sounded upset.

"Let's forget about that. Did you find any correlation that might suggest that ECO Academy needs the power built into this plane?" Parker asked.

JCubed shrugged, "Maybe. The Premier is using about half of what was recommended by ECO Academy. Three of our ideas, but as a percentage, ECO Academy scientists are providing just over 68% of what the Premier is going to try."

Parker nodded, "I would think then that the world expects a little more from us and Dr. Phillips-Lee wants to be sure that he can support that. Publicity. He does not want to fail. Not after spending so much money on the school."

Priya understood. "Then we best get to studying all the notes JCubed has been collecting for us to try and do better. If the water is contaminated, I have to design some new collection and analysis devices that can index the CDC databases faster." Her thoughts showed why they were such a good couple.

"And I have to help my father with the research on the various symptoms those who have died displayed, and those who got really sick and survived. There may be a vaccine amongst those who survived."

Parker nodded, "We have a lot of research to do, and we have to get some sleep as well, else we will have a lot of jet lag. We best get at it." The others, even Guillermo, agreed and they settled in to study. They would reach Chile soon enough.

-Chapter 12-

Stefan had things as ready as they could be for Zedadiah Carter's arrival in Santiago. His first concern had been that of security. The boss had pushed back against the Cartels when he had found they had been meddling beyond what had been agreed to years before.

Kutuzov had tried to explain once before that the leaders of the Cartels wanted to be thought of as businessmen once they reached a certain level of wealth and success. They however would never distance themselves far enough from the streets they had come from. And no Cartel, despite the intentions of those running them, seemed to pass onto the second generation in their family, the reins of power.

The children of the leaders had been born to luxury in almost every family. Those children could not show that they were enough of a hard-hitting thug to keep the criminals and murderers who made up their army of workers in line.

Zedadiah understood the words Stefan said when describing the men who ran the Cartels, but he thought they were similar to him. That men who had become billionaires and ran multibillion dollar companies could relate to one another. The leaders of the Cartels understood hard men like Stefan more than men who could push money around like Zedadiah Carter.

It had taken real examples but now the boss understood things. He had given Stefan a free hand. Zedadiah did not mind Stefan's tactics as long as results were acheived. Stefan, when he had a free hand, also meant he had access to the company bank account. Well bank accounts, for there were a lot of places ZED Corp hid money. Assets that did not show up on the balance sheet any longer. Money that no longer could be taxed by the regulators, since that always sucked.

"I want another sweep of the perimeter. Just because we were told there were three rocket launchers in Santiago, and we found three, does not mean that our informant didn't lie, or didn't know about others," Stefan said.

"Yes sir, I'll take the north quadrant," that was one of the lieutenants leading two jeeps scanning the flight path into the airport.

"Dimitri and I have the terminal and all other parts of the airport under observation."

"Michael and I are in Sanhattan and we have the route to the villa covered." A third voice said.

Others on the communication network checked in. Stefan had over forty men and a few women with weapons and scanning equipment about the city. Then the military and police had been brought in as well. The officers had not been told that Mr. Carter was about to arrive. They did see that the Z Men were stepping up their presence in Chile and helping to clean up against some of the criminals who thought they could operate without restriction in the country.

The Z Men had hit the Cartels hard. Stefan had made good on a promise he had made years before. That if the Cartels exceeded a certain line in order to seek riches, then ZED Corp would respond. His men had spent liberally, and mercenaries, and assassins, had killed many of the soldiers near the bottom rungs of the Cartel. When the regular soldiers died it seldom mattered, but when they died in large numbers, new recruits became hard to find.

Then his men had blown up drug processing plants. More dead. Millions of dollars of product destroyed. And then to make the point very much something that the leaders of the Cartels would notice, close family members of the leaders were kidnapped. Alive and being held against the good behavior of the Cartels, especially while Zedadiah was in South America. A tactic out of the Cartels very own game book. The cartels must learn not to mess with ZED Corps business.

The leaders knew that should one retaliate, then all the hostages would lose their lives. And they also had been shown that what security they had to protect their loved ones could be defeated. It was something that Stefan sweated over about his protection of Zedadiah. If the fools in the Cartel did not know that he would carry out his threat, they could go after the boss, and eventually someone would succeed in getting Zedadiah.

The Z Men had shown the Cartels that they were very prepared to go to battle, and that they could hit hard and fast. Faster than the Cartels could respond. The men who ran the organizations understood that kind of power. They knew better than to fight against it, unless they had to.

"Sir, the boss has landed," one of the other lieutenants said. This one had binoculars watching the airport terminal. They had used secrecy to make Zedadiah's arrangements. His private jet had actually travelled to South Africa, the boss doing business in Cape Town before flying to Chile. Then none of the Cartels, if they had been feeling the least bit challenging, were in a position to know of the travel plans of the boss, Stefan hoped.

Stefan had impressed upon Zedadiah that he had to be circumspect in his plans. Zedadiah had to be spur of the moment and make one call on a secure phone when he had been airborne on the last leg of the journey.

Stefan still tried to insulate the boss from the security team, which he knew several of the Cartel teams were tracking. Stefan had hired a few consultants to keep an eye on the airport where the private jet would land. Those were watched for signs by other consultants, who then signaled to a third group, that were watched from a distance by Stefan's men at the end of the chain. They had now seen the signal. Zedadiah had landed.

A cordon of security from his team, as well as the Army would surround the boss and whisk him to a secure villa. All this was still against protocol. Zedadiah was at risk in Chile.

But the boss wanted to take matters into his own hands. Matters that were becoming more complex and potentially damaging each day.

"Right, lets get down there, and have our allies surround the plane. When it goes into the secure hangar, you know the protocol on access," Stefan said.

"At any time the plane is on the ground, it is vulnerable to be tampered with. Pretty easy to get a bomb onto the plane and activate it once in the air." His lieutenant said on the com network. Stefan nodded. He had shown his team many times how easy that could be. A skill the Cold War had taught him, and the years after, when he and his comrades had gone after the new enemies of the state, they had then perfected the tactic. To think that the enemies of the state were the former republics that had once comprised the Soviet Union, or former operatives from the KGB who had left to become the oligarchs of Russia made Stefan shake his head.

He had nothing against a man who could make a few billion rubles, as long as they had not forgot who their motherland was. At least, not until the motherland had turned against him Stefan thought. When Russia had turned against him, Stefan knew it was time to sell his skills to the highest bidder. A skill that included placing bombs aboard luxury jets poorly guarded in hangars, waiting for their owners to board and whisk them away.

Stefan led his team to the reinforced security ATVs. These cars were hardened against attacks. Watching one of Harrison Ford's old movies ensured that all public figures travelled in heavily reinforced vehicles when in potentially dangerous countries. Stefan had a wolfish smile. The world was a dangerous place and they had to take precautions. That was a shame. But it meant that a man with his skill set had a job.

A very good job.

"So the head of our national office killed himself. And he did not leave much of a note."

"No Señor. We only found that he says it was all his fault, though we are unsure what he meant." The man in charge of all the police in Santiago said.

Zedadiah nodded, "Thank you commissioner. I shall look into the matter as well to see if we can understand it. You know we have made quite a bit of money on the water rights, and now with so many dying in the south, well perhaps that has something to do with it. Señor Valdez y Gonzalez we have found, has had problems with the Cartels before. This could have bearing on things as well."

"Si, your associate Señor Kutuzov has been very helpful. For a short while we thought that there may have been foul play, but we have found nothing to suggest that there really was such."

Zedadiah did not think that there would be any clue to suggest foul play. Kutuzov and several of the men who worked for him had killed quite a few men and made those murders look like suicide. Deaths that would only be found to be murders by the best of the television coroners. They of course always were able to identify such deaths as murders and find the killer in an hour on the TV. Somehow he doubted that far more murders were called suicide because those who spent their time looking at dead bodies really could not tell when there was a murder being masked as a suicide.

"Well, if we find anything that suggests the man had something to do with the Cartels and his remorse over it, we will let you know at once." There of course would be evidence over the next few days to show a connection. It was what they had already planned.

The policeman saluted, and Zedadiah rose to shake the man's hand. Many men would remember the times they spoke to the world's billionaires. It would be a significant event in many people's lives. How many would look back at the end of their days and be able to count the number of encounters with world leaders and the superrich on more than the fingers of one hand. Not many.

Kutuzov nodded and then escorted the police commissioner from the room before returning. Zed had opened his computer to scan some email before turning his attention to his security chief.

"That went well," Zedadiah said. He was glad Valdez was taken care of.

"He doesn't know anything." Kutuzov said. "And he won't."

Zedadiah knew to trust the former KGB agent when he said things that emphatically. At times Zedadiah had been tempted to see if there were any other men in the field of security who might be even better than Stefan. He knew to be discreet in his enquiries. Those who were on the market looking for work, or could be hired from other well paying jobs were few at Stefan's level of skill. The times he had checked, there really were few alternatives to replace Stefan. The KGB trained well.

The CIA, MI-6 and the Mossad had some former agents that might do just as well as Stefan. But then they would have to get acquainted with the organization that Stefan had built. Instead, Zedadiah just asked that Stefan ensure that he had a depth of leadership that meant the Z Men could put someone in command and be super effective quickly in the event that Stefan was incapacitated.

In the line of work the man engaged in, that was a possibility. Not a certainty, but it was more probable than remote.

"Aside from the death of 'Cisco, I have removed six others so far." Zedadiah swallowed. He usually had to approve such drastic measures.

Stefan laughed a short little bark. "No, I didn't have them killed. Two have gone to the Madagascar office. That was punishment. The other four have new plum jobs in Europe and the US. Rewards for good service and knowing something that they shouldn't. As long as they don't know they aren't supposed to know, they probably will never speak of it. At least as long as no one finds out about ZPakCad-1328."

Zedadiah actually wiped his forehead. It felt a bit damp. "Good. Though necessary, Francisco is a loss to the corporation. His greed propelled profits down here well beyond what any other manager seemed capable of attaining. That was somewhat admirable. Even if he got into bed with the devil."

"Devils. We have four very nervous drug lords who are worried about how we will react. Or what we will do to the hostages we have taken. They made a great deal of money riding on the bus that 'Cisco made for them, and we have ensured they understand we are not pleased. They will be purchasing a great deal of whatever you wish so that they can make some restitution for their misdeeds. I suggest ZED Corp take about half of the profits they made. They will understand that. It will be a show of respect."

Zedadiah shook his head. "It will be a show of their fear."

"Same thing. That is what is needed now. They will ask for permission from someone you designate if they step into your sandbox ever again. That is what we wanted to have happened before," Kutuzov said. Stefan often acted as if he thought Zedadiah tended to forget that they had both let Francisco Valdez y Gonzalez keep the lines of communication to the Cartels open. That they knew he was giving them company secrets in the hope that they did not interfere with their operations.

"I want to wrap up this problem with the Cartels so we never have to deal with them again," Zedadiah said.

Stefan said, "This time I will put one of my people in charge in the Bogota office. They will ensure that the Cartels know what they can and can't do when they want to piggyback on our operations."

Zedadiah nodded, "Very well. Can we limit them to only one access point to the United States through our transportation channels?" So totally illegal that Zedadiah sometimes wondered how many times a month he had such decisions to make.

"One each, but yes. After this they will accept that," Kutuzov had one of his feral smiles again. Zedadiah knew the man actually liked conducting the operation against the Cartels. His men attacking the soldiers, and destroying the operations were the ex-KGB agent's way of slapping down the unruly dogs. Stefan was showing the other animals who was the leader of the pack.

'Fine. Now we need to concentrate on this disaster. Have we gotten all traces of ZPakCad-1328 out of the country?"

"None of our databases now show it ever came into Chile. Every drop that was not put into the water supply is gone and being destroyed back in Pakistan. Three of the Docs in Pakistan were stupid though. One even thought he could hide in an al-Qaeda cell. The one who went AWOL in Afghanistan and sought to work for the Taliban we extracted and are sitting on. The Taliban, well we didn't feel we had to be too clean about that."

Zedadiah had read the report that had been filed internally about that extraction. As retribution for long ago actions, Stefan had ensured that only his Russian operatives were chosen to enter Afghanistan and wreak havoc there. The western news agencies credited an errant attack drone nearly wiping out a border village. In reality, the Z Men had annihilated every male of adult age, and sequestered all the other villagers until they could take the Pakistani researcher away. Fourteen dead. Fourteen violently dead. This year was certainly the worst year for ZED Corp in terms of dealing with those who opposed them.

In all the previous years, if the number of people who were killed to ensure that ZED Corp continued to thrive was more than a dozen, it would have been remarkable. Now with the dead from the attacks on the Cartels, those in the Near East and of course, all those dying here in Chile, the number was in the mid hundreds, and destined to rise.

"I know that you felt that you were doling out justice, but should this ever come back to attach to us, you know what is going to happen."

Stefan laughed, "All my men know that. Don't worry. We are extra careful. Worst case it will look like some stupid American security contractor has messed up once more. We may stage an operation because we want revenge. These American's, they are just stupid and don't care how many they kill. After a few weeks in these dark places, all sense of American justice and altruism is gone, if there ever was any in the first place."

A sad commentary about the country that Zedadiah was born in. But Zedadiah believed that was true as well. He could not say that England was any better, but for tax purposes, his international living arrangements worked out well when he didn't spend more than a couple months in the land of his birth. "Very well. Now Chile. The lab reports said that the enzyme has infected the crops and should any of this food be ingested, the chances of being riddled with the disease is about eight percent."

Stefan said, "On this scale, and Chile being an exporter of food to the world, that is quite a disaster. No way to profit by it either."

Zedadiah was not going to admit that he had tried to think of ways to profit by it. He was an investment banker of the first order. He had thought often of how he might profit by it. But acting on the information he had, that no one else in the world had, meant that someday, someone would link ZED Corp to the disaster. That was never going to happen. Kutuzov had full permission to terminate as many people as needed to keep that a secret.

"The WHO is bringing in as many scientists as they can to figure out what is going on. Somehow we need to get the information, once they see that the water is leading to these deaths, to that of the future crop failure. Or we need to get as much of the regions infected with other pathogens to see that all crops are destroyed. Livestock is dying as well now." The ZED Corp team was much more attuned to look for deaths connected to the release of the enzyme.

"About three in 1,000 of those who are exposed to the water die. Same holds true with animals. But the crops intensify that by 25 times. You're right, we need to find a way to support this and get the word out without anyone seeing that it is us. We can seed a few journal findings and documents so they start showing up in science blogs and that might get the notice of the scientists who are flooding into the country."

Zedadiah looked to Stefan. Zedadiah was trying not to make any puns that tied water to the tragedy, but Stefan had no such compunctions.

"I can not emphasis how critical it is that no one finds out that we manufactured ZPakCad-1328. I have asked Sung Ling Chou to tear apart the research facility, and ensure that all mentions of the work in water based enzymes disappear from journals and publications as well." Zedadiah said.

Stefan shrugged his shoulders, "That is not as easy to do as you would wish. Once it is in the cloud, well it is impossible to tell which hard drives have made a copy of the information or not. What we can do is overwrite information. We have asked a few scientists who worked on the initial project and who saw that their interests lay with cooperating with us, that they identify all such posts. If we have the exact wording, and punctuation of a subject title, then we re-upload a piece with that same header. Servers think that all you are doing then is putting in a comma, taking care of a misspelling. Then they overwrite the body in almost all instances."

Zedadiah caught the last part. Stefan, was either totally sure of something, in which case he said so, or not sure, as he was just then. "What happens in the instances where the body of the material is not overwritten?"

Stefan said, "Then we point a finger and misdirect saying we were hacked. We have a great many ways we can deny culpability. It will be fine. No one will ever be able to suggest that we are doing anything. Or have done anything. Our humanitarian efforts are beginning to prove worthwhile. I don't know if I like the idea that we are calling the charitable fund the Valdez y Gonzalez memorial, but I suppose 'Cisco started this fool stunt."

Zedadiah had thought Penelope had been inspired, for it was her idea to start a campaign to help the sick. ZED Corp had quickly come to the aid for it was no secret that they owned a majority of the water rights in the Regions affected.

Millions had been collected, mostly internally by the rank and file employees of ZED Corp. Then the Corp matched funds, though, it really allowed Zedadiah to allot money that was needed to target getting fresh, untainted water to all the places where the illness had occurred.

"Fine, whatever it takes." Zedadiah had little patience for the details when they were awful no matter how he thought about it. This tragedy was something he could not sugar coat. However, a few years from now, when it was over and a memory, he would forget the decisions he was making now to deal with it. He would put this all behind him so that he need not ever remember that he so callously dismissed the lives of those who had died, were going to die, or who needed to die, in order to keep the secret that had started with the foolishness of his employees.

Great corporations were not in the business of killing people. ZED Corp was in the business of making money. A lot of money. They had a diversified portfolio of products and companies that they owned and marketed, with the desire to control national and international monopolies on those products, or commodities. That gave Zedadiah power.

That he had one employee who saw the business model as a way to feather his own nest egg, did not mean the Francisco had been the only employee who had done so. Part of what Zedadiah was now devoting time to was the investigation of every employee who had the authority to spend money in a way that could lead to the same type of aberration that had been Francisco.

It was clear that all his national office leaders were men and women of ambition. But that could not be unbridled ambition. They had to follow rules. It was hard enough to deal with the one crisis that ZPakCad-1328 created. To think that the leaders he had under him might have created other foolish schemes to become rich that might also have blown up only led to restless nights.

"We've really got this, Boss. You did not need to fly in…"

"Good publicity. You know it is all about the public's perception. We own the water rights where people are dying, saying they are not thirsty. Then dying of dehydration. Water. It looks good if we take the lead and make sure people get clean fresh water, etcetera."

"No one has linked that there is anything in the water, but the researchers are suspecting that water is at the root of the epidemic," Stefan said.

It was that now, an epidemic. "Sung wrote earlier today that they had analyzed the half-life, and the incubation time. This should crest in the next two weeks. Then taper off, at least until the harvest. That will make this seem like a picnic."

Kutuzov said, "Don't worry about that. Nothing will leave this country from the infected area. Nothing will be harvested or consumed. Once we squash this bug, my people are already at work on ensuring there is no harvest. But you are going to have to write a big check to ensure all the fields are aerated."

Zedadiah nodded. "Sung Ling Chou is working hard on a neutralizer. We will have to spray heavily, but they think that next year the land's deadliness will fade below three parts in a thousand, which the water is at now.

-Chapter 13-

"Look at the reports again," JCubed said.

Parker scanned them. The death toll had crested over eight hundred but the last two days, the numbers of new cases had begun to decline. That was a victory.

Jennifer and her father were busy, as were most of the other medical doctors trying to come up with treatments for the stricken. Nothing seemed to work. Not only were those afflicted convinced that they were not thirsty, their body seemed to process all forms of water at a hyper level. If one hung an IV and tried to keep the patient hydrated, the bag drained around three times as fast as it should have.

These patients were at rest. Any combination of drugs or other treatments so far had proven fruitless. Yet something was causing the disease, which had no name as yet, to take root in a wide swath of people.

"I will look at the reports again. I have looked at them three times. But I will read them once more." Priya smiled at him. Guillermo stifled a laugh. Parker had not spent all his time with the team, but was often called into a meeting with Dr. Phillips-Lee, or pulled off to the side by the Colonel to be talked at.

Always talked at, and not talked to. Parker could tell the difference. It was the same way his father always treated him.

Parker was nearly eighteen and going to graduate from the Academy. Some of the students would go onto other universities to study in their fields and add to their knowledge. Some would go out into the world and work as scientists for large organizations. And still others would go forth to proceed on their own. To stand on their own feet and see if they could make a difference. Parker was thinking that the last option was what he was going to do. His Grandpa had promised him some money. Enough to set up a lab in Kansas City, and travel to do his research. At least for a short time.

Parker's father thought it was foolish and had many ways of saying that. The Colonel, when it came to security, had ways of saying that he alone knew what he was talking about.

The Colonel was quite concerned that Parker sanctioned Jennifer going off to the southern Regions and the hospitals with Dr. Smythe-Lytton. If he had been consulted, the Colonel said, then it would not have been allowed. Jennifer was too young, and even though she was with her father, her mother would surely cause some trouble over taking the girl into what was a plague zone.

Parker had so little that he could speak to the Colonel about that, that he didn't say anything. He may have been the oldest student, but no one was treating him like much of a leader. In any case Jennifer had recently called to say she was headed back to their base. They stayed at a small hotel in Coihaique. Their laboratory vans were parked out in front, and a platoon from the army not only guarded them, but the other scientists that the WHO and UN had sent to this part of the world.

Coihaique was a small town with a little over 50,000 people. The crisis in the region was overpowering, and though they were in a town, fear seemed to have taken hold. More than 150 were dead who had lived in the city itself, and much more than that from other parts of the Aisén Region.

"Priya, about the computers? Is there still no correlations between who is stricken?" Parker asked.

"Still a bell curve with young and old being afflicted more than those in the prime of their lives. So the doctors think some immunities come into play." Parker glanced out the window and saw another truck drive past that bore the ZED Corp logo. They, and a few other multinationals, were trucking in water each day.

"Why do we think this has something to do with water?" Parker asked again.

Guillermo was quick to bark out, "Because they are dying of thirst." Parker knew the boy wanted to add, you idiot, to the end of his sentence.

They were all drinking bottled water. Their food was made with bottled water that had been shipped in from areas well north of any of the areas where the disease had ever shown to be. If it was a disease. Parker was not fully convinced that there would be such a large scale localized disease.

Not only did they drink with bottled water. They washed with it. Every faucet in the hotel they stayed at was shut off. When they used the toilets in their bathrooms in the hotel rooms, they had a bucket they ladled water into the basin before flushing. That water was shipped in as well.

Dr. Phillips-Lee thought that learning what was often normal conditions while doing field research in third world settings was a good experience. Dr. Phillips-Lee though had begun to speak about returning to Santiago, which was of course, urban and not having problems with water. The Colonel laughed whenever the Doctor seemed to want to return to the luxurious life of the capital.

Parker had to agree that he didn't think there was much novelty after the second day of inspecting every thing that you drank. Every time you wanted to reach for water or something with water that was part of it. There was no going to get fast food because you could not be sure the restaurant was cooking with good water. You had to wash yourself with a sponge that you squirted with water from a bottle.

You had to dry wash your clothes. Dampening them, and then rubbing in detergents and sparingly rinse them. There was not a lot of water for all those who lived in Coihaique for luxuries. Washing your clothes was a luxury. The ECO Academy students, professors and security team could use their plane to fly in and out twice daily and on the way out, the plane took their soiled laundry every third day, returning it cleaned the next. The Colonel had the students wash their clothes though, with the most minimal use of water for a week, because he said it was good training as well.

"Like being in the Golan waiting for the Hezbollah to do another of their stupidities. You move at night then, and stay hidden in the day. The terrorists think we never know what they are up to. Fools, we always know what they are up to." Parker had found that the Colonel had many stories about his service in the IDF as well as his time working in the Israeli Intelligence service. The Mossad. Many stories, most of which the Colonel was not about to tell him.

Parker said to the other classmates, "Lets think about this. Water is pretty much a static combination of elements."

JCubed said, "Yeah. Two hydrogen atoms, one oxygen."

Parker nodded, "Right. We know that it can taste different. We know that it can feel different, like when it comes out of the tap with so much hydration that there are bubbles everywhere."

Priya said, "So?"

Parker continued, "We haven't been looking at the water for things that we don't know exist but for things we do know exist and eliminating them from our equations. We have been running tests for every known water bourn disease that there is. Starting with concentrations of water based infections that are specific to Chile and South America." That was a summary of the last week they had been in the country.

The students and the other scientists had been doing just as Parker had said.

"Yeah, that is exactly what we have been doing. And it has not been doing much good." Guillermo, Parker was sure, wanted to add, 'stupid,' to the end of that sentence as well. Parker could tell that the boy was resentful that Parker had been put in charge, and had time with the Colonel and Dr. Phillips-Lee about managing the team of other youths. Guillermo could not see that next year, when Parker had left the school and Guillermo was a senior, that he would then be in charge of such a field team.

JCubed stood up, "I'm no biologist. And I don't know a whole lot about the biochemistry of water, but look at the reports."

He had been saying that for a while now. "What do you want us to look at?"

"Oh… Oh!" Priya said in surprise, and then she buried her head down at her own tablet and her hand got busy really fast. She was swiping and pinching and pulling on her tablet. "No. That's terrible."

Parker knew better than to stop her, or interrupt her with a question. But he jerked his head to JCubed and then pointed at the tablet. The other boy understood and swiped at his own tablet until on the wall which served as a big screen for all of the team, the images from Priya's computer started to show. What she looked at and manipulated was now displayed for all.

Parker said, "Priya we are following you on the big wall…" He tried to be quiet as he spoke. He wanted her to know that what she saw, they all saw. He knew that Priya had a picture of him when he was taking off his wetsuit somewhere on her tablet. He had one of her in her bikini, though she had her big bulky t-shirt on as well, since she did not like to take it off.

Parker knew that Priya looked really good under that t-shirt. Well, he took Shelly Botha's word for it. Shelly had no qualms about showing how well her own body was when she wore a bathing suit. She had assured him that Priya had a very well developed body. All Parker had seen were her legs, and they were very nice. It left him imagining that the rest of his girlfriend's form was just as nice. One day he was determined to have a picture of Priya in her bikini without the t-shirt on his tablet.

Watching Priya work, Parker saw that she was identifying research and then sending it out to all the other members of the team. He could hear the pings as his own tablet and phone registered that mail was arriving in his inbox. He knew it was from Priya so he could either look at what she was still doing, or look at the information she was sending him.

Priya spoke, though, "JCubed, didn't you know what this was? You keep saying read the reports, so you had to suspect?"

"Nah, I know that we have been getting the information, but I don't know a lot about it. But we have identified hundreds of things in the water down here. Why? Why so much stuff in this water? Isn't water just H_2O? Most of what has been found is harmless. But there are a lot more things we need to analyze. Some things though, the scientists haven't figured out yet," JCubed said.

"And that is what we have to look at. Or at least isolate and test. We think that we will find something we already know about that triggers such a sickness in all these people. But of course it won't be something we know about," Priya said.

Parker nodded, "Call Jennifer and conference her in please, JCubed. If it was something that anyone had ever seen in water before, then such a disease would have been documented."

Even Guillermo put aside his animosity for a moment, "I get it." He then started to look at his own tablet. No doubt looking at the emails he had just gotten from Priya.

Parker was focusing on putting together a spreadsheet of the chemical compositions of all the organic compounds found in the water that had not been previously identified. Some of the compounds looked like they could easily be proteins, including enzymes. With so many unknown compounds in the water, he had to find something that stood out from the others.

Guillermo though spoke, "Look at this document that Professor Johansson from Stockholm wrote. Three days ago he found a very long amino acid chain in a sampling that he thinks is not naturally organic. He requests that should the Coihaique team find at least a milliliter of bad water, he can perform numerous analyses. The problem is that only a few PPMs of this compound have been found."

"A few parts per million?" Parker deciphered.

"Perhaps." Priya said. "It could be a lot less than that. The team analyzing the water, which is a lot less than the scientists who are looking at the sick patients, are spending the bulk of their time on known particulates and looking for the interactivity that they already know about."

Guillermo said, "But that's stupid! If we already knew the interactivity of anything, then we would know what produced these results that we are seeing. We know how people who get this disease end up, but we have never seen it before, so we have never seen the cause of it before."

Priya looked down at her tablet again. Parker knew she did not want to argue with the other boy. He said, "What are there, thirty scientists in all of Coihaique including us. And then in Santiago another thirty? Most of them medical doctors looking to find a cure. We were briefed on this. With so many dying, saving the patients is the first thing that they are all working on. Not finding out why people had gotten sick and looking down that path to see if they can fix things once they know why."

Parker could see that it made sense to look at the symptoms of a disease and try to fight those symptoms with the protocols that beat back similar diseases. Especially when the death toll now stood at over 1,000 and new cases were reported daily. Thankfully though it was less cases each day.

There had been debate whether he and the other students should visit a morgue to see the sense of urgency that the adults were dealing with. Jennifer, who was conferencing in just then, had seen several of the dead now. She said it was not pleasant. Especially when she saw that there were children their own age who had died as well. She had broken down when she had seen, not the first, but the second dead person.

Jennifer had told Priya that she had been comforted by her father then. Priya had told Parker that. It took a few minutes but they told Jennifer that they had found some very big proteins that stuck out on a long list of items that they were identifying from the water sample.

"But you are only using the samples in Coihaique. What about other parts of Aisén and the other Regions where people have been stricken. Shouldn't you see where these items in the water show up?" She said.

Parker was already manipulating his tablet, but JCubed was much faster. "I am getting reports but we are getting samples from all the locations that perhaps we should," the internet genius said.

Priya, who had ways of manipulating hardware that was a mystery to him said, "But they have been installing meters to sample water at many of the places where there has been this disease. Over 70 percent of the locations where there have been deaths reported, have sensors we can log into. Let me write some programs and start checking. We should see a spike and correlation on some of these proteins soon."

By soon, Parker translated, she meant in minutes. He thought it would take much longer. The one that showed up on the report he saw was from an instance that came in at a few PPMs. A lot of water would have to pass by a sensor to be seen, and the sensors were seeing everything.

"Urgh, this may be more than a few minutes." Priya said. Parker believed she just saw how daunting the task was.

Parker asked, "JCubed, how many proteins do we have here that no one really knows about?"

"Well, it's water. There should really not be any proteins incorporated into water, but if these are naturally occurring proteins, then there is information in various databases."

Guillermo said, "Not once we start looking at all the particulates in it. If it was laboratory pure, then we would only have our base H_2O. If it was so–called pure drinking water, then a few other items could be there. Nutrients and minerals that might be incorporated into water, but just a few parts per million or billion. There should not be any proteins in drinking water. Let me write you a program that separates out all the items we really do know about already." JCubed walked over to where Guillermo sat at his laptop.

Parker added, "So for there to be polypeptide chains in the water suggests that someone put them there." Parker had done some research and found that these were not natural.

Soon those two were quite engaged, while he could see Priya equally busy. Jennifer had said she was already being driven back to the hotel. Her father was doing an autopsy, yet again, on one of those who had died. Jennifer was due to be back in half an hour.

For the next hour, or longer, since Parker did not look at his watch, everyone was busy. Parker placed monitors on his screen to see what everyone was involved with, while he then went and looked through correspondence with the international community and the protein discoveries to see if there was any comments on them. He found none but the one questioning report from Dr. Johansson.

He sent an email to the scientist in Stockholm, but did not know when he would get a response. Email did make things proceed faster, but people often did not look at their emails. That meant that things slowed down.

Texting also made things speed up, unless you didn't have your text device on and could text back. During lectures at the school, or study groups, everyone turned their phones and other mobiles to quiet mode. It meant that if someone needed you for an emergency, you couldn't respond until class was over. And then you had to remember to turn everything back on.

Sometimes you just forgot to do so. Parker knew that his parents didn't like to text, though they had mastered cell phones and making calls all the time. His father, Prescott came home with an earbud and often rubbed at his ear at dinner. He said it hurt to wear it almost all day. He also said that sometimes he had to have a private conversation and he was in public. He had to explain that so he could have the private conversation later.

"I have about half of the sensors I need online analyzing things. I think statistically for a sampling we don't need all the water sources to have sensors on them. There are so many rural areas where there were wells, that it would be very hard to do," Priya said.

"Impossible to do," Parker said. Nothing was impossible, but he knew that to place a sensor on every water source in the three affected provinces would be a herculean task. More thousands would die before they could ever do that, so in practice it was an impossible task. Though if they had the luxury of unlimited time and resources, it would be possible.

Parker continued to the other members of his team, "In any case, you are right, we will get enough data to make some informed study. The question is when? When will we have enough data to know what is going on?"

"Tomorrow morning?" Guillermo said, but he seemed unsure.

JCubed nodded and so did Priya, "We did some modeling and it will be early in the morning when enough water has been sampled, and the other sensors are on line to give us a majority. We also have some data from Santiago and other places north where there has been no deaths, or sickness. That can be a control."

Priya added, "There are a few unidentified compounds in the water elsewhere, but it is the one that is unique to the affected region we need to watch for."

Parker nodded. He had sent them both a text about a control group which would highlight the problem they were looking for. "Now, do we tell Dr. Phillips-Lee and the others what we are doing with this, or present them our findings when we are done."

He knew the answer he wanted to go with. But it was important that they all be on the same page. Especially Guillermo. He always was such a problem, that if he wanted to be a pain, he would be.

Guillermo was the first to speak, "They really don't care what we do. They think we are just here to learn and observe. Nothing that we do will really make a difference. I say we collect our data and show them we have found something."

That actually was what Parker wanted to do. Jennifer however, "If this will help, I say we tell my father and the other professors now."

Priya was more practical, "But we really don't have anything to tell them yet. We will later, but we don't at the moment. We have some questions we are trying to get answers to. It would just be a lot more on their plate that would make them chase what we are already chasing."

They heard from three, Parker said, "JCubed, I guess this is like a vote, what do you want to do? Tell the professors or wait until we have enough data to show them what we have then."

JCubed made it tough, "I don't want to get in trouble. You know we are like spending a fortune to get all these sensors to get the data. I think we should tell them."

It meant that the others had tied things up. Parker was going to have to be very obvious and make a decision. Not that he was not capable of making a decision, but what he did decide would cause two of the group to be against him, while two to support him.

"Well we aren't going to be unanimous that is for sure," Parker said. It provoked a little laugh from Priya. It did not help that Jennifer and JCubed were the youngest members of the team and still had something to learn. Maybe he could teach them a little.

"We'll tell Dr. Phillips-Lee and the others tomorrow, when we have the data to back it up." He knew he was nodding as he spoke.

Priya was either mimicking him, or he was mimicking her.

Guillermo said, "Good. That's what we should do." Guillermo was just not sensitive to the others at all.

Parker held up his hand, "Jennifer, please don't tell your father about our tests and data collection. Here's the thing, if we are wrong, and we don't see these compounds in the places that others got sick, then we have nothing to really report. But say we do speak to Dr. Phillips-Lee, your father or others today. If they think that we are onto something and we haven't found a thing, then they might leave something important that they are doing to chase our little hypothesis. If we do find something, then it is only a few hours before we tell them that we've got a mystery that we need to solve."

Jennifer nodded, but it seemed that she was reluctant.

JCubed just smiled and shrugged his shoulders. "What do we do until then?" JCubed asked.

That was easy. "We take a look at this weird compound and see if we can decipher where it comes from and what it does. Doesn't biochemistry and the way elements bond together provide all the answers? Find the right strand, mix it with another strand, and you can make a baby!" His enthusiasm and the joke didn't carry to the others well, though Priya smiled.

Parker might have to admit that since she was his girlfriend, he had some moments when he thought that if they were a couple long enough they would be married and have babies. But he wasn't going to make them in a test tube. He wanted to get back to Malibu so they could go back on dates and then explore the traditional way of practicing how people made babies.

It was not easy to work with Priya on this trip all the time. They had kissed a few times and each time it seemed to lead to more passionate moments. Moments that lasted longer. It was much more than fun to hold her close. To let his hands wander where they wanted to, and to kiss Priyanka. It was the greatest thing he had ever experienced.

And without water and feeling grungy almost all the time here in Aisén, he was sure that she didn't want to find time to go on a date. They had sat close one time and kissed a bit, but both of them felt dirty while doing it. Not dirty for kissing, but dirty because of the limitations on using water.

Putting the matter to rest, the team broke up to start analyzing all the information they had on the strange compounds that had been found in the water. Parker started to check on the history of such compounds, finding the information he needed. But for one particular protein, there was no information on the exact amino acid sequence. He then looked more at the Regions where the occurrence was taking place.

"Mr. Thornton, you are late for an appointment at the gun range," Colonel Ben-Levi was leaning over his shoulder. The security team had set up a range a few feet outside of the hotel, for their had been an open field next door.

An earthmover had dug a wide and long trench, where targets were put at one end. The citizens of Coihaique had not liked the noise of the guns at first, but when the death toll had continued to climb for no reason, the additional security forces in the city to keep order had seemed a relief. With the water rationing, many sober heads recognized that rioting could break out. Parker had that explained to him, and he had also been shown footage of how people acted when there was such rationing for basic necessities.

Here, water really was the stuff of life.

"Sorry Colonel, we have been really busy. I need to reschedule."

The Colonel said, "Normally son, if we were some place secure, I would allow you to do it. Not today. You have to shoot at least four magazines, and do so well, before you can return to your work. Come on. I'll shoot with you. Won't take but a half hour at the most."

Parker shook his head, but he got up. There was no way he could tell the Colonel no, and there was no use wasting time arguing about it. Parker did know that if the Colonel only allocated a half hour, than it would only be that long. The Colonel never added or padded the time anything took.

As they walked out of the hotel, a convoy of water trucks with the ZED Corp logo drove by. "ZED Corp has been very helpful about getting water to us here and to the other Regions."

The Colonel smiled, which looked a little feral. "They have to be. If this thing has something to do with the water, it is their water that's the cause. They own all the water rights, or at least most of them. Owning water rights. God causes the rain to come and gives all man that. It takes a great deal of chutzpah to say you own what Ehyeh has given."

Parker stopped. It was like there was an invisible wall in front of him as he thought quickly and then yanked out his phone so he could use the computer in it to quickly get information.

The Colonel noticed, "Son, I want to get your shooting done now."

"Wait a second, please Colonel," Parker said. He had begun to like that he was signaled out to lead, and to learn to shoot. But right then he didn't want to be interrupted because he was sure he was onto something that was important.

"Mr. Thornton. A half hour I said, and all the rest can wait."

Parker looked up then, and spoke. "You have made me the team leader of the other students. We are scientists and our bursts of inspiration and insight come when they come. Even if a half hour at the range is scheduled. We have to write down these things before we forget them and they disappear for who knows how long. Now Colonel, please be quiet." That was the diplomatic way to say things. He wanted to tell the Colonel to shut up and let him concentrate.

Parker had a text out to JCubed. Then, thinking about it, hacking ZED Corp, if that could be done, would probably be useful as well. He had to bring Priya in on that as well. She though had more scruples then JCubed.

He dialed Priya on his phone, "Priya, there is some connection between ZED Corp and the water. They own well over half of all water rights in each of the three affected Regions. They do not own any rights in the rest of the country. Just here. That is strange for if they were going to do something like corner the market, they would have a presence in the entire market."

Priya said, "So? They are a business, aren't they?" He could see her in the video phone. She was very pretty.

"Yes, but it doesn't make any sense. I was doing a timeline and they have been very supportive. More so than any other company, and always they were first to step up during this crisis. Can they be involved somehow?" That was what was in his thoughts. But how? As the Colonel said, the water came from God. How could a company have any effect on the water? Especially since the aquifers for such a large area were not interconnected.

"I don't see how they could be involved, and we just can't break into their mainframe."

The Colonel leaned over his shoulder, "Ms. Zadari, I know you can do things my team can not, as well as Mr. Jefferson. Perhaps you might consider this a project and see how far you can get. I should imagine the most secretive of information that the company you mentioned has is well protected. But Mr. Thornton has a point about how quickly the various elements of that company have responded to the crisis. It takes time to organize such relief efforts. Please see what you can find out."

Parker said a little more to Priya who was still reluctant, but agreed to take a look and see if she could find a way to breach the computers of ZED Corp. Then he turned back to the Colonel who had gotten on his own phone to speak to his subordinates.

"You were a little deflective about ZED Corp," Parker noted.

"ZED Corp? I do not recall mentioning any company by name. I assure you, philanthropists such as ZED Corp must assuredly be beyond any reproach at this time. What would the world think were we to be found rummaging through their files when they are the lead in the humanitarian efforts addressing this catastrophe." Colonel Ben-Levi looked very serious to a point. The point that Parker knew masked his true thoughts. Parker did not know what those thoughts were, but he could see that the Colonel had secrets as well.

"Right. Well I think there is something there. Like you said." Parker pointed down the street to where long lines of people were standing in line to get their water rations from the ZED Corp caravan, he continued, "They did seem to respond quickly. So quick that it would have taken super human achievements to have been ready to help so greatly."

The Colonel nodded. "Good, now that you have gotten your thoughts out, time for shooting practice. But we'll add the assault rifle today as well. I think things just got a little interesting." Leading the way to the firing pit, the Colonel added, "Now I am not singling out ZED Corp though there security is run by ex-KGB, but there are some organizations that believe in shooting first to protect themselves. Yes, the assault rifle as well today."

-Chapter 14-

Zedadiah hung up his phone. He was not that happy. Kutuzov said that there had been taps the last four days on the computer system. He was advising that they allow one or two of them to have the low hanging fruit.

Computer warfare had become more advanced in the twenty-first century. Millions of Chinese soldiers sat in front of terminals trying to hack their way into every organization in the world. They were the world's biggest identity thieves. And no doubt profiting by selling credit card numbers on the black market.

Zedadiah would abuse the workers of China every single day, for their masters were abusing the rest of the world. He sent millions each year to charities working towards making the Chinese care more about democracy. The only way to get any fairness out of them was to overthrow communism and get them to be as openly corrupt as any western capitalist was.

His security chief and he had also talked about the Penelope situation. She had called before Kutuzov and so it was natural that Zedadiah mention their conversation to Stefan. Penelope had reported two things. One was the offer to leave and work for another company. That was no surprise since Zedadiah knew she was giving out subtle hints she was ready to leave ZED Corp. The other was the requests by Dr. Phillips-Lee, nearly every day, for a few minutes to speak to Zedadiah.

Dr. Phillips-Lee had been in the southern part of Chile and had returned to Santiago with all his students in tow. Kutuzov thought it was time for Zedadiah to leave. He had been putting on the corporate game face of being a help to the people of Chile, but should the scientists now wish to probe why, then Kutuzov was correct. Zedadiah had to be elsewhere. No one in ZED Corp was going to speak as to why they were helping out. Penelope's team carefully worded why they were in Chile helping. He did not want a comma misplaced that might lead a reporter to start asking the wrong questions.

As well as Kutuzov clamped down on the knowledge of

ZPakCad-1328, there was the possibility that someone knew something that they had not hidden, or covered up. Deaths were slowing. New cases of the mysterious illness were much less now then when the crisis had peaked. But they were still coming and the scientists, once they had determined that this was a water-borne disease, would find that it had germinated into the coming harvest season. That it had to be eradicated into the gestating crops.

Kutuzov said his spies watching the scientists in the Regions and here in Santiago looking into the matter had now isolated several chemical elements in the water, amongst which ZPakCad-1328 was hidden. That it was merely a matter of time before it was discovered and a solution could be applied against it. And should all the other scientists fail in this, Sung Ling Chou out of the Asian office had three scientists on the international team. They would identify the enzyme should the other scientists be too dim to see it.

Dialing quickly, "Michael, we are leaving. I want to be out of here in the next hour if we can. Time to go home," Zedadiah said to his assistant.

"Sir, I can have a helicopter at the top of the building ready to take you to the airport in ten minutes. Colonel Kutuzov has given me several quick exit strategies for you that meet his security criteria."

"Do it. The sooner we are back in London, the better." Zedadiah knew there was a great deal to consider with the Cartels, but they had been very docile the last few weeks. It was either the hostages, or they believed the threat that Kutuzov had left with them. That enough evidence could be fabricated to tie the Cartels into having tampered with the water supply.

If the Cartels were linked to such a disaster, governments around the world would step up their efforts to eradicate them. It was one thing to allow them to be violent upon themselves. To fight and kill each other, and then the occasional crooked law enforcement officials. But to attack innocents so far out of their normal sphere, would make them a target as big as Osama Bin Laden had been for the US.

Less than twenty minutes later Zedadiah was aboard his plane, and five minutes after that, it was in the air. He had done what he humanely could to help those who were suffering in Chile. Zedadiah had also seen to justice being served, ordering the termination of Francisco Valdez y Gonzalez who had been motivated by greed and governed by his own stupidity and limitations. Of course in a corporation such as ZED Corp, termination could have more than one meaning, as in this case.

Francisco's sudden death, ruled a suicide, closed one chapter of the event. It was time to let Kutuzov ensure that ZED Corp was not seen to have any tie to the rest of the matter. Even as he left Chile, an announcement to the press was made. It said that the root cause of so many deaths having to do with the reliance on water, which the corporation owned the most rights to in the stricken areas, caused ZED Corp to feel compelled to set up a multi-million dollar fund for the survivors. The announcement went on to say that they hoped other charitable aid foundations and the Chilean government were encouraged to join in ZED Corp's efforts. The proposal of a multi institutional board to keep the fund honest, he had told Penelope who had drafted the idea, was a nice touch. Zedadiah was sure most of the money would end up in corrupt politician's hands, but he still thought it was a nice touch.

ZED Corp would of course make Penelope Vruder their representative to such a board and should she leave the company, as she planned to do, Zedadiah was sure she would find a way to siphon money into her own personal accounts as well. It had been a few very intense weeks in Chile and leaving, Zedadiah felt a sense of relief. He had to confess to himself his fear of the water issue. Not that the corporation would be caught out and blamed.

Corporations had been singled out in such cases before. They had survived. Their executives had survived. Zedadiah was no longer truly worried about the Cartels, for none of them were truly stupid enough to attack him. The retaliation from such an attack would see their families killed first, before his security teams eradicated the leaders. The media often talked of dirty nukes. At the level ZED Corp operated, since they sold refined plutonium, they could make rather small clean bombs, should they choose. Then lob them at the leaders of the Cartels. Nukes though were somewhat inelegant in the vast arsenal of destructive devices that ZED Corp could not only make, but get their hands on.

ZED Corp supplied nine of the top ten weapons producing defense contractors. Even owned vast positions in seven of them. To revenge an attack on Zedadiah, virtually any weapon was available to ZED Corp security. He was not worried about being killed.

Zedadiah got out his phone and sent a text to Kutuzov. The man had wanted to start stockpiling such weapons against future need. It was time to give him the official okay to do so. Though knowing the ex KGB operative, the man had already probably done so.

What terrified Zedadiah was that someone might have found a way of getting the horrid killing enzyme into the Santiago water supply, and that he would ingest it. Bioterrorism was a real and scary issue. Not that it would be a form of poetic justice. Zedadiah would have never, probably, released such a beast as ZPakCad-1328 onto the market. But others might think it just. That was the nightmare that now he could put to bed as he flew away from Chile.

"Are you sure about this, children?" Dr. Phillips-Lee asked. Parker noted that he had asked that once before when they had demanded to see him and go over their findings. Parker thought that the man would have shown them more respect.

It had been four days since they had proven that there was an unnatural protein component in the water. Man made and surely the cause of the illnesses that had spread so quickly throughout the country. Dr. Phillips-Lee was a scientist. He should know that they all subjected their discovery to the scientific method before coming forth with their proofs.

"If it's alright with you, Dr. Phillips-Lee, we could take you through all the steps we used to break this down and model it, then test it, but that would take a great deal of time to present. We feel very strongly that we have isolated the problem chemical and know why people are getting sick. Now we think we need to adopt treatments to cure them," Parker said.

Dr. Phillips-Lee swiveled his gaze to Parker. They wanted him to be the Team Leader, and so he was acting like it. So often when an adult looked at them, seeing only children, they discounted that they had already done a task, and done it well.

"It is not that I do not trust you, but we have to be sure," the adult Dr. Phillips-Lee said.

Without even looking Parker could sense JCubed's shoulders tense up. Even his own were tense.

"Dr. Phillips-Lee, really, when we isolated and analyzed the amino acid sequence and brought it to your attention, you thought we might have things wrong." That was what the Doctor had said, but he had also ordered they, and the other members of the ECO Academy team to return to Santiago to really test the findings about the chemical. They were calling it CHI-One, or C1 as the first thing that the ECOAgents had said needed to really be studied.

Now four days later the adults were still working through their protocols on handling a drug. Parker and the others amongst the students were very much ahead of that. Priyanka and JCubed had isolated and sequenced the amino acid chain and determined it had homology to known enzymes, and then in minutes, rather than days, ran simulations of the sequence to determine activity.

Combining with the chemical substrates in the particulates that one found in Chilean water helped accelerate the water into what was surely something that caused the disease. The adult chemists hadn't bothered to see if there was interaction with the particulates that were concentrated in Chilean water, but were still testing, slowly, how the enzyme acted on human cell structures. They would need weeks before they could see what his team had already found.

Guillermo, he and Jennifer had been taking the testing results that Priya and JCubed had deciphered and applying it to common and not so common drugs to see if there could be some reverse of the damaging effects of CHI-One. Autopsies had clearly showed that there was alteration in the biochemistry in the brain of those with the illness, those who had died.

It had suggested that they needed to neutralize the enzyme first before it compromised a person's brain. Then find a way to affect those whose brains had begun to alter and believe that they were in no way thirsty, when their bodies were dehydrating rapidly. Their simulations also showed that without further ingestion of contaminated water and without replenishing CHI-One, the enzyme would only stay active for about a month.

Now that they knew what to look for, purifying the water completely of the enzyme was easy, with proper protein filtration techniques, albeit on a large scale. What was not so easy was ridding the enzyme from people who had already ingested it. JCubed had hit on using compounds of common treatments in the testing phase and an antihistamine combined with nervous system medications such as propranolol and Xanax, and a low dose of anti-diuretic hormone seemed to restore normal brain activity, overriding the enzyme if it hadn't taken hold. The simulator showed that the concoction, in a dose the size of a pill, daily for a month, or six weeks just to be safe, would allow the body to rid itself of the enzyme without any detrimental effects.

"There is a great deal relying on this, children. How many times did you verify your results?" Dr. Phillips-Lee asked.

Parker knew without looking at the paperwork in front of him, exactly how many times. He had set the parameter up and had Priya and JCubed implement it. But he glanced at the papers on his clipboard to make Dr. Phillips-Lee think he needed to look at them for reference.

Turning a few pages, he then pretended to study for a moment, "Twenty times. Twenty times at each level of permutation, so the simulators and the sequencers ran approximately six hundred testing protocols in the last two days on this mixture of medicines."

That was so. In all the simulations, still churning in their section of the laboratory, they were currently on the ninety-sixth thousandth testing sequence. Fortunately they did not have to explain to Dr. Phillips-Lee how their devices were working today. They had already done so earlier.

"We need to do some animal testing."

Jennifer said, "We have done so on animal cells. And father has injected a few mice that are now fine. We don't have a great deal of time to immunize the rest. But we have to get into production and prevent others from getting sick. There are about one and half million people in the infected area."

Dr. Phillips-Lee then pointed to his tablet and what he was referencing showed up on the main wall. "It says here that we might be able to deliver this, antidote? By the water we are exporting to the Regions. That would be a very effective distribution system until we can be sure that the water is pure again."

That had been Guillermo's idea. Jennifer had not liked it because she wanted the medical professionals to disperse the pills and ensure that all registered inhabitants had them. There were still areas that might not be receiving bottled water.

"What happens if this doesn't stop the disease's growth? These drugs in and of themselves this way have some side effects surely?" Dr. Phillips-Lee asked.

Jennifer then sent to the wall her findings on that issue. Some, a small percentage, would still have reactions just to the drugs. And of course with any protocol, the drugs might not be effective for all the patients covered. Though JCubed and Priya's analysis showed a great deal of success. Since identifying the unnatural protein and being sure that it was what was at the heart of the crisis it had become a race to best it.

With this cocktail, it felt that they had won the first lap of the race.

Jennifer finished explaining the down side of the drugs and now had a chart up showing that the adverse effects seemed to be minimal. Guillermo was ready to place his own work showing the returns of the various ways of distributing the antidotes. Guillermo liked it, Parker was sure, because his suggestion seemed to be the favorite for success.

And if it was, that was fine.

Parker said, "This is only the first leg. It should stop the disease that has been leading to so many deaths. But anyone who has advanced to the point where their brains have begun to be altered, needs some other cure. We have to still find that. We have to make sure this enzyme is eradicated entirely from the water, and that an inhibitor is included in the aquifers and rivers so that it never arises again."

Priya added onto his words, "And we have to see if it has affected next year's crop. We have had no time to analyze that yet, but now our computers are going to have time, since we have found a cure to stop it metastasizing any further. And this has to be checked in more animal species for we know we have protected humans. We have to see about livestock as well as other animals.

"The imported water has been given to farm animals, but no animals in the wild. And they have drunk from the water sources. Many being found dead around the Regions." Priya finished.

The Colonel cleared his throat and when everyone looked at him, he just shook his head. Parker though nodded and added, "It looks like this enzyme, being structured the way it is, is man made. That this is an act of terrorism."

Dr. Phillips-Lee said, "Yes, you have raised that point before. About its nature. And about ZED Corp seeming very proactive in helping during the situation. I have tried to speak to the chairman. He purchased one of my companies so I have met Zedadiah Carter before. But his office has put me off many times."

If Dr. Phillips-Lee could not get a meeting with the man, then it would be hard for anyone else to.

"He's left the country. He was here for the last few weeks, but he flew out this morning," Colonel Ben-Levi said.

Dr. Phillips-Lee just nodded, though it was clear he was not too happy about it. "Very well. I will make calls, though I see you already have figured out whom we have to call to get the ball rolling. You are right, there are a whole host of answers we need. So, let me get the drugs we need so the antidote is fabricated, and we get our other scientists to follow your lead and concentrate on the parts that affect the brain."

Parker agreed. "Jennifer should work with her father on this. She had been isolating things he would need to solve the problem."

Dr. Phillips-Lee held up his hand, "You go ahead and do all you need to, let me get on this."

The Colonel then said, "Come ECOAgents, leave the Chancellor to his duties now. You all have a lot of work ahead of you still." The Colonel ushered them out even as Dr. Phillips-Lee was telling his phone to dial the President of Chile.

When in the hallway, the Colonel said, "Well done Mr. Parker and team. Now you must focus on those other items you mentioned. It seems that you are all much more able to reach a solution to these problems than some of the others who are called experts in the field."

Parker said, "Priya and JCubed can wire up the machines and the data we need faster than anyone else. And speeding up the test results is what leads to the conclusions that lead to a cure."

The Colonel smiled, probably indulgently Parker thought, "In any case, now find a way to save those who are really dying, and a way to clean the water of this thing forever."

Priya said, "And cure the animals, and see if the crops are ruined... We have a lot to do."

Parker agreed, "Yes, back to work everyone. There are thousands of sick people relying on us." He did not include the adults in that thought. They had not seemed to have done a whole lot of anything. But that was not entirely fair. Dr. Johansson had found the mysterious long chain of amino acids, asking for more clarity by the team at ground zero. Dr. Smythe Lytton had done autopsies which gave them cells to use in their analysis.

There were other scientists in Chile who had done work that was fed into their use of the data. But it was the ECOAgents who had made the discoveries so far.

"JCubed, how long is it going to take Dr. Lee to get the drugs we need?"

"I had a spider check that. Check stocks, production figures, tooling so we can make this. It can't be done in Chile, not yet. But the US, elsewhere, we could have the first batch flying on it's way to us by tomorrow. Or in a month if Dr. Phillips-Lee doesn't get through to who he has to."

Parker nodded and said his thanks. He walked a few feet away and looked at his phone and then the time it would be where he was placing his call. He dialed anyway, it was that important, "This is Parker Thornton. The Premier said I was to call this number if there ever was an emergency."

"Thornton. The young American man from the Ural. I shall wake the Premier for you at once. Hold, please..." A heavily accented voice said in English.

No matter how much work and effort the entire team put into studying the chemical that they had found contaminating the water, and killing people, more died even as answers became clear. Parker noted that if they talked about the deaths, the other students became upset.

People were dying and they were racing to find ways to save them.

"You are not Gods," Dr. Smythe-Lytton said to Jennifer and he, bringing Parker out of his reverie.

"What?" Parker said.

"Dad…"

Dr. Smythe-Lytton cleared his throat, "Everyone, come here for a moment. You two Jackson." He never called JCubed by the nickname that almost everyone else did.

"Good. Now look. If we had left you in Malibu and had you analyze all this from home, people would still have been infected and still be dying. If we hadn't brought you or even put you on this project, people would still be getting sick. It is terrible. There is nothing as horrible to a family as something like this. But hundreds of thousands will be so thankful that we did bring you here."

Dr. Smythe-Lytton patted his daughter's hand. "You all have found the cause of this and an inoculation that stops it spreading. That is tremendous. Dr. Johannson of Sweden's Royal Institute of Technology called me to say he was surprised that you found the enzyme so quickly. He said with his research team, he would have needed two or three more months. Thousands more, tens of thousands, would have become infected and died as he searched for answers. Thousands that you saved. And the work you are doing now, the best minds might not find a cure for those already infected. If you do, that is a miracle. If you don't, you are no less human than the hundreds of researchers around the world trying to figure this thing out. And all based on your discoveries."

Dr. Phillips-Lee walked into the laboratory. "Simon is correct. I forget that you have not had a lot of time in science and don't realize how hard it is to find such solutions. Decades can be spent trying to find cures. Look at AIDS, or various Cancers. We research cures and still thousands die from these diseases each year. I am sorry children, but it is possible that those who are already sick, may never recover. That we may not be able to help them, and it is not your fault."

Parker spoke, "It is someone's fault. The protein in the water is absolutely man-made. There is less than an eight sigma chance that it is natural."

Dr. Phillips-Lee raised his hand "Yes, I have read those findings. It may be so. It will be hard to find exactly who is at fault for such a crime, but rest assured, several people are trying to find out who is responsible. The Chilean government, Interpol, our own security people. A lot of people want to know who is at fault for such mass murder. We though need not get involved in that. We will continue to look for a cure, but I want to also tell you that we will be going home as well. I spoke to some of your professors back at campus. I have been a little lax. I have not pushed you as hard to maintain your coursework in your other classes because you have done so well here."

Parker grimaced, and he saw that he was not alone. He could see Guillermo do the same. "Ah, Dr. Phillips-Lee, I know we have all missed a few due dates on papers and tests, but we cleared it with our professors back at the Academy that we could make things up…"

Dr. Phillips-Lee smiled. "Yes, and they have been quite understanding, but there is an overall time line that we must respect. We have other classes that will start soon enough and if you fall too far behind, all of you, then it will be very hard to keep things on track later. So we leave for home in two days. I know you may not have finished all you have to do here. There will be plenty of other scientists though who will be staying here to try and find the solutions that we have been looking for. That will be building on the solutions you already found. You are heroes. Again."

Dr. Smythe-Lytton said, "Yes indeed. Russia and the US teaming together to make the pill and get them rushed to us in quantities that will make a difference. That was the greatest piece of medical cooperation I have ever seen in all my years. We had prototypes last night and they were perfect. By tomorrow we will have batches for tens of thousand, and by next week enough that almost everyone in the troubled Regions will be defended against CHI-One."

Priya raised her hand, "Dr. Phillips-Lee, sir."

"Yes Ms. Zadari?"

"Uh, the crops for next year. Guillermo gave me a few formulas to try on the soil samples, but we needed more, so I've tried to get more soil to analyze. But even with what I have, the analysis looks like next year could be bad. We are unsure of the stability of this protein in plants."

Parker looked down at his tablet and saw among all the emails that were marked urgent, and most of which he hadn't had time to read, three from Priya. He had been sending her encouragements every few hours, though he hadn't marked them urgent. They were little notes saying how he liked her. How he had plans for their next date. How much he liked the last time they had kissed. And that was last night for about five minutes.

Her notes had a subject line saying soil samples.

Opening one up, he could see that preliminary analysis showed that the ground was saturated with the enzyme and it had transferred into the seedlings. Could it be sustained in the plant? Though the plant could not produce more enzyme, what about the enzyme that was already in the soil and plant? Will additional enzyme be incorporated into crops as water is pulled out of the soil? What happens when people and animals eat these plants? Could the coming year see levels of infestation many times higher than the current year? And these crops are many times exportable crops. The disease could go international.

Colonel Ben-Levi had come into the room and perched himself against a table. He adjusted his assault rifle, which he had taken to carrying since they had found the enzyme to be man made. He said it was an affectation. But it helped him make his point with the Chilean Government officials who did not think that the matter was really as serious as it was.

The Colonel said, "Ms. Zadari's analysis points to what we thought might be needed. We are going to have to recommend that all farming for next year be destroyed. And in future years until this enzyme is completely eradicated from the soil. Is that not so?"

Priya nodded, "That is what my research points to. Guillermo said that if we can't find not only a cure, but something that neutralizes the enzyme in crops and the soil, then we must continue to monitor the area. It is like mad-cow disease but a lot faster acting. It doesn't eat away at the brain so much as makes the brain really sick."

Dr. Phillips-Lee did not look happy.

Parker spoke, "Ah, the Vice President asked me how bad it really was the other night. When I talked to the Premier and him. I told him that we hadn't yet developed any real data on the food supply here, but that it was really a possibility that the food could be contaminated and if that was the case, then I thought it would be troublesome since Chile exports so much." He paused. The Vice President was very smart. He knew what it meant.

The Colonel knew he had called and talked to the Vice President and Premier of Russia. He now said, "Go ahead and tell them Mr. Thornton."

Parker swallowed and said, "The Vice President said he would talk to the President. That first they would have to quarantine the troubled Regions, and if Chile was not cooperative, then all of the country. The UN would definitely be involved. That the entire harvests would have to be burned and destroyed if our hunches were right, and it looks like they are."

It was Guillermo who spoke. "For this year. We have to destroy the crops for this year, but we don't know about next. We can still find a cure for those who get sick. We know how to purify the water supply that entirely removes the enzyme. We just have to make sure it gets done. Knowing the amino acid sequence will allow us to find an inhibitor and kill it. Once that has occurred, we should be able to find a way to saturate the ground with this CHI-One killer, counteracting whatever traces of this chemical are in the ground for the following harvest."

Or not, Parker thought. He was not going to say it aloud. It was very likely they would solve those three problems. He did speak, "Dr. Phillips-Lee, if you have trouble with the Chilean government over this, the President will step in. That is what the Vice President said. It is far too important to not have him ensure that tainted food gets out of Chile. Even that tainted food is allowed to be harvested and consumed by anyone."

Dr. Phillips-Lee nodded. "No, you are right. We won't let that happen. Ms. Zadari, lets review what you have found. And children, work on your projects. But tonight, after dinner, we start summarizing everything for other colleagues to take over. Tomorrow we wrap everything up and then go home. Everyone understand?"

The team nodded. Dr. Phillips-Lee was right. They had done a lot of work. They may not have solved every problem on their list. They might not have found the cure for those infected, yet. They could still work on the plane, they could still have sequencers and computers run simulations even as they were back in class. The ECOAgents had found the most important things. They had stopped further infection completely. They had started the world's scientists on the right road to solving all the remaining problems. It was a victory against a horrid problem.

-Chapter 15-

Stepping out of the Applied Sciences building, Parker looked towards the Descartes library clock tower. He knew it was probably three to five minutes later then when he had closed his testing book, and glanced at the clock in the classroom. Strange that he hadn't looked at his watch since then, or at the time on his phone. That thought reminded him to fish out the phone from his pocket and return it from silence mode to normal mode. He also could check for messages that had come in while he had been taking his last final of the quarter.

One quarter of his senior year done, two more to go. As a senior he would not be taking classes in summer unless he failed a class and had to repeat. No student of ECO Academy had ever failed a class yet. He didn't expect that he would be the first to do so.

He saw Priya in the quad waiting for him. She was talking to JCubed and Shelley Botha. Parker was the last of them all to finish taking his exams for the quarter. He had worked as hard as the rest of them to catch up so they could complete finals together with the other members of the Academy. He still had two reports to finish and turn in, but he was allowed the time during break to do so. He wasn't going back to Kansas City for Christmas. There was a quick trip to Washington DC scheduled for him and the other ECOAgents.

All the parents were being flown to the capital as well, though Jennifer's mother refused to come. A quick meeting at the White House and a dinner at the Chilean embassy that night. Then a flight on Saturday morning back to Los Angeles.

His grandparents, both sets, were going to meet up with them all in Washington. The Chilean embassy was going to really put on a big shindig for them that night. A great many of Washington's elite had been invited, as well as others, Parker had been told. His father, according to his mother, did not know what to say. Grandpa had walked into the headquarters of the bank and was telling everyone how Parker and the other ECOAgents had gone and saved all of Chile, which was not really the case. Though close, maybe if you wanted to be really generous with praise.

Mother said it made his father proud. Parker was sure that was not the way it was at all. Grandpa might be saying how great it was, but Parker's father probably wanted Grandpa to be saying something about how loans were performing better this year than last. Something about Prescott Thornton's efforts. Grandpa often said great things about Prescott Thornton and how the bank had grown. Parker wondered if his father ever said anything about how well Parker was doing. Getting As was great, but isolating a deadly enzyme that had the potential of making more than a million people deathly sick, was an achievement. And in the three weeks since they had returned to the Academy, the team's efforts had helped the scientists that remained in Chile, further.

"Hey," he said approaching the two girls and JCubed.

"Finally done, stud," Shelley said.

"Shells, really," Priya said quickly.

JCubed just laughed. "Stud…"

Parker thought his face might be turning red. He and Priya had gone out twice since they had been back. Not further then the strip mall to get something to eat, or to the bluffs to look at the ocean. They had a date tonight though. They were going down to Pacific Palisades and eating at the fish house on the coast there.

"Thanks Shelley," he said. Parker knew being called 'Stud' was a compliment. At least it should be.

"Don't encourage her. She's just terrible," Priya said.

"Not that she has any practical knowledge, Priya, but when you can confirm for Shelley that she is guessing right, she'll only be jealous." Even as he said it, he was laughing and Shelley was the first to laugh also. Even Priya giggled. Tonight was not the night he had planned to let his girl know that he was a stud, well he hoped she thought of him so. But soon. Each week they had been getting closer to something that would bring them as close together as two people could be. And he did think about sex with Priya a good deal. They were staying in the St. Regis, just two blocks from the White House when they were in Washington. The first night was before their parents arrived.

Parker had casually mentioned to the Vice President's aide that the parents would fuss over them all something terribly once they arrived. The Vice President then called two hours after Parker and the aide had talked.

"Parker, you weren't blowing smoke at my aide, were you? It's alright, you can talk. Aside from the government record keepers, only you and I are on this call."

Parker could see that the Vice President looked like he was alone. Parker had solid relationships growing with the Vice President and the Premier. Even the President of Chile was now in his speed dial list. "I am just trying to get some private time with Priya. If all the parents are around that will be hard to do."

The Vice President shook his head then, "You are away at school there in Malibu. You can't get any private time? Well never mind. You are all supposed to come to dinner at Number One the first night. I'll just make it for you ECOAgents, and another guest that will be in town that day. No Dr. Lee. Though I suppose your Colonel will want to tag along, despite my Secret Service detail."

Since working with the Security team, Parker knew a lot more about them. "You are probably right sir. Colonel Ben Levi respects the Secret Service, but he doesn't trust any other security detail but those he has trained."

"It's the Mossad in him. They are all like that. I'll keep your parents away the first night. Will that give you the time you need to be with your girl? I did something similar when I was in college to get time with my wife."

"Thank you sir. That would be great." The Vice President chuckled and by the next day it was all arranged. Just the students were to spend the first night at dinner at Number One Observatory Circle, the home of the Vice President of the United States.

Now back with Priya and the others, Parker hoped that after that dinner at the Vice President's they would have a chance to sneak off, and complete all the facets of their relationship that still remained a mystery. So much emphasis was placed on sex that getting that over with would probably accomplish two things. One that they both crossed the threshold into the mysteries of adulthood that it locked.

Parker was sure that Priya also was a virgin, like he was. But that, once having done it, and hopefully finding opportunities to do it again many more times, then they would not have the question whether they would like doing it with each still left unsettled between them. Parker was a scientist and knew that there was empirical proof that people liked having sex. If not, there would be no babies all over the place.

So sex was fun. It was time to start exploring that because in a few more months, he would have graduated and he might drift so far from Priya that it would be hard to schedule time to see her. As for his future, he had received letters of interest from several world-renown university scientists, and then also phone calls from people highly placed in think tanks and governments with preliminary offers. Dr. Phillips-Lee said he must wait to accept any of them. Even though he had already accomplished alot, Parker knew he had to finish his doctorate to be truly an accepted part of the scientific community. But he still wanted to keep his ECOAgent status.

The other 19 seniors weren't getting that type of cautionary advice. He knew that more than half of his senior class had already lined up what they would do in the coming year once they graduated. But Colonel Ben-Levi also told him that he should wait. Until he decided after he met the President. He would wait till then.

"Hey, stud, you are wandering again," Shelley said.

"I have another text from the head of the Russian Academy of Sciences. I think they are determined to offer me the best deal of anyone, and Dr. Phillips-Lee says I shouldn't take any offer yet," he said.

Guillermo and Jennifer were approaching Parker saw, as were some of the other students.

JCubed said, "Well Dr. Phillips-Lee seems to be right if every time someone calls you to offer you a place they offer you more money then the last phone call. It's all because of Chile, though."

Parker shrugged his shoulders. Priya said, "And the Ural Sea. We did good work there also. And if the RAS wants Parker it is because he impressed the Premier when we went to Aral'sk."

That had occurred to Parker as well. That a few of the offers he was receiving were because the Premier wanted him to work for the Russians. "I think the offer from the Russian Academy of Sciences is to not only attach myself to their faculty, but to be a part of the international coalition that is saving the Ural Sea."

Guillermo was quick to speak. "Why? Because of the paper you read? You had two ideas and your science was shoddy. Only your idea that some projects need international cooperation and control was what made an impression."

Jennifer said, "Sometimes leadership trumps science. If we didn't have goals and objectives we might putter around in the lab for years. But look how having defined goals and time pressures helped in Chile. We may not have saved everyone, but we certainly found a way to save more than a million people this year, and Priya's analysis of the soil came in so fast that we know destroying the crops is going to save tens of millions."

"That doesn't have anything to do with Parker," Guillermo said.

JCubed shook his head. "Would you like me to show you the calls, emails, and texts of what Parker did to help us find the time to get the answers that quickly?"

Shelley, who hadn't gone to South America said, "Gui, babes, you have to let this fight thing go. Everyone else says that Parker got everything that was needed including presenting the material to the Professors that got them to sit up and take notice. That is very often no easy task, as you well know. I keep telling you that you have to do more than PowerPoint slides in giving your oral reports. That is so twentieth century. Interactive supplemental apps streamed to an audience engages the Professors now."

Priya said something quietly to Shelley that Parker couldn't hear. Parker guessed though that since Shelley was wandering off topic, Priya pointed that out. Shelly said, "Right. Gui babes, your team needs a leader, and this year Parker is it. Next year, well Parker will graduate so the ECOAgents will need some of us others to join. I'm going to make sure Dr. Phillips-Lee has my CV."

Parker smiled, "That's great Shelley, but I am not sure that he looks at your Curriculum Vitae when he chooses who goes on these field trips. The first time, to Kazakhstan we all know how that worked. This time, I think he did not have the time to think very long about which students to take. And then we had already met some world leaders. I think he wanted to show that the Academy had the ability to augment the worlds leading scientists in the missions that they are needed for."

Now Guillermo turned and nodded. "Yeah, that I agree with. This really helped the Academy. I know that we get a lot of applicants each year, and that we are going to have three times as many freshmen next year as this, but I heard administration is swamped because applications are already forty percent higher than last year."

Parker smiled, "They probably also don't like being moved all around to make way for the construction work the Colonel keeps doing under the building." He thought it was funny.

Parker had told his friends only a little of what he had seen being done below the building. The security force had impressed on him that some of what was going on below the building was not for anyone else to know.

Lately, though the expansion had taken another turn. There was now tunnels being built under all the buildings of the campus. Then access points for security and a few others were going to be built from the tunnels up to the buildings. Under Descartes Library, a security restricted laboratory was being built. The Colonel had once again asked JCubed and Priya to specify everything that was needed to be state of the art, and then he had asked Parker last week to check it, and lay out a floor plan. Parker had cut a few of the instruments that JCubed and Priya had wanted to purchase for the lab.

Those were very expensive, they took a lot of space, and took a great deal of energy to run. What could be done was rent the use of the machines, for there were a few around Southern California of each. Parker had asked the Colonel with his connections if he could do that discreetly and anonymously.

The Colonel grinned then, "Now you are making me proud. We can do that Mr. Thornton. Oh, and of course there is no need for a supercollider just yet. Though I think that in a few years, like everything else, it will be smaller and cheaper and perhaps then we can put one in."

Parker had to look up how much a supercollider cost. Over four billion dollars, and it was over 27 kilometers in diameter.

There was enough room on the campus for it, but they were not high enough above sea level at the coast. And the California Coastal Commission might have a problem building something that caused nuclear reactions built so close to the city. The Colonel though did have a point. Each year technology became cheaper, smaller, and more powerful. One day everyone might have a collider in their back yard.

Parker smiled when he had researched the machine. It was just the type of thing that Priya would invent in the next ten years. Something the size of a washing machine that every home would then have. If she had been an American scientists she would find a way to share patents for her invention and become fabulously wealthy, but as an Indian, she might end up gifting the whole thing to some corporation like General Electric or ZED Corp.

He still wondered about ZED Corp and how quickly they helped with the crisis in Chile, but that was weeks ago now, and the adults were trying to figure out the answer to that question. He had other things to worry about. Or to plan for, like his date with Priya when they were at the St. Regis.

Sitting down on the Quad, it wasn't long before well over half of the student population had gathered as well as several of the faculty and staff. As was the case whenever the students were together and the adults came, the students were always outnumbered by those who made the campus run. With all the work going on, the construction crew that was working on the security expansion project even outnumbered the students.

Parker thought that perhaps he was going to graduate at the right time. That next year there were going to be 60 freshmen. Then the year after Dr. Phillips-Lee had announced that the Academy planned to add more than one hundred new freshman as it expanded to it's full potential. Now Parker knew every student's name, and every one of the faculty. Even the professors and their assistants in disciplines he didn't study. In a few years he would not be able to say that, so the entire culture of the Academy would have changed.

Dr. Phillips-Lee was making his way towards the cluster of students and adults. "Please, everyone, please. Dr. Michaels still is conducting a final for three of your colleagues. He has called to complain that you are becoming a distraction."

Parker, along with almost all gathered turned to look towards the Chemistry building. That was where Dr. Michaels had his lecture hall and lab. Parker wasn't absolutely sure, but Dr. Michaels would have had a second floor room, and with such a small class, it had to be the left corner, where the lights were on. It was still an hour before sundown, but there was very little chance that anyone taking a final in that room could see all gathered in the quad.

Knowing Dr. Phillips-Lee, he was using the final test as an excuse to get all their attention. The man could have just said, 'Your attention please.' But that was not really Dr. Phillips-Lee's style.

"Young ladies and gentlemen, please." The Colonel was close behind Dr. Phillips-Lee and when he spoke, it became quiet instantly.

Dr. Phillips-Lee turned to the Colonel with a look of displeasure. Then he turned back to the crowd of students and adults. "Very well. A quarter is drawing to an end. I see that many of you are gathering again in the quad to celebrate. This seems to be a tradition."

They had done so at the end of Spring Quarter in June, and also last September when the shortened Summer Quarter ended. Perhaps it was a tradition now.

"I have some good news. As you know your fellow students who accompanied me to Chile were very instrumental in the efforts to aid the sick there. They were instrumental in stopping an epidemic and now we have news that arrived an hour ago. The analysis of compounds and medicines to attack this horrid water based enzyme has succeeded. We now have a formulation that is arresting the attacks on the brains of the infected. Their bodies, when they have this inoculation, no longer believe it doesn't need to hydrate. It is stopping the disease in all but the cases that were the worst."

Parker let out a very long breath. That was the most important thing. Naturally they needed to do some other things against the Chilean enzyme still. They had to totally see that it had been removed from the water supply. They had to ensure that future crops, once they had destroyed the coming years harvest, could be grown without the enzyme continuing to be produced in future iterations.

Dr. Phillips-Lee was still speaking. "Now this is good news. I think a celebration is in order, and since it is finals and the end of the quarter, with the last test in Dr. Michaels' chemistry class finishing, we will have a party at the cafeteria."

Parker smiled. They always had a special dinner at the cafeteria after the last final. Often many of the faculty came as well as those who worked on the campus. The cafeteria had a few moveable walls since it had been designed for over six hundred. The student body of eighty, and those who administered their houses usually meant that at any meal there was just over 100 people always being served lunch or dinner while the faculty and staff often ate lunch on campus, they seldom ate dinner there.

The last day of a quarter was different. Especially as the catering service brought in special desserts and other treats to eat. Dr. Phillips-Lee knew all that.

And all the students knew he knew. It was a very long running joke, but usually they only had the end of the quarter to celebrate. Not stopping this horrid enzyme that was causing people to die.

That was a win for everyone. And it was the ECOAgents who had shown the rest of the world the way to the cure. They had identified the cause. They had set up the analysis and protocols that led not only to the recognition, but to the first cure that fought back against it.

"Even though this is Southern California, it is getting a little cool. What say we take this party into the cafeteria? Don't tell your parents, but the Chilean government sent some Sparkling Wine from their country for us to celebrate with."

Parker smiled. He had champagne before, and thought it like a funny tasting soda pop, but with a dry taste after. He liked soda pop better. And there were several kids who wouldn't drink anything alcoholic, though with the Academy supervising, they would not get much anyway. One glass perhaps. One small glass.

The adults though were sure to over indulge. Parker had noticed that most of the professors made a point of drinking at the end of each school week. At least those that lived within walking distance of the campus hung around each other's houses and tied it on.

As all the students walked towards the cafeteria Parker found his way to stride along with Priya at his side. He felt a slight vibration as his phone received a text. And he heard a sharp ping as Priya also received one. Fishing out his phone to see what it said, he saw a message from Dr. Phillips-Lee saying that he needed to hold back and go to the Regents Room in the cafeteria complex. It was a room that had wood paneling and nicer tables and chairs. It was where Dr. Phillips-Lee entertained visiting dignitaries to the school.

Priya said to him, "Did your text say Regent Room?"

He nodded and said, "Yes. Dr. Phillips-Lee wants us, so I bet he wants all of the ECOAgents there."

"Here comes JCubed. He probably has hacked the address list on the text, even though mine only has my name," she said. Parker was pretty sure that Priya could hack the address list of the text as well.

"JCubed, are you to go to the Regent's Room?" Parker asked as soon as the other boy got close.

He nodded back at them, "Yeah. We all are. Just those of us who went to Chile."

Parker said, "Just the ECOAgents then. It won't last too long, since Dr. Phillips-Lee will want to be with all the Academy to celebrate. Let's hurry. Guillermo will be there first and probably make some crack about us coming late."

They stepped up their pace, even though there were not that many feet between them and those students who were at the very front of the pack. But Parker was correct, for they found Guillermo speaking with Dr. Phillips-Lee, Jennifer, Dr, Smythe-Lytton and the Colonel when they arrived in the hall.

Dr. Phillips-Lee was nodding steadily as Guillermo talked but noticed Parker and his friends and waved them to come close. "I shall think about that young man. Good. Now that we are all together we must talk, though of course we will have many chances to talk when we travel to Washington. I have arranged an airplane to rent, much like when we travelled to Kazakhstan. The new plane is just so bulky and we are not going to see the President and need our labs with us."

Parker thought they could have travelled by the regular airlines, but then you had to arrive at the gate early. You had to check your luggage and had the body search lines. When they travelled with Dr. Phillips-Lee and his private jet, they still had to go through a TSA check point, but it was routine. There was no line and the TSA attendant, though thorough, was pretty sure that they were not going to blow up or hijack the plane they were getting on.

Parker had to think it was pretty cool to get on a private luxury jet. Maybe he needed to tell those who were trying to recruit him that it was a condition of his being hired. Elite flying arrangements. Everything else was just so yesterday.

Dr. Phillips-Lee said, "Well now that we are here, just us, I thought I would talk about our trip though. You all did exceptional work. I really mean that. I knew that we were onto something extraordinary with the idea that some young people are very capable of great things. That no schools really addressed the needs of people your age, or myself when I was your age. Most of our Professors, I think feel the same, as most were hired to be a part of our faculty because they too were brilliant at an early age and had no place that could help them reach their full potential."

He continued, "The second thing that is extraordinary is that we as adults founding the institution knew that the Earth needed our help to cure its ailments. More so than many governments have realized, or acknowledged. That principle happily has found adherents in your generation. Or at least in you amongst your generation. We have needed you and the other students to tackle the problems that so many of the world's governments think that their children, or the children of their children will solve, but by then of course, as we teach you in your first weeks, it will be too late.

"Governments will pay to heal the planet if it cost them little, a rounding error from their tax monies. And will not cause any of their big contributors to their reelection to ask that they not follow the sciences we bring to cure the world of its ills."

Parker knew that was true. He had heard a lot of that from his father. A man reluctant to really want to change the status quo in regards to how things worked. Upheaval and change would mean uncertainty and that would cause businesses to think twice about getting loans. Bankers made money on people taking out loans. Whether it was to buy a house, which they needed a good job to do, or a business wanting to expand and hire more people. Which Parker knew would lead to those people wanting to buy a house since they had a job. And then they would buy companies stuff, which led to those companies wanting to hire more people. His father called that the business cycle. And then he said no politician had the right to mess with it.

Dr. Phillips-Lee was saying, "We never expected that we would put you into situations like the Ural Sea, or Chile. I knew we needed to show the world that your learning here was worth it to all nations. But you exceeded beyond everyone's expectations. What you did when we went to Kazakhstan was more than enough. But what you accomplished in Chile certainly has earned you the sobriquet of ECOAgents. Just as the media has called you."

Jennifer's father said, "Daniel, you are doing it again. These young people do not need a history lesson."

"What? Oh right. Of course. I have been talking to the media so long that I can't seem to forget that I am doing it. They labeled you ECOAgents and we are going to make it official. A few hours each week, next quarter, and on our trip to Washington, the public relations people are going to talk to you and coach you. You are our best image of what the future of science should be. To help us get the best and brightest and to pay for this campus and future campuses, we want to present to the world that image."

JCubed asked, "Are we going to get special uniforms, or something."

The Colonel chuckled and said, "Yes. That is exactly what is going to happen. Well, maybe just special shirts, blazers and jackets, and of course, lab coats, but we'll call them uniforms. We are having an insignia designed that will be embroidered on all ECOAgents garments. There is a certain esprit de corps when there are uniforms involved. And Mr. Cordovan, you should get used to acknowledging Mr. Thornton as your leader. Even should you not like it. If the media finds that you are fighting amongst yourself, that will send the wrong message." EcoAgent-in-Charge. It was hard for Parker not to grin just a little.

Parker looked at Guillermo. The junior did not like hearing that at all. Guillermo had too big a chip on his shoulder. Parker did not think he was spoiled, but of course to Guillermo's background from Costa Rica, he was.

"We would like you all to have the uniforms for next weekend, so tomorrow at 10 there will be a fitting by my tailor in the Administration building. The Colonel will have clearances for you." Dr. Phillips-Lee said.

The Colonel said, "They are in my section, which only Mr. Thornton has had access to. Tomorrow we shall also give the rest of the team an introduction to the security features. We have been asked by the President to be prepared for any situation in which the ECOAgents are needed. That Presidential request was accompanied by a significant endowment to the ECOAgent operation of the Academy. So, sometime in the next month or so, a permanent lab for the ECOAgents shall be ready. At that time I shall give you a tour of your new nerve center. As for our trip, aside from your uniforms, pack for warm weather. It snowed last week in Washington, and this week there is a heat wave that should last until after we have been and left. But with weather you never really know."

"Hey, give me a minute and I can tell you what the weather will be exactly when we are there," JCubed said.

Parker could not hide a grin for that was global warming, and that was his specialty. The other news commentators had covered that issue the last few days. How it was early December and it should be cold back East, but weather in the nineties was wrong. Each year that was happening more often. A freak reversal in the midst of a season. Cold and even snow in summer for a brief few days. Heat waves in winter.

Someone needed to look into it closer, and the international community was not taking point on the issue. Dr. Smythe-Lytton cleared his throat to speak, "I have some more information about Chile. The enzyme in the water, we are finding, seems to have a half-life, and it's potency passes from affecting people, and animals after about a month, just as you all predicted. Or, all the samples that we have left viable are too weak now to cause harm."

That was good news. Parker understood the Doctor to say that if no new enzyme was found in the water, the older enzyme that was there was now ineffective and too powerless to harm anyone. The Doctor continued. "With Priya's sequencers and her and Jackson's programs for analysis no longer working on a compound to help us with the medical solutions, I got an email today that they now can run testing on the soil samples and they predict by the time we get to Washington, they should have solutions on the damage to the soil and know what they have to do for the future. The crisis is just about over."

"Good, now let's go to the party. Another quarter done, and we have shown the world we can do tremendous work." Dr. Phillips-Lee said.

Parker supposed it was all right for the man to take some of the credit. His smarts had led to inventions that gave him a lot of money. Money he used to build the Academy. And the Academy had given Parker and his friends the place they needed to learn enough to have solved the problems that they had. A place where they could solve even more of the world's problems in the coming months.

As he reached for Priya's hand, and she squeezed his, Parker knew that things were pretty good. And then next weekend, when they got to the St. Regis in Washington DC, things should get even better.

THE END

Find Out More

You can explore more about the mission of the **Ecological Conservation Organization's Academy of Higher Learning and Scientific Achievement**, or the ECO Academy.

Become a part of the team and learn how you can be admitted to this institution of higher learning. See what the students are studying and what environmental conundrums they are solving.

Explore what Parker, Guillermo, Priya, Jennifer and JCubed are up to by visiting the website.

http://www.ecoacademyagents.com/Home.html

Search for the entry to the basement security complex and see if you too can become a member of the ECO Agents.

About the Authors

David W. Wilkin

A graduate in history, Mr. Wilkin has been writing in various genres for twenty five years. Extensive study of premodern civilizations, including years as a re-enactor of medieval and renaissance times has given Mr. Wilkin an insight into such antiquated cultures.

Trained in fighting forms as well as his background in history lends his fantasy work the ability to encompass mores beyond simple hero quests. His educational focus adds the depth of world structure and political forms to these tales.

Connect with Mr. Wilkin Online:
http://www.regencyassemblypress.com

His Blog:
http://thethingsthatcatchmyeye.wordpress.com/

Or follow Mr. Wilkin on Twitter at @DWWilkin

His other published work includes The Trolling Fantasy Series:
    A Trolling We Will Go
    Trolling Down to Old Mah Wee
    Trolling's Pass and Present
And
    Colonel Fitzwilliam's Correspondence (A Pride and Prejudice continuation)

Dr. Douglas J. Wilkin

Dr. Wilkin earned his Ph.D. in Biological Chemistry from UCLA. He currently directs the Cleveland Science Initiative at Grover Cleveland High School in Reseda, CA, where his students focus on ecological issues, human genetics and forensic science.

Prior to teaching high school, Dr. Wilkin held faculty positions at the National Institutes of Health in Bethesda, MD, Cedars-Sinai Medical Center in Los Angeles, and the FBI Academy in Quantico, VA.

Dr. Wilkin also serves as the Life Science expert for the CK-12 Foundation, and is the lead editor of their "Understanding Biodiversity" on-line journal. He also sits on the Education and Learning Panel of the Biodiversity Heritage Library.

He can be followed on Twitter @d_wilkin.

ECO Agents: Save the Planet is his first novel.

www.ingramcontent.com/pod-product-compliance
Lightning Source LLC
Chambersburg PA
CBHW060923180626
46817CB00004B/1376